House Revenge

House Revenge

MIKE LAWSON

Atlantic Monthly Press
New York

Published simultaneously in Canada
Printed in the United States of America

FIRST EDITION

ISBN 978-0-8021-2523-1
eISBN 978-0-8021-9039-0

Atlantic Monthly Press
an imprint of Grove Atlantic
154 West 14th Street
New York, NY 10011

Distributed by Publishers Group West

groveatlantic.com

16 17 18 19   10 9 8 7 6 5 4 3 2 1

For Dan Caine (1942–2015)
Lawyer. Naval officer. A good husband. A good father.
A good friend. We all miss you.

Author's Note

———◆◆◆———

To the best of my knowledge, there is no Delaney Street in Boston.

House Revenge

Prologue

It's impossible to know how Ray and Roy McNulty might have turned out if they hadn't been raised by two violent, ignorant drunks.

And maybe nothing would have happened at all if Sean Callahan had just pretended to show John Mahoney the respect Mahoney felt he deserved.

But when the McNulty brothers tried to kill Elinore Dobbs and cracked Joe DeMarco's skull . . . Well, after that, things just spun out of control.

1

It was humid and almost a hundred degrees outside, the day John Mahoney met Elinore Dobbs—but Mahoney was feeling about as mellow as a man can feel.

On the way to his district office on Boylston Street, he'd stopped for a massage at an establishment he visited occasionally when he was in Boston. The masseuses were all tiny Vietnamese women and reminded him of bar girls he'd enjoyed in Saigon when he was a marine, a lad of just seventeen, fighting in a war he didn't understand. The masseuse he had that day was a lovely lady named Kim with coal-black hair and sparkling black eyes and breasts the size of apples. She started out with his back, pummeled and rubbed tight muscles, making him moan with pain and pleasure, then her soft lips brushed his ear and whispered that he should turn over.

Then it was off to lunch at L'Espalier, also in the Back Bay, also on Boylston Street. L'Espalier was one of the most—if not *the* most—expensive French restaurants in Boston. Mahoney had lunch in the Crystal Room, a room bordered on three sides by bottles of wine resting in striking steel and glass cases. The tables were covered with linens whiter than fresh-fallen snow—and certainly whiter than John Mahoney's soul.

Mahoney had L'Espalier's signature Maine lobster bisque with garlic flan for an appetizer, followed by Amish chicken, roasted with herbed cannoli, rum raisins, and pine nuts. This fine repast was preceded by a tumbler of A. H. Hirsch Reserve, one of the priciest bourbons sold in America. With his lunch, he had a bottle of Chardonnay that he guessed went for over a hundred bucks a bottle. He had to guess the cost of the wine, of course, because he didn't pay for a thing. L'Espalier's owner comped him, as he always did, Mahoney being who he was: the senior congressman from Boston, a former Speaker of the House and currently the House Minority Leader—arguably the most powerful Democrat on Capitol Hill, and a man sensitive to the needs of his friends in the restaurant business.

At three p.m., he finally sauntered into his district office. He was supposed to have been there at two. The lobby was crowded with about twenty people, ordinary citizens—and John Mahoney's constituents. Sitting behind a desk overflowing with correspondence was a stout woman with unruly gray hair and a noticeable mustache. Her name was Maggie Dolan and she'd worked for Mahoney for years. She ran the office, was intimately involved in Mahoney's ongoing reelection efforts, and acted as boss and den mother to three or four summer interns. Maggie glared at Mahoney, letting him know she wasn't the least bit happy that he was late and that she'd been forced to deal with all the whiners.

Also present was one behemoth, a guy with a shaved head who would have fit right in on the New England Patriots' offensive line. He wore a navy-blue blazer, never-press gray slacks, a blue button-down shirt, and a blue-and-green-striped clip-on tie. He was security. He wasn't armed, except for a can of Mace, but was so damn big it looked as if it would take a bazooka to knock him down. He was present in case any of Mahoney's constituents violently disapproved of the way he represented them.

"Hey, how's it going," Mahoney said to the citizens. "Sorry I'm late. I had to take a call from the president, some flap going on with Iran. I'll be with you all in a minute, and I'm looking forward to talking to you."

Mahoney was five foot eleven, broad across the back and butt; he had a big hard gut that swelled his shirt. His hair was snow white—it had been that color since his forties—and he had bright blue eyes and handsome features. When he turned on the charm, people were charmed. The folks he'd kept waiting for an hour instantly forgave him now that they understood he'd been assisting the president in a matter of national security. Had they known he'd been getting his nob polished, they might have been less forgiving.

Mahoney stepped through a door and walked back to his office. On the way he passed the space where the interns sat, two boys, two girls, all about twenty or so, all Harvard undergrads. Mahoney was sure they had IQs that went off the chart but he had no idea what they were doing on his behalf; Maggie Dolan gave them their assignments.

He stuck his head into the interns' office and said, "Hey, guys, how's it going?"

The interns leapt to their feet like Mahoney was an admiral and somebody had called out: *Officer on deck!*

"Congressman!" they all cried in unison.

"Thanks for being here," Mahoney said. "Keep up the good work." Whatever the hell it was.

He finally reached his office. He took off his suit jacket and hung it on a wooden coat tree, loosened his tie, rolled up his sleeves, and took a seat behind a large mahogany desk. The desk was old, battered and scarred, as was all the other furniture in the room. Mahoney didn't want anything fancy in the office; he didn't want the citizens to think he was squandering their hard-earned tax dollars.

On the wall behind the desk were photos of Mahoney posing with various luminaries: presidents, movie stars, and athletes who played for the Sox, the Celtics, the Bruins, and the Patriots. One picture showed him standing on the Great Wall of China next to his wife, Mary Pat, and their three daughters. The women in the photo all looked wonderful; Mahoney's family was good-looking and incredibly photogenic.

Mahoney, however, looked pale and his smile seemed off center. He appeared to be ill, which he had been that day. The night before the photo was taken he'd stuffed his face with every delicacy the Chinese cooked while drinking about two gallons of Tsingtao beer—and when the sun started to beat down on his head the next day, he'd upchucked everything he'd eaten. He figured he was probably the highest-ranking American politician to ever throw up on the Great Wall of China.

He picked up the phone, punched a button to speak to Maggie, and said, "Send the first one in. Oh, and have one of the kids bring me a Coke. I'm gonna need the caffeine to stay awake."

At least once a month, Mahoney would fly up to Boston from D.C., where he'd attend fund-raisers, make speeches, and try to get on local talk shows. Most important, he'd meet with his big-money donors and see what he needed to do to keep them happy. As Mahoney ran for office every two years, he was constantly scheming and groveling to keep the campaign money rolling in. But about every fourth month, he'd do what he was doing today. He called it Open House.

Mahoney didn't care at all for the town hall meeting format used by some politicians. He'd tried it once and hadn't liked the unruly, disgruntled crowd that gathered—yelling out questions, booing his responses—not to mention the Republican-planted hecklers trying to shove political sticks in his eye. Then there were the reporters writing down every word, taking things out of context, pointing out every inconsistency with things he'd previously said. So instead he held Open House, where he could meet with his constituents one-on-one—without the media jackals present—and listen to their problems. He did this partly to give the impression he cared—which he actually did—about the ordinary slobs who voted for him. He'd take the temperature on how they were feeling about certain issues, listen to them bitch, and assure them that he was fighting for them body and soul down there in Washington. The other purpose of Open House was that he was always looking for something that would play well in the press, something to remind the voters that the man they'd elected was really on their side, and not on the side of the people who contributed vast sums of money to him.

Politics was a cynical game. But what can you do?

Most of the people who showed up for Open House were old folks, which was understandable as Mahoney held it on an afternoon, during the week, when everyone else was usually working. The first old guy wanted to bitch about his property taxes, which kept going up and were killing him as he was on a fixed income. Mahoney could have said that property taxes were a local issue and he should be tossing eggs at the mayor and not at him—but he didn't. Instead he told the old coot that he was meeting with the mayor and the city council that night (he wasn't), and he would give them a piece of his mind.

The next old guy, who was about the size of your average jockey, complained that Social Security cost of living increases weren't keeping up with the cost of living. So what else was new? But here was an issue that Mahoney could handle. First, he blamed everything on the Republicans, then he picked up the phone and said to Maggie: "Have one of the kids bring in a copy of the speech I gave at the Knights of Columbus over in Charlestown a couple months ago."

Two minutes later one of the interns, one of the girls, ran into the office with a copy of the speech. Mahoney couldn't help but notice that the young lady had an outstanding rack on her. He handed the little guy the copy of the speech and said, "Read that, Mr. Compton. You'll see that I'm on top of the issue, that I'm all over the bastards."

The third person who entered his office was Elinore Dobbs.

2

Elinore Dobbs looked like she was in her seventies; Mahoney found out later she was actually eighty-two. She was wearing a 2004 Red Sox World Series T-shirt, baggy blue jeans, and cheap running shoes. She was a slender five foot one and had short gray hair she didn't bother to dye or perm; she probably had it cut at a men's barbershop. Bright blue eyes twinkled behind wire-rimmed bifocals.

The first words out of her mouth were: "I know you're basically a useless shit, but I figured I didn't have anything to lose by coming here."

Mahoney laughed.

"What's your name?" Mahoney asked.

"Elinore Dobbs," she said.

Elinore Dobbs immediately reminded him of his maternal grandmother. Mahoney's parents had both been working stiffs. His father had been a machinist in a shipyard that had closed down decades ago and his mother had been a waitress, a secretary, a clerk at various stores. His mom took whatever job she could get to send her son to parochial schools. So Mahoney's grandmother had largely raised him. She babysat him when he was too young to go to school and when he started school, he'd go to her house afterward and stay there until his folks got home from work. And like Elinore Dobbs, his grandma was a tough old bird. She made him do his homework, wouldn't let him hang around with boys she considered riffraff, and wouldn't take the least bit of guff from him. If he annoyed her she'd box his ears and many a night Mahoney went home with ears as red as Rudolph's nose—or as red as his nose would later become thanks to all the booze he consumed.

"So, Elinore, what can I do for you?"

"I live in an apartment building on Delaney Street and they're trying to force me out. Two years ago, I signed a five-year lease to fix my rent because I didn't plan to move until they carried me out in a coffin. But not long after I signed the lease—"

"A five-year lease is kind of unusual, isn't it?" Mahoney said.

"I suppose," Elinore said, irritated that Mahoney had interrupted her. "But the guy who used to own the building was a good guy and getting old, and some of the long-term tenants like me convinced him to give us longer leases. Anyway, like I was starting to say, not long after I signed the lease, the owner died and his kids sold the building to this damn developer. In fact, this guy has bought up all the real estate in the entire neighborhood, and now he's trying to force everybody out of my building so he can tear it down and put up a fancy new one with high-priced condos."

"I see," Mahoney said.

"No you don't. Let me finish. This developer, the first thing he did was triple the rent for everybody whose leases were expiring even though we did everything we could to stop him. We filed a suit in housing court but his lawyers kicked our ass. I organized protests. We protested in front of his house on Beacon Hill—there was a picture of me in the *Globe*—and protested around his construction site to keep the trucks from going in, but the cops made us move. Anyway, by the end of the first year, he managed to get rid of about eighty percent of the people who used to live in my building.

"The next thing he did was try to buy out the folks with long-term leases like me and offered to help us relocate. By the time he was done with that, all but four tenants had moved out."

"But I take it he couldn't buy you out," Mahoney said.

"You're damn right he couldn't. And that's when he started playing dirty. He fired the building super, a great guy who'd been there for twenty years, and replaced him with these two thugs, the McNulty brothers. Now the elevator hasn't worked in a year, and some of the tenants aren't in good shape like me and it practically kills them to take the stairs. The power goes out half a dozen times a month, and it'll be out for days, like we're living in some third world country. The front door doesn't lock anymore so junkies can get in and steal things, although I don't think it's the junkies who are doing the stealing."

"Geez," Mahoney said, the grimace on his face real and not feigned.

"It gets worse," Elinore said. "The hot water isn't hot about half the time and the air-conditioning stopped working the first summer this all started. Today it's like a blast furnace inside my apartment. They took out the washing machines and the driers in the basement so I have to go to a Laundromat four blocks away. Mail gets stolen. My apartment's been vandalized twice. And the McNultys, these thugs the developer hired, they just hang around the building intimidating folks."

"I get the picture," Mahoney said, but Elinore still wasn't finished.

"I've complained to everybody. The mayor, the city council, the cops. I hired a lawyer but this developer's got slick lawyers coming out his ass, all of them smarter than the guy I hired. Right now, I'm the only one keeping the few tenants remaining from moving, but they're not going to last much longer. Within the next couple of months, I'm sure I'll be the only one living there. So what are you going to do to help me?"

Instead of answering her question, Mahoney said, "I'm just curious. Why don't you take the money this guy's offering you to relocate? I'm guessing you're costing him a bundle, so he should be willing to pay quite a bit, and in the end, three years from now when your lease expires, you're going to have to move anyway."

"I told you. I don't want to move." Her lips compressed into a thin, unyielding line the way his grandmother's used to when she got her back up over something. "I like where I live. I like the parks I can walk to. I like the bakery a couple blocks over where I go for bagels in the morning. There's a T-stop just three blocks away so I can get around town. But those aren't the main reasons I won't move. I'm taking a stand against this guy and all the other guys just like him."

"You're taking a *stand*?" Mahoney said.

"That's right. This kind of crap is happening all over this country. Places like Manhattan and San Francisco and Boston are becoming the domains of the ultrarich. The poor folks are being forced out and replaced with people who can afford to spend millions on condos or five or ten grand a month for rent. The rent on little mom-and-pop stores is set so high that none of the small shops can afford to stay in business and they're being replaced by swanky boutiques where only rich people shop. I read just the other day in the paper, out there in Seattle, some developer is trying to force a bunch of tenants out of an apartment complex and an old lady like me is taking the guy on. So I'm taking a stand."

"Huh," Mahoney said.

But Mahoney actually liked this problem. He didn't really think he could stop the developer from renovating the area where Elinore lived, but he could take her side on the issue. He'd give a speech about the need for affordable urban housing and how developers can't be allowed to do what this guy was doing: cutting off the heat and power and using scare tactics to force her out. Yeah, he'd hold a press conference with Elinore at his side; she was articulate and photogenic in a feisty, little-old-lady kind of way and would look great standing next to him. He'd rant about income inequality and show how he was on the side of all the poor folks like Elinore Dobbs.

Then he'd go see the developer and get the guy to knock off the bullshit, at least for a while, so Mahoney would look like he'd made a difference. He'd tell him to blame what was happening on his employees, like these McNulty goons, and say that they'd been overzealous and doing things he didn't approve of. Then he'd tell him to make Elinore a deal she couldn't refuse; hell, a place on Cape Cod would probably be cheaper than what Elinore was costing him by delaying his construction project. Yep, Mahoney would champion the little people and would look good doing so, and when Elinore was eventually forced to move . . . Well, he could show that he'd done his best—and find some way to blame the Republicans.

"What's the name of this developer?" Mahoney asked.

"Sean Callahan," Elinore said.

Mahoney almost smiled. This was perfect. He knew Callahan well. He also knew a little about Callahan's development in Boston. It was huge, and Elinore Dobbs's building was just a small part of it.

But he didn't smile, and he didn't tell Elinore he knew Callahan. Instead he said, "Callahan. Yeah, I've heard about him," making it sound as if Callahan was evil incarnate.

He called Maggie and told her to send in one of the kids. He was hoping she'd send in the good-looking coed again. Instead she sent in one of the boys—a tall, gangly dork who was probably a genius as Maggie only hired geniuses, and he was probably rich as she only hired kids whose parents were likely to contribute to Mahoney.

"What's your name again?" Mahoney asked the boy. He'd never known the kid's name.

"Mason Stanhope," the kid said.

What a yuppie fuckin' name! But Mahoney knew Stanhope's father; he was a lawyer who'd made his money filing class action lawsuits against airline companies and had a house as big as a medieval castle on Martha's Vineyard—another place where only rich people can afford to live.

"Mason, this is Elinore Dobbs. I want you to sit down with her and write down all the stuff she's going to tell you. Elinore, you give Mason the facts. Dates, specific people you've contacted, details about the things these McNulty creeps have done. And Mason, you tell one of the guys you work with—like maybe that young lady who brought me the copy of my Knights of Columbus speech—that I want to understand the law on evicting folks from their apartments. You'll understand after Elinore explains to you what's going on. And I want you to move fast on this, Mason. Elinore and I are going to hold a press conference tomorrow, so you move chop-chop. Got it?"

"Yes, sir," Mason said.

"You're really going to help me?" Elinore said, sounding incredulous.

"You're damn right I am," her champion said.

3

Mahoney asked Maggie to send in the next citizen, but he also told her to call Sean Callahan. "Tell Sean I want to see him this evening, have a drink over at the Copley about six or seven."

The next citizen was an old woman who was wearing her Sunday go-to-Mass clothes, including a feathered blue bonnet and white gloves. She brought a plate of chocolate chip cookies she'd baked herself, and they were good. She surprised Mahoney when she said she wanted to talk about how Comcast had a monopoly on Internet service in Boston and kept jacking up their rates and forcing people to bundle services to get a decent price. She said the Internet ought to be a public utility like sewer and water, and that poor people—because of that demon Comcast—had to go to a library to get online to look for a job or apply for one. She wanted to know why Mahoney didn't give that wimp who ran the FCC a kick in the pants, a guy who, according to her, was basically on Comcast's payroll.

Mahoney pointed out that the FCC had just blocked a merger between Comcast and Time Warner to prevent Comcast from dominating the market but the old lady said that didn't do a damn thing for cities like Boston where Comcast *already* had a monopoly. Mahoney knew she was right but he was thinking he'd just as soon not piss off

Comcast, who contributed to him—and maybe to everyone else in Congress. He was trying to come up with a way to blame this one on the Republicans, too, but at that moment, Maggie stuck her head into his office and said, "Sorry to interrupt, Congressman, but Mr. Callahan said tonight isn't convenient for him and asked if he could meet with you some other time."

"Not *convenient* for him?" Mahoney said. "Why, that arrogant little . . ."

He'd been about to say "prick," but stopped himself as the old lady was still in the room. If Mahoney needed to meet with the president of the United States, and if the president was in town, he'd make time for Mahoney. Yet here was this punk, Callahan, who thought that because he was now worth a few hundred million, he could blow Mahoney off.

"You call him back and tell him that if he doesn't meet with me tonight, he'll hear at my press conference tomorrow how I'm gonna shut down his project on Delaney Street."

"Yes, sir," Maggie said.

"Now what were you saying, Mrs. Waters?" Mahoney said to the Internet crusader.

A couple minutes later, Maggie came back and said, "Mr. Callahan will meet you this evening at the Copley at six."

"That's better," Mahoney said, and reached for another cookie.

———◆———

The Fairmont Copley Plaza Hotel was constructed in 1912 and is across the street from Copley Square. A block away is historic Trinity Church, founded in 1733, and a place where generations of Episcopalians have knelt and prayed. A bit farther to the west is the Old South Church with its magnificent bell tower. It seemed as if the first thing the old

New Englanders did when they stepped off the boat was to build a church; Mahoney would have built a tavern with an adjoining bordello.

To enter the grand hotel you pass under a large red awning and between two stern-looking seven-foot lions made of stone and painted gold. The lobby is as big as a football field but instead of AstroTurf, the floor is covered with thick blue-and-red Oriental carpets. Hanging from a twenty-one-foot ceiling is a chandelier that might have come from the set of *The Phantom of the Opera*. Mahoney thought it was the most impressive-looking hotel lobby in the city.

The OAK Long Bar, just off the lobby, has brown leather high-back stools in front of a bar that wraps around a kitchen so you can watch the chefs prepare your meal if you're so inclined. There are also comfortable cloth chairs—some red, some white—in front of small marble-topped tables, which was where Mahoney was seated: in a red chair, drinking Wild Turkey, and growing increasingly annoyed at Sean Callahan, who was now twenty-five minutes late for their meeting.

At six thirty Callahan arrived, pretending to be breathless from sprinting to their appointment. "I'm so sorry I'm late, John," he said. "Damn traffic in this town gets worse every year."

Bullshit. Mahoney knew that Callahan's office was a ten-minute walk away on Exeter Street. But instead of saying how he didn't appreciate Callahan deliberately keeping him waiting, he said, "That's okay. I just got here myself, two minutes ago." *And fuck you.*

Sean Callahan was forty-seven and looked as if he might have descended from a Beacon Hill, Boston Brahmin clan. He was six foot two, had a longish nose, thinning dark hair with just a sprinkling of gray, and thin lips best suited for expressing disapproval. His face was unlined due to the skills of a top-notch cosmetic surgeon, and he appeared to be in terrific shape thanks to tennis, a personal trainer—and a very young new wife. He was dressed casually: dark blue sport jacket, tan slacks, a blue cotton shirt with his initials monogrammed over the pocket but no tie—sort of a preppy, rich kid look, similar to what the

Harvard interns in Mahoney's Boston office wore. But Mahoney knew that Callahan wasn't a Brahmin and hadn't attended Harvard; he'd been raised in Charlestown, had gone to a community college, and it had probably taken him half his life to eradicate his boyhood accent.

Callahan ordered a tonic water and lime; apparently alcohol wasn't part of his current fitness routine. "So how are Mary Pat and the girls all doing?" he asked.

They spent ten minutes chatting about nothing before Mahoney got to the point. "A little old lady named Elinore Dobbs came to see me today."

Callahan shook his head and smiled without humor, as if chagrined. "She's a nut, John."

"Maybe, but she tells me you've been putting the screws to her to get her out of her apartment."

"Did Elinore tell you that I offered her two hundred grand to move? Did she tell you I found her an apartment six blocks from where she is now that's twice as nice as the one she's in?"

"No, she didn't tell me that." Mahoney was actually shocked that Callahan had offered Elinore so much; she must be costing him a boatload. "What she told me is that you've been cutting off her heat and hot water and power, vandalizing her apartment, and stealing her mail. She told me you got two creeps named McNulty terrorizing the old folks like her who still live in the building."

"I offered her two hundred grand, John! Two hundred!"

"Well . . ."

"Do you have any idea what it takes to put a project like Delaney Square together? To get the investment money, buy the properties, get all the permits, make all the deals with the city? I've been working on this for over seven years, and that woman is interfering with a development that's bringing new businesses to Boston, providing construction jobs for a lot of people, and, after that, jobs in all the offices and retail stores that will be there. She's also standing in the way of the city collecting millions in taxes because the people who will move into that area actually pay taxes."

Mahoney noticed that Callahan was talking about how much good his development would do for Boston—like he was some kind of philanthropist—but he didn't bother to mention how much money he was going to make.

"Goddamnit, John! I've tried to reason with that woman but—" Callahan stopped ranting and took a breath. "What do you want, John?"

"I want you to find some way to work things out with her."

"You're not listening to me! I've tried to work things out with her. She won't budge. She'll tell you the reason why is because she likes where she lives, that she likes going to all the places she's always gone to, that she likes to be near her friends. But do you know what, John? Most of the places she used to go to are gone already and her friends have moved away—and she *knows* that. Do you want to know the real reason she's screwing with me?"

"Yeah, what's the real reason?" Mahoney said. He already knew the reason—Elinore had told him about the stand she was taking—but he wanted to hear Callahan's spin on the issue.

"She has an agenda, a political agenda. She says guys like me—the ones who create all the jobs and pay all the taxes—are making the city unaffordable for working-class people. And that's what this is all about. It's about the one percent depriving the ninety-nine percent of affordable housing. That's the drum she's beating."

"Well, she's got a point."

"No! She doesn't! People with money—the ones with the brains and the drive and the education—have a right to live in decent places. Even *luxurious* places. And I have the right to build the places where they want to live. Do you want this city to become like Detroit, John? Do you want the people who create jobs and pay taxes to go someplace else? I'm sorry, but this is the way it's always been and the way it will always be. This country doesn't support communism, and everyone isn't guaranteed the same standard of living. You get the standard of living you earn. And nutcases like Elinore Dobbs, goddamnit, don't have some God-given right to stop progress."

By the time he finished talking, Callahan's face was as red as the chair Mahoney was sitting in, but Mahoney said, "I can't be on your side on this, Sean. I'm sorry, but I can't appear to be supporting a guy as rich as you while people like Elinore are getting hurt. At least not publicly."

"How much did Elinore Dobbs contribute to your last campaign, John? I contributed fifty grand."

"And I appreciate that, Sean. I really do. But when I'm running for reelection every two years, I have to at least pretend that I care about people like Elinore because there are a lot more of them than there are guys like you. And the fact is, I do care about them. So I'm asking you to find a way to work it out with her, and to knock off the strong-arm shit. It may take you a little longer to finish your project but in the end, everybody wins. And tomorrow, instead of me holding a press conference where I say Sean Callahan's a bad guy and a bully, I'll say I've talked to Sean Callahan and he's a *good* guy. I'll say he had some people working for him who behaved in a bad way, and he's going to fire those guys and do right by Elinore and the rest of the tenants in that building."

Callahan didn't say anything for a minute, as he stared into Mahoney's bloodshot blue eyes. Then he said, "No."

"No, what?"

"No, I'm not going to do right by her. I've tried to do right by her but she's screwing me over. And I've got investors relying on me to get this project completed. I've got schedules to meet and every day I'm delayed from knocking down her building is adding to my losses."

"You mean it's cutting into your profit," Mahoney said. "You're not going to lose money on this thing."

Callahan didn't respond.

"Sean, I'm asking you to be reasonable here."

Callahan stood up. "Go to hell, Congressman. And when you come around next time with your hand out for a contribution, I'll tell you the same thing. And I'm going to talk to my friends and tell them that John Mahoney is a man who'll take your money then screw you to make himself look good. So go to hell. You need guys like me a lot more than I need you. I'm going to help your opponent in the next election beat you, and when I do, he'll show some gratitude."

Callahan spun on his heels and left.

Sean was furious as he left the Copley, so mad he could barely see. Delaney Square was the most complicated development he'd ever taken on and now, on top of everything else, he had that hypocrite Mahoney meddling in it. But in the time it took for him to walk back to his office on Exeter, he realized that he shouldn't have lost his temper with Mahoney. He certainly shouldn't have said what he did. He could have been more diplomatic. He could have even lied and said that he'd try harder to come to some agreement with Dobbs. Then he thought: *Screw it.* Like he'd told Mahoney, Mahoney needed him a lot more than he needed Mahoney. And there was a larger problem: the people who'd invested in Delaney Square were not the kind of people he could afford to disappoint. He needed that old bitch out of that building and out of his way now.

Mahoney ordered another drink after Callahan left. He was steaming.

What he was really pissed about, more than anything else, was the lack of respect. *Go to hell?* Who did Callahan think he was talking to?

But more and more these days, rich guys like Callahan didn't even *pretend* they were impressed by politicians. Not anymore. These guys knew their money controlled politics, not the people who held public office.

Just the other day, Mahoney had watched a Senate hearing on television. The Senate Banking Committee had summoned a couple of Wall Street bankers down to D.C. to grill them on some outrageous, risky thing they'd done that resulted in about ten thousand ordinary people losing all the money they'd socked away for retirement. But those bankers, surrounded by a platoon of lawyers in pin-striped suits, weren't the least bit intimidated. In fact, they sat there *smirking*. They knew they weren't going to jail. They didn't break the law—they just bent it a little—and a bunch of senators, half of them in the banking industry's pocket, wouldn't do a damn thing to stop them.

Well, Mahoney was sick of the disrespect—and the guy that was going to find out how much power he still had was Sean Callahan. Normally, he'd be worried about the threat Callahan had made, about how he'd rally his fellow developers to contribute to his opponent, but this time . . . This was no longer about Elinore Dobbs. This was about an arrogant punk with money who needed to be taught a lesson, the lesson being that you didn't tell John Mahoney to go to hell.

4

Mahoney called Maggie Dolan, who was still toiling away in his district office, and told her not to let the interns leave. He said he was coming back and wanted a briefing on all the things they'd learned. He also told Maggie to call the *Globe* and the TV stations and tell them that he'd be making a speech at ten a.m. tomorrow—in time for it to be on the twelve o'clock news—down there on Delaney Street, right outside Elinore's building, with Elinore by his side.

And that's what he did.

John Mahoney had always had the ability to give a rousing speech and he usually did it off the cuff because he was too lazy to prepare a speech and practice it. And the next morning he stood next to Elinore and ripped Sean Callahan a new asshole. He said people like Elinore had rights, and developers like Callahan couldn't be allowed to violate those rights just so they could get richer. He described Callahan's harassment campaign against Elinore, cutting off her power and water, trying to force her to move. He said he'd be talking to city officials, like the mayor, to find out why he was allowing Callahan to treat people this way. And the speech worked—at least in the sense that Mahoney came across as a man who cared about the plight of all those like Elinore Dobbs.

The following day, a spokesman for Callahan read a statement to the media saying that Mahoney was grossly exaggerating Elinore's situation, and Mr. Callahan *deeply* resented the implication that he'd done anything illegal. If any vandalism had occurred in Elinore's building, it had been perpetrated by the criminal element who currently lived in the neighborhood—the sort of people who would migrate elsewhere when Mr. Callahan's project was complete.

The spokesman said that, sure, there'd been a few maintenance problems in Elinore's building. It was an old building, and since most of the tenants had moved out, there was less rent money coming in to pay for maintenance. But there wasn't any sort of ongoing harassment campaign against an old woman. That was ludicrous. Things just break and it takes time to fix them.

The spokesman also said that Mr. Callahan had done everything humanly possible to relocate Elinore and her fellow tenants. He'd made very generous offers to buy out their leases and relocate them to apartments much nicer than the ones on Delaney Street. In fact, Ms. Dobbs had been offered two hundred thousand dollars to relocate. For Christ's sake, how much more generous could Mr. Callahan be?

Speaking of generosity, the PR flack said, just look at Mr. Callahan's record, how he and his wife contributed more than two million dollars last year to organizations like Big Brothers, the Boys and Girls Clubs, the YMCA, and Habitat for Humanity. Yeah, the spokesman concluded, Sean Callahan was a *good* guy and he resented a powerful congressman, for purely political purposes, saying he was otherwise. And by the way, the spokesman said, Mr. Callahan's project was providing jobs for a whole lot of working folks and, if anything, Elinore Dobbs was taking a paycheck out of those workers' pockets.

In short, Callahan's spokesman sent a message to John Mahoney. The message was: *Go fuck yourself.*

And Mahoney responded accordingly. He called the police commissioner and told him if he wanted any more of those federal antiterrorism funds, he'd better get off his fat ass and protect Elinore Dobbs. Mahoney wanted big guys with nightsticks patrolling the neighborhood. He wanted these McNulty clowns who were intimidating the old folks leaned on and leaned on hard.

He called the secretary of the Treasury and said he wanted Sean Callahan's crooked development company audited. The secretary informed him that the last director of the IRS had been forced to resign for auditing Republicans to make the Democrats happy. Mahoney's response was that this wasn't about partisan politics; in fact, the guy he wanted audited was a registered Democrat. The secretary said, "Man, I don't know," to which Mahoney said that maybe it was time to review the secretary's last trip to Jamaica, the one where he'd flown in a government plane, accompanied by a secretary that everyone knew was his mistress, and then spent the whole time playing golf and hide-the-pickle in his hotel room. "You're right, Congressman," the secretary said. "A man like Callahan who would push an old lady around is very likely to be defrauding the government out of its rightful share."

Mahoney's called the chairman of the SEC, saying he wanted Callahan investigated for insider trading. He didn't know if Callahan was guilty of this particular crime but suspected a man with his money and connections might be. Mahoney, in fact, had been guilty of insider trading many times but as a member of Congress, and despite recent changes to a vaguely worded law called the STOCK Act, he could get away with it. But Callahan couldn't. So unless the chairman of the SEC wanted to be dragged in front of a House committee to explain why his commission was so damn useless . . .

He contacted the director of the FBI next, and told him that he wanted the bureau to investigate Elinore's claim that Callahan's people had stolen her mail. Stealing mail was, after all, a federal crime. The head of the bureau languidly said, "Not my job, Congressman. You need to talk to the Postal Inspection Service." Mahoney had never dealt with the Postal Inspection Service in his life. He looked them up on the

Internet and found that, yep, they were the guys who investigated if your mail got stolen. They also investigated mailbox destruction, letter bombs, identity theft, lottery fraud, and a whole bunch of other stuff. They had over a thousand inspectors, seventeen field offices, and even had their own forensic laboratory. No wonder the price of stamps kept going up. But when Mahoney learned that the postal service's top cop had started off his career as a mail carrier in Mississippi, he "imaged" a guy with a wandering eye, in those shorts mailmen wear, one of those white safari hats on his head—and decided not to bother.

Lastly, Mahoney called the mayor of Boston and the city councilman representing Elinore's neighborhood. He told them one thing he wanted done immediately was to have the right people inspect Callahan's project looking for building and safety code violations. He wanted inspectors crawling over Callahan's development like red-hot ants. He also wanted to know why the civil suits Elinore and other tenants had filed to stop Callahan's terrorist tactics hadn't prevailed. He screamed at the mayor, "You tell the useless son of a bitch who's supposed to keep Callahan from breaking the housing laws to do his goddamn job!"

The mayor and the councilman said they'd do what they could but their response was noticeably lukewarm. It was apparent to Mahoney that those two jackals were in Callahan's pocket, either getting a kickback from him or a promise to contribute to their next campaign—and Mahoney couldn't help but wonder if the mayor might actually be thinking about running against him.

Two days after meeting with Elinore Dobbs, a disgruntled Mahoney sat in an uncomfortable plastic chair at Logan Airport waiting for his plane to D.C. to board. On one hand, he felt good that he'd done the right thing by siding with Elinore against Callahan. Maybe his reason for siding with her had more to do with pride than anything else—but he'd done the right thing. On the other hand, he had this queasy feeling in his stomach that his next run for the seat he'd held for more than three decades might not be so easy.

The other thing was, in spite of all the bureaucrats he'd leaned on, Mahoney knew that eventually Callahan was going to win and Elinore was going to lose. There was no way she could hold out for three more years against Callahan. He also knew that after a couple of weeks the media would become bored with the story, if they weren't bored already. So he needed to do more. He needed to find some way to keep the heat on Callahan, and what he really needed was to find some legal way to stop him from harassing Elinore. Then he thought: *Who says it has to be legal?*

He called Mavis, his secretary in D.C. "Track down that lazy bastard DeMarco. He's probably playing golf. Tell him I want him in my office tomorrow, and to pack a bag. He's going to Boston."

5

———◆———

Ray and Roy McNulty were Irish twins, born eleven months apart. Sean Callahan met them when he was in the ninth grade.

The McNultys were raised by two violent, bigoted drunks, and their mother was just as bad as their father when it came to smacking them around. The smacking stopped when the boys entered their teens and were big enough to fight back. And you never fought one McNulty brother; you always fought them both simultaneously. Their parents got the picture one fine night when the boys sent their dad to the emergency room with a broken nose and dislocated shoulder.

Their mother, who was morbidly obese, died of a heart attack when they were seventeen and their father died of lung cancer compounded by liver problems a couple years later. Sean vividly remembered the McNultys weeping at their mother's funeral. It had been like watching hyenas cry.

Sean's parents were nothing like Ray and Roy's. They were decent people who doted on their only child. Sean's dad worked for the MBTA as a maintenance man and his mom was a substitute teacher. The problem with them was that they were weak people and Sean learned to manipulate them at an early age. They never approved of Sean being friends with the McNulty brothers, and could never understand why he was their friend. What Sean's parents didn't realize was that the Mc-Nultys made life interesting for a bored, discontented kid who didn't have anything better to do.

Sean wasn't a good enough athlete to make the first team and he had too much pride to ride the bench. He had no desire to hang around with the losers on the school marching band, the debate team, or the chess club. Nor was he—in those days—cool enough to hang with the A-list kids, most of whom were either athletes or had money coming out their ears.

So the McNultys filled the vacuum. They introduced young Sean to pool and pinball machines and bowling alleys thick with smoke. They initiated him in the urban sport of shoplifting. (Sean would be the diversion while the McNultys would go through a Kmart like a plague of two locusts.) The McNultys knew older guys who would sell them weed and booze. They also knew girls who would give it away for a six-pack of beer; these same girls would later understand that they were significantly undervaluing a moneymaking asset.

The amazing thing was that Sean was never arrested for the things he did with the McNulty brothers. He graduated from high school, and went off to college. Ray and Roy were not so fortunate. Ray spent most of his senior year in jail for stealing a car. Roy dropped out of school, as he didn't like to do anything without his brother.

Sean met the McNultys at their bar in Revere the day John Mahoney flew back to Washington.

At the ages of forty-seven and forty-eight respectively, Roy was maybe ten pounds heavier than Ray, and Ray's hair was disappearing faster than Roy's, but those differences were barely noticeable. They were both five foot eight, stocky, thick necked, and had the muscles one gets doing forty-pound curls while watching pro wrestling on TV. They had short, broad snouts; small, close-set eyes; lips as thin as knife blades. Their hair was cut within a quarter inch of their knobby skulls and they shaved dark, heavy beards a couple times a week. The easiest way to tell them apart was Ray's right ear: a piece was missing from the lobe, the piece swallowed by a drunk in a bar fight.

The brothers were proud of their bar in Revere; in fact, owning a bar was the pinnacle of their ambition. They did wish that their bar was in Charlestown where they'd been raised, and people they knew could say, "Hey, let's go to Ray and Roy's place for a beer." But thanks to developers like their friend, Sean Callahan, they couldn't afford a bar in Charlestown.

Sean, however, did "loan" them the down payment to buy their bar for a favor they once did for him, knowing they'd never repay the loan. The bar was called the Shamrock. The brothers desperately wanted to change the name of the place to McNulty's—never mind where the apostrophe was supposed to go—but they never seemed to have enough cash on hand to afford a new neon sign.

The Shamrock was the sort of place you see all over America in small towns and in the not-so-classy neighborhoods of large cities: twelve stools in front of a scarred mahogany-stained bar, the stools padded with cracked and split red Naugahyde; four wobbly tables with three or four mismatched chairs per table; a much-abused pool table with cushions so soft you couldn't make a bank shot. Neon BUDWEISER and MILLER HIGH LIFE signs occupied the two small windows facing the street.

The previous owner of the Shamrock had been a Boston Celtics fan, and three-decade-old pennants were thumbtacked to the walls, the pennants moldy and curling from age. Prominently and proudly displayed behind the bar was an autographed photo of Larry Bird, arguably the most famous white guy who ever played the game. Had it been Bill Russell's picture, the McNultys would have removed it the day they bought the place.

The other thing about the Shamrock was that the McNultys now owned the bar, free and clear. They'd initially gotten a mortgage with a little help from Sean, and struggled every month to make the payment, then a *real* miracle happened. This was a miracle on par with Moses parting the Red Sea, comparable to Lazarus rising from the dead. An unmarried uncle—and maybe the only McNulty in generations born with a brain in his head—made a lot of money during his lifetime, then died unexpectedly and without a will. The McNultys inherited a hundred and fifty grand from a man they barely knew and thought might be queer, and that was enough to pay off the mortgage on the decrepit, narrow, two-story building in a bad neighborhood in Revere.

The Shamrock had a regular clientele of maybe twenty people, but most of the time there'd only be two or three customers in the place, old-timers with nothing better to do, alcoholics who went there because it was the closest place to home. The only time the Shamrock did a booming business was the day people got their Social Security checks and St. Paddy's Day. The main reason the place stayed financially afloat, if just barely, was the McNultys had a lady named Doreen who was, just possibly, tougher than the brothers and she managed the place. To compensate for her irregular salary, they let Doreen live in the small apartment above the bar.

But the McNultys were perfectly satisfied with the Shamrock the way it was—except for the sign over the door. It may not have been the grandest bar in Beantown, but it was *their* bar.

Sean took a seat with Ray and Roy at the back of the main room, near a dartboard that hardly anyone used. The people who patronized the Shamrock rarely had the hand-eye coordination to throw a dart and hit a target. Sean had a draft beer in front of him that he had no intention of drinking; he could see a lipstick smudge on the rim of the glass even as poor as the lighting was. There was only one customer in the place, a guy in his eighties who'd gotten there when the place opened at eleven a.m. and he'd been sipping beer for four hours since then.

Sean had dressed down for the meeting, wearing a wash-faded golf shirt, old jeans, and running shoes. The McNultys were wearing camo shorts with cargo pockets, white V-necked T-shirts that were tight on their bulging biceps and across their muscular chests, and high-top black tennis shoes without socks.

"About the old lady," Sean said. "You gotta back off her for a while. Just leave her alone. Don't mess with the power or the air-conditioning or anything like that. Thanks to that fuckin' Mahoney . . ."

Sean had noticed—he couldn't help himself—that when he was alone with the McNultys his manner of speech changed: he swore more, tended to drop his *g*'s, and his boyhood accent emerged, if only slightly.

"There'll be cops comin' around," Sean continued. "A couple of building and fire inspectors will probably drop by, and even some TV and newspaper guys. But after a week or so, everything will go back to business as usual. But guys, I need that woman out of the building. She's killin' me."

"What are you sayin', Sean?" Roy McNulty asked. "We've been doin' everything you told us to do."

"I'm saying, do whatever you have to do to get her out of there."

"Yeah, but what's that mean?" Ray asked, his small eyes glittering with amusement. He knew exactly what Sean meant.

———◆◆◆———

The first time Sean used the McNulty brothers was ten years after he graduated from high school—and he hadn't seen them once in the intervening ten years. After Sean acquired a business degree and a real estate license, he had the good fortune to be taken under the wing of a man who was a much, much smaller version of what Sean Callahan would later become. Thanks to his mentor, Sean started flipping houses and buying properties that were later torn down to make way for more upscale residences. Then he took a major risk, and invested everything he had in a development where he made his first million. Sean Callahan *was* the American Dream: he came from a middle-class family, and thanks to brains, hard work, and ambition, he pulled himself up by his bootstraps. But nineteen years ago, at the time of his ten-year high school reunion, he'd had a problem.

He attended the reunion that year mainly to show off: At the age of twenty-eight, he was certain he was worth more than any other man in the room. He was accompanied by his second wife, Adele, who was only twenty-three at the time and as lovely as any starlet likely to grace the red carpet on Oscar night. Sean was surprised to see the McNultys at the reunion, as they hadn't graduated. He figured they hadn't been invited, but found out about it, and no one had the balls to tell them to leave. And as soon as he saw them, he decided they were the right guys to solve the problem he had.

The McNultys were standing alone by the punch bowl; everyone attending the function was doing their best to pretend they weren't even there. They were dressed in sport jackets that were too tight across the back and too short in the sleeves, polyester slacks, and black shoes so shiny they looked like they were made from plastic. Sean figured they came to the reunion just to see him; they'd had no other friends in high school, and there were at least half a dozen men at the reunion who the McNultys had kicked the crap out of when they were teenagers.

Sean and his new bride had been talking to another couple—a couple who'd been the homecoming queen and king his senior year; the woman had really packed on the pounds—when he saw the McNultys by the punch bowl. After thinking about it for a couple of moments, he told his wife and the other couple that he'd be right back, and walked over to greet Roy and Ray. On his way toward them, he made up his mind about how he was going to act, and when he reached them, he let out a whoop and clutched them in hugs. The McNultys were as startled as everyone else in the room.

They started to ask Sean how he'd been and what he'd been doing the last ten years—they couldn't keep their eyes off his wife—but he cut them off and said, "Look, we need to get out of this place and go somewhere and get a real drink. I never liked any of these people when I was in high school, and I don't like 'em now. I'm gonna hang around for another hour or so, then I'm going to drop my wife back home and I'll meet you guys over at McGill's so we can catch up."

When he met with them at McGill's—a bar they used to go to in high school and where the owner tended to be flexible when it came to underage drinkers—Sean downplayed his success. He just said that he was in real estate and asked what they were doing these days—and got the answer he'd expected: "Aw, you know, just this and that." Which made him wonder what sort of criminal records they'd managed to acquire in the last ten years.

After thirty minutes of bullshit, reminiscing about the good old days when they'd tormented the weaker sheep in Charlestown, Sean got to the point. He told them he was trying to renovate an apartment building in Chelsea, turn the small apartments into decent-sized units, and there was a building inspector who was fucking with him. And that was the only way Sean could describe it: "This guy, he's just fuckin' with me," he told Roy and Ray.

For some reason the building inspector had taken an intense dislike to Sean, and the renovation had practically ground to a halt with the inspector identifying every small code violation he could find with wiring, plumbing, sprinkler systems, and so on. According to this inspector, not a single thing had been installed correctly, and Sean was constantly having to rip out work that had been completed; then, after he redid it, the inspector would find more problems. The guy was costing him thousands of dollars per day, and Sean couldn't find any way to get him out of his hair. He'd tried to bribe the guy—that almost got him arrested—and then he said he was going to sue him, maybe even file a discrimination complaint. The inspector was black and he was going to say that the inspector was picking on him because he was white. The inspector laughed in his face.

"I need to get this guy off my back," Sean told the McNultys the night of the reunion.

"We can do that," Ray said.

"Yeah, we can do that," Roy said.

Sean was worried that they might actually kill the inspector, which he didn't want; that would be going too far. But the problem with the McNultys was the always-present *rage*. Imagine a teakettle, the water in the kettle simmering, almost to the point of boiling, the kettle spout barely whistling—and then, with a slight increase in temperature, steam comes billowing out of the kettle and it begins to *scream*. That was the way the rage simmered inside the McNultys: it was always there, and it took only the smallest provocation—an imagined slight, just a hint of disrespect—and all that barely contained fury would erupt like a volcano.

Sean remembered once when he and the McNultys were sitting on the stoop of a three-decker in Charlestown, drinking beer, and these two teenagers a little older than them walked by. The teenagers looked like kids who came from money—nice sweaters, expensive tennis shoes—so they weren't local guys. Well, one of the kids made the mistake of glancing over at the McNultys.

"What the fuck you looking at?" Ray said.

"Nothing," one of the kids said.

"Nothing!" Roy said—and immediately stood up and threw a full can of beer at one of the kids, hitting him in the forehead. Then he and Ray came off the porch and just pounded the snot out of those boys. That was the McNultys.

A week after Sean spoke to them at McGill's, the McNultys caught the building inspector alone at another construction site and beat him so badly he was in the hospital for a week and would be getting physical therapy for six months after that. Satisfied with their performance, Sean gave them the money for the down payment on the Shamrock and threw them work whenever he could: demolition jobs that didn't require much skill—and certainly no explosives—moving furniture, hauling trash away. That sort of thing. And the job he currently had them doing for him—driving reluctant tenants out of a building—wasn't the first time they'd performed this function for him.

But back to the present in the Shamrock and Elinore Dobbs.

"So exactly what are you saying, Sean?" Ray said.

"Yeah, what do you want us to do with the old broad?" Roy said.

Sean's answer was: "How come you guys haven't changed the sign on this place to McNulty's like you're always talking about?"

"Because it'll cost us a couple of grand to get a new sign, pay an electrician to wire it up, rent a cherry picker to take down the old one, and have a new one installed," Ray said.

Sean pretended to study the room they were in and said, "In fact, this place could use a total makeover. New sign outside, paint the exterior and interior, buff up the floors, that sort of thing. Yeah, I think I might be able to help you with all that."

6

That lazy bastard DeMarco was not goofing off playing golf when Mahoney's secretary called and said that the big man was upset, wanted to see him, and that he was being deployed to Boston. DeMarco, in fact, was working on an assignment that Mahoney had given him and had apparently forgotten about due to whatever had happened in Boston.

DeMarco was sitting with his friend Emma on the patio of her expensive home in McLean, Virginia. DeMarco had known Emma for years—and knew very little about her. She was the most private person he'd ever encountered. He knew she was gay, a cancer survivor, and absurdly rich. How she came to be so rich, he had no idea. The reason he was visiting her today was because he also knew that she'd spent thirty years with the DIA—the Defense Intelligence Agency. As near as he'd been able to figure out, she'd been a spy but she never talked about what she had done before she retired. Because of her past employment, however, she had contacts in places where DeMarco didn't—places like the Defense Department, the CIA, and the NSA—and DeMarco asked for her help sometimes when he needed her connections. Today what DeMarco needed was a back door into the Pentagon.

"I'm not sure you're going to find the proof Mahoney's looking for," Emma said. "This happened over thirty years ago and everything wasn't as computerized then as it is now."

Emma was sitting in a lounge chair sipping ice tea. She was wearing white shorts that reached her knees and a pale blue blouse that matched her pale blue eyes. She had short hair that was a blondish gray, and she was as tall as DeMarco, almost six feet. And although she was several years older than DeMarco—she was almost Mahoney's age—she was slender and in incredible shape because, for one thing, she ran in marathons. In fact, she'd been in the Boston Marathon the year the two terrorists set off their pressure cooker bombs, but fortunately had not been near the finish line when they exploded. When DeMarco heard about the marathon attack, the first thing he did was call Emma's cell phone and when he didn't hear back from her for several hours, he made a reservation to fly to Boston to see if she'd been injured. When she finally called him back and said she was fine, he hardly whined at all when he couldn't get a refund on the ticket he'd purchased.

"But you'll take a look. Quietly," DeMarco said.

"Yeah," she said. "But don't be surprised if there's no record and then you'll have to decide if the absence of a record means he's lying."

DeMarco had been pretty sure that Emma would be willing to help him in this particular case but he could never be positive because she despised John Mahoney. She thought Mahoney was corrupt, which he was; she loathed him for cheating on his wonderful wife, which he did; she believed he was a man totally lacking a moral compass—although Mahoney's compass was no more defective than those of his fellow politicians. But in this case, DeMarco figured that Emma and Mahoney would be in total agreement.

DeMarco's assignment had to do with an Alabama congressman named Clayton Sims. Sims represented Alabama's Seventh District— the only congressional district in Alabama represented by a Democrat. Sims, who was fifty-five, had held the job for fourteen years and in order to get elected, and stay elected, in a state that voted overwhelmingly Republican, Sims was basically purple—the color you get when you mix red and blue. He voted with the House D's, however, at least most of the time, and Mahoney had always thought he was a pretty good guy, although not the sharpest knife in the drawer. The problem was that Sims claimed to be the recipient of a Purple Heart—and Mahoney suspected he might be lying. And if he was lying, this was no small matter to John Mahoney.

There was nothing unusual about men—and it was almost always men—claiming to be recipients of military medals they'd never earned. There were in fact numerous documented instances of men showing up at public events wearing a uniform, their chests bedecked with phony medals they'd purchased online—sometimes even the Congressional Medal of Honor—when, in fact, these imposters had never been in the military at all. Most men who lied about their military service did so because they wanted to impress people. They wanted the slaps on the back; they wanted to hear "Thank you for your service"; they wanted, these least heroic of men, to be thought of as heroes.

Others, however, lied for financial gain. In one case a guy who'd never been in the military claimed to have been wounded in Vietnam and racked up over two hundred thousand dollars in VA benefits before he was caught. DeMarco had initially thought that the VA should easily be able to verify if a guy had served or not, or had been injured in combat or not, but the fact was that the records were so screwed up that this wasn't always the case.

The practice of people lying about their military service was in fact so egregious and offended so many veterans—John Mahoney being one of those veterans—that Congress, in a rare act of bipartisanship, passed the Stolen Valor Act in 2005 saying these liars should get up to a year in prison. But the act was overturned by the Supreme Court in 2012 in a 6 to 3 decision, the Supremes essentially saying the right to lie was protected by the First Amendment. In 2013, Congress, still pissed, passed a second Stolen Valor Act saying that if someone benefited in some tangible way by lying about his service, *then* he could end up in prison. Which made DeMarco wonder why they bothered passing the act at all since fraud had always been a crime.

Anyway, like all politicians who'd served in the military, Congressman Clayton Sims was proud to be a veteran—and made a big deal of his service record when he was campaigning. Sims, like Mahoney, had been a marine, and in 1983 he was in Lebanon. He was there the morning Hezbollah exploded two truck bombs destroying buildings housing American and French soldiers. Of the 241 American servicemen who were killed, 220 were marines. According to Sims, he'd been walking toward the barracks to meet a friend for breakfast, and had been less than a block away when the bombs went off. He was knocked briefly unconscious and was struck in the leg by a long piece of glass that he said was curved "like one of those Muslim daggers." He pulled out the piece of glass, used his shirt to bandage up a wound that was bleeding profusely, and then spent the next thirty-six hours trying to save marines buried and dying in the rubble.

When Sims first came to Congress, while Mahoney was still the Speaker of the House, Mahoney met the freshman congressman, and during their initial meeting, they talked about their shared experience as marines. The thing Mahoney remembered from that conversation was that Sims said he'd been injured in his right leg. Well, Mahoney had also been injured in the right leg. His right knee had been shredded by a Vietcong grenade, and on cold days, and on days when he was on his feet too much, his knee ached liked a bastard. Mahoney remembered Sims saying it was the same with him, how, for whatever reason, his leg also bothered him when the temperature dropped. Fourteen years then passed without Mahoney giving much thought at all to Sims's military record, although one year, when Mahoney went to Alabama to stump for Sims, Mahoney praised Sims for his service to his country—and the blood he'd shed in Lebanon.

But then, just a week ago, Mahoney and Sims happened to be seated at the same table at a fund-raiser for men and women who'd been severely injured in Afghanistan and Iraq—men and women missing legs and arms and eyes, men and women whose brains had been so badly damaged from the concussion of IEDs that they were but shells of their former selves. Being among these veterans who'd sacrificed so much, John Mahoney's eyes had welled up with tears more than once.

At that dinner, one young man—a young man using two high-tech prosthetic hands to hold his knife and fork—asked Congressmen Mahoney and Sims about their military service. Both politicians, being in the company of people who'd suffered so much worse than them, didn't say much and played down what they'd done. Sims told about being in Beirut when the marine barracks was demolished and said, "I can't believe to this day how lucky I was, with all the debris flying, that I was only hit in the leg." Then he slapped his thigh and said, "This baby still aches once in a while, but I'm not about to sit here with a guy like you and whine about it."

The problem was, he slapped his *left* thigh.

One thing Mahoney knew for sure is that you didn't forget which leg was injured in a combat-related injury, even thirty-plus years after the fact. And not when the injury was caused by a piece of glass that Sims had described as looking "like a dagger." Mahoney was appalled at the thought that Sims might be lying about a Purple Heart. He suspected that Sims—when he was just starting out his political career—had felt the need to embellish his military record and gave himself a medal he hadn't earned.

But Mahoney had a dilemma. In fact, he had two. First, he didn't really know if Sims had lied about the Purple Heart. Although it seemed unlikely, maybe Sims had just slapped the wrong leg by mistake. The bigger dilemma was that Mahoney didn't know what he was going to do if Sims had lied. If Sims had been a Republican and Mahoney knew that he'd lied about a Purple Heart, Mahoney would have pounced like a puma, ripped Sims to shreds, and raised enough hell that Sims would have been forced to resign. But Sims was not only a Democrat; he was the *only* Democratic congressman from Alabama and holding on to his district by the skin of his teeth. The last thing Mahoney wanted was another Republican in the House. At the same time, he couldn't bear the idea of serving with a politician who'd lied about a medal he hadn't earned. John Mahoney had many faults but when it came to the military and veterans, he was above reproach. It was the only area, as far as DeMarco could tell, where he was above reproach.

So Mahoney had told DeMarco he wanted to know the truth about Sims's supposed Purple Heart. He didn't, however, want DeMarco to contact the Pentagon directly or officially. Mahoney was afraid if an official inquiry was made, the media would learn about Sims's deceit and then Sims's fate would be out of Mahoney's hands. If Sims had lied about the Purple Heart, Mahoney would punish the man; he just wasn't sure what the punishment would be. And in order to accommodate his boss, DeMarco had gone to Emma because if anyone could find a way to look at Sims's service record in a quiet, under-the-table way, it was her.

"Thanks," DeMarco said. "I'll give you a call in a couple of days. But right now I gotta go find out why he's so hot for me to go to Boston."

DeMarco met Mahoney at his office in the Capitol. He started to tell him where things stood with Congressman Sims, but Mahoney said, "Forget about Sims for now. I'll deal with him later."

Mahoney proceeded to tell him about Elinore Dobbs. The thing that surprised DeMarco wasn't what Callahan was doing to Dobbs; that was hardly a unique story, a greedy developer doing underhanded things to move a tenant out of his way. What surprised DeMarco was Mahoney's demeanor. Mahoney was angry, of course, but he also seemed depressed, and Mahoney wasn't the type who got depressed. Mahoney, in fact, prided himself on causing depression in others. And he wasn't depressed about what was happening to Elinore Dobbs. He was depressed by his inability to help her. He ranted to DeMarco about how guys like Callahan—guys with real money—had no respect for Congress or the law or anything else, knowing they could buy their way out of almost any situation.

DeMarco almost said: *So what else is new?*

"She's got three years remaining on her lease," Mahoney said, "and her plan is to fight Callahan for all three of those years. She knows she'll have to move when her lease expires but until then she's going to make his life as miserable as she can. The problem is, what I did up there in Boston isn't going to help for long. In a couple of weeks the media will lose interest and the cops will back off on patrolling the place. On top of that, the mayor and the city council guys are in Callahan's pocket, and they don't really want to help. This means that before long, Callahan will go back to doing everything he can to force her out unless you can figure out some way to stop him."

"How the hell am I supposed to do that if you couldn't?" DeMarco asked.

"I don't know. Figure something out. That's your goddamn job!" Mahoney screamed.

Oh, boy. He could tell that Mahoney was in no mood to listen to reason.

But that *was* DeMarco's job: fixing things that Mahoney wanted fixed. DeMarco had worked for Mahoney for years, starting out right after he obtained a law degree he'd never used. Instead of practicing law, he'd become Mahoney's troubleshooter. Or at least, that's the way DeMarco preferred to think of himself. Mahoney's staff in D.C. handled the day-to-day political shenanigans related to passing laws—or not passing laws—but DeMarco was the one Mahoney used when he wanted something done that required a certain degree of tricky underhandedness. To put it another way, DeMarco was the guy Mahoney called when the law itself became a roadblock and Mahoney needed a way around the barricade. DeMarco was also the man Mahoney sent to collect campaign funds from those donors who wished to remain anonymous and preferred to pay in cash, which meant DeMarco was also Mahoney's bagman—a job description he didn't like. He had no idea, however, what he was going to do when it came to Elinore Dobbs. If a politician with Mahoney's clout couldn't deter Callahan, and if the people who ran the city of Boston were on Callahan's side, then what could he possibly do? But he knew this wasn't the time to debate the issue with Mahoney, so he flew to Boston.

7

———◆———

DeMarco checked in to the Park Plaza Hotel off Arlington Street, picking the hotel primarily because it was centrally located and reasonably priced.

DeMarco liked Boston. He liked the harbor where Old Ironsides anchored at the pier, the food stalls at Faneuil Hall, and the Italian restaurants in the North End. He liked the churches and the cemeteries built before the War for Independence, and seeing the university crew teams sculling on the Charles in the morning mist. And then there was Fenway.

For a baseball fan, Fenway was like the Vatican for Catholics, like Mecca for Muslims. Fenway was a cathedral and the Green Monster—the thirty-seven-foot wall in left field—was its high altar. Yeah, De-Marco was happy to be back in Boston, although not so happy about the reason he was there.

He decided the first thing he'd do was go see Elinore Dobbs. She lived in west Boston on Delaney Street, a street that ran roughly parallel to the Massachusetts Turnpike and was only a few blocks from the Charles River. When Mahoney had told him that Callahan was a developer and trying to force Elinore out of her apartment, DeMarco had assumed that Callahan was just knocking down a building or two and erecting more modern ones. He was completely wrong.

Callahan's development was enormous, taking up several city blocks. Dump trucks, bulldozers, and cement trucks were all over the place, and the *beep-beep* of large vehicles backing up was almost continuous. There were six large buildings at various stages of construction and DeMarco could see at least a hundred workers in hard hats, and he imagined there were a lot more he couldn't see. Five tall yellow cranes, like one-armed giants, loomed over the site. In a couple of the buildings workers were using nail guns to install interior framing and it sounded as if a military engagement was taking place.

Delaney Street cut through the heart of the development, and on the eastern edge of the project, where DeMarco was standing, there was a ten-by-ten-foot poster that showed an artist's rendition of the completed development and provided a few helpful facts. The project was to be called Delaney Square, and it would occupy fourteen acres and cost approximately five hundred million dollars. There would be a twelve-story corporate headquarters for a solar energy company; a twenty-story hotel with 175 rooms; four office buildings with 850,000 square feet of office space; a three-acre public park called Delaney Commons; and retail shops and restaurants too numerous to count. All the work would be completed in about two and a half years if everything stayed on schedule, and Delaney Square would generate twelve million dollars in property taxes annually, and provide jobs for six hundred construction workers at its peak and three thousand permanent jobs for the people who would occupy the office buildings and retail stores. Lastly, the project would include two hundred luxury apartments at the far western end—which was where Elinore Dobbs lived.

Because of all the construction work taking place, DeMarco had to walk around the site to reach the block where Elinore's apartment building was located. He had no idea what had been there before because almost every building on Elinore's block had been demolished. Now there was one massive hole in the ground that took up three-quarters of the block, and at the western end of the street were four old triple-deckers that were vacant, the doors and windows missing, the interiors gutted. It appeared that they were just waiting for their appointment with the wrecking ball. Across the street from the triple-deckers, on a corner, stood Elinore's apartment building, the only habitable structure remaining. To DeMarco it looked like Custer's last soldier, just waiting for the arrows to start flying.

DeMarco walked over and peered down at the large hole in the ground where the new building was being erected. All he could see were concrete foundation pieces with rebar sticking out. On the cyclone fence surrounding the hole, however, was another large poster showing the residential units that Callahan was constructing, and there were photographs of model apartments with walk-in closets, kitchens with marble countertops, high ceilings, glossy hardwood floors, and large balconies where the tenants could sit on pleasant evenings sipping their martinis. The new building would also contain a fitness center, a pool, and a rooftop garden/party area. DeMarco figured the penthouse units would sell for a couple of million, maybe more. Retail stores would be located on the ground floor of the building. In addition to the inevitable Starbucks so the yuppies could start off their day with a nonfat latte would be a yoga studio, an art gallery, and a hip bistro that sold vegetarian gluten-free meals.

Also included in the design was an interior landscaped courtyard that would be inaccessible to the unwashed masses. The courtyard would have stone benches, shade trees, and a fountain, and would be a fine place for the nannies hired by young working couples to sit with their charges and gossip about their employers. It was clear that Callahan's luxury apartment complex would be an urban paradise—a private Eden minus the serpent—for anyone who made two or three hundred grand a year.

DeMarco headed across the street toward Elinore's place. The street in front of her building had been ripped up, the sidewalks had been replaced by muddy sheets of plywood, dust swirled in the air, and the noise of a nearby jackhammer was almost deafening. DeMarco considered himself to be a fairly stubborn guy, but he was thinking that if he were Elinore, he would have given up a long time ago and taken whatever Callahan was offering to move to somewhere clean and quiet.

Elinore's building was five stories tall, made of brown brick, and had probably been constructed around the time of the Second World War. DeMarco found it charming with its Paris-like mansard roof, dormer windows, and marble cornices. It had been built in an era when workers still took pride in their work and cost wasn't the only consideration. He noticed that some of the units on the upper two floors had small balconies enclosed with black wrought iron, the balconies barely big enough to hold a lawn chair and a barbeque.

He walked up the stone steps leading to the front door and saw that the latch assembly on the door had been removed so the door would no longer lock or stay shut. DeMarco entered a small lobby that was littered with trash—fast-food cartons, beer cans, bottles, and one tired old army blanket probably crawling with lice. There were about thirty mailboxes on one wall in the lobby, but the boxes had been flattened as if someone had smashed them with a hammer. There was also a small, ancient elevator, which surprised DeMarco as most places as old as Elinore's building didn't have elevators—not that it mattered. There was an OUT OF SERVICE sign on the elevator door and when he pushed the UP button, nothing happened.

Elinore lived on the fourth floor, so DeMarco trudged up a wooden staircase with a dark oak banister and ball-topped newel posts. The steps were shiny and a bit concave from age and use. None of the lights on the stair landings were turned on, but there was enough illumination coming from the stained glass window on each landing that he could see. Barely. If any of the tenants had to take the stairs at night, they would have needed a flashlight.

As he walked down the fourth-floor hallway toward Elinore's unit, he noticed the doors had been removed on all the vacant apartments. He passed one apartment that still had a door with what looked like a new lock. The door had been spray painted with graffiti, meaningless swirls of red paint. He could hear a television playing on the other side of the door and remembered Mahoney saying there were three or four other tenants in addition to Elinore holding out against Callahan.

Elinore lived in a corner unit. The first thing DeMarco noticed was that although her door was tagged with graffiti, too, it was made of metal not wood and the frame around the door was also metal. The door appeared to be indestructible. There was a peephole in the door and it looked as if someone had sprayed paint directly onto the peephole, but the paint had been cleaned off the glass. He could hear a radio playing inside the apartment but when he knocked, no one answered. He knocked again, and the peephole darkened.

"What do you want?" a voice said.

"Elinore, my name's Joe DeMarco. John Mahoney sent me."

"How do I know that?"

"I'm going to hold up my congressional ID. Will you be able to see it through the peephole?"

"Yeah. Show it to me."

DeMarco did, and a moment later the door opened.

"That blowhard really sent you?" Elinore said.

DeMarco laughed and said, "Yeah, he really did."

"Well, I'll be damned. I figured I'd never hear from him again after that photo op."

Like Mahoney, DeMarco liked Elinore Dobbs the moment he met her. He liked her boyishly cut gray hair and her bright blue eyes and the Springsteen T-shirt she was wearing. On her feet were red Converse tennis shoes, about a size five. She came across as Mahoney had described her: tough and feisty but with a sense of humor; she struck

48

DeMarco as a person who almost always enjoyed life—or would enjoy it if Sean Callahan gave her the chance.

"Mahoney cares, Elinore," DeMarco said. "Plus Callahan really pissed him off, and that's even better than him caring about you."

"Well, okay. Come on in. You want a beer?"

"Sure," DeMarco said.

Elinore's apartment was small, as he'd expected. The living room was no more than two hundred square feet, but there was a window with a dormer seat facing Delaney Street, and on the side perpendicular to Delaney, there were French doors allowing access to a tiny balcony, like the ones he'd seen from the street. He imagined the place had only a single bedroom, and the kitchen was compact and had appliances that were twenty years old. He'd seen galleys in powerboats that had bigger kitchens.

The living room was painted eggshell white and there were large photos on the walls of nature scenes—a New England country road in the fall, a stream flowing over boulders, tree trunks bright green with moss—and he suspected that Elinore had taken the photos. There wasn't much furniture in the living room, however—just a brown leather recliner facing a late-model television set—and the reason why was because this was the room that Elinore had staged to withstand Sean Callahan's siege.

Along one wall were at least ten cases of bottled water and canned food. There was a propane camp stove sitting on a small folding table so Elinore could cook her meals when Callahan cut the power to her electric stove, and a large cooler she could fill with crushed ice to keep her food cold. There were two fans for when the air-conditioning system didn't work—both fans were on now, pushing warm air around the room—and an electric heater and three or four blankets for when the heat was cut off. And a couple other items of note.

"Is that a generator?" DeMarco asked.

"Yeah, ain't it a beauty? It's got electronic ignition so I don't have to yank my arm off trying to start it with a pull cord, and enough juice to power everything I need."

"You can't use a generator inside," DeMarco said. "You're going to kill yourself with carbon monoxide fumes."

"I'm not a total idiot," Elinore said. "I roll the generator onto the balcony if I need it and in the winter, I run the cord through the door and seal the opening with duct tape to keep from losing heat. I keep the gasoline out on the balcony too."

Jesus. "What's in the boxes?" he asked, pointing to two large, white cardboard boxes stacked against one wall.

"All my records of the things Callahan's done to force me out, and my correspondence with all the bureaucrats and lawyers who haven't helped me. I keep copies of everything, including a letter I sent to Mahoney that he never answered."

Then DeMarco saw the gun.

"Aw, man, you got a rifle?"

"Shotgun. That's a Ruger over-and-under twelve gauge. I've never had to fire it, but I know how."

DeMarco figured if she ever did fire it, the recoil would knock ninety-pound Elinore flat on her back.

"I got it before I replaced the wooden door with my new metal one. I've been vandalized twice. If anyone tries to break in while I'm here, I'll blow their asses to kingdom come."

"Well, that door should keep them out," DeMarco said. "But . . ."

Elinore laughed. "A SWAT team couldn't get through that door."

"But I think you should get rid of the shotgun."

"Hey! What would you do if someone broke into your apartment and trashed all your stuff and shit on your bed? Almost all my furniture's new—well, new secondhand from Goodwill—because they destroyed everything I had."

"And you think these guys you told Mahoney about are the ones who broke in? The McNally brothers."

"The McNultys. And I know it was them. I just can't prove it."

"Has anyone bothered you since Mahoney held the press conference?"

"No. But it's only been a few days. And a cop stopped by once and asked if I was all right. But that won't last."

"How many other tenants are still in the building?"

"Here, let me get your beer and a chair so you can sit."

She handed him a Budweiser and a folding lawn chair. She took a seat in the recliner; she was so short her feet didn't reach the floor. She popped the top on her beer, took a sip, and said, "That hits the spot. I usually have one a day." She looked at DeMarco for a moment as if she was studying him. "You sort of remind me of my husband. He was a good-looking guy, too, and built like you."

DeMarco was a broad-shouldered five eleven. From his Italian father he'd inherited thick dark hair he combed straight back, a prominent nose, and a square chin with a cleft in it. His Irish mother's only genetic contribution was his blue eyes. He had a hard-looking face—and although he'd been through a few tough scrapes working for Mahoney he'd never thought of himself as a hard man.

"Is your husband still alive?" DeMarco asked.

"No. Pete died when he was fifty-two," Elinore said. "He was a fireman and had a heart attack one day going up a flight of stairs carrying a coil of hose that weighed a hundred pounds."

"How long's he been gone?"

"Well, we were the same age and I'm eighty-two, so he's been gone thirty years now. He was a lot of fun. But hey, life goes on."

"And you never remarried?"

"Nah. Who wants to start dating again at fifty? I mean, I know lots of women do. They go looking for a man on those computer-dating sites because they're lonely or need somebody or something. But I've never been lonely. I've got lots of friends and I keep busy. I used to be a nurse but after I retired, and before Sean Callahan came along and tried to destroy my life, I did charity work—helped teach kids to read, helped out at a soup kitchen. Don't have time for that stuff these days, of course."

DeMarco couldn't believe she was eighty-two. She didn't look it. And there was obviously nothing wrong with her mind.

"I was asking how many other tenants are still in the building."

"Only three now. There's Mrs. Polanski, down the hall from me."

DeMarco remembered the one door that was closed when he walked down the hall.

"She's only seventy-two but she's got dementia and she really should be in an assisted-living place. Her daughter's been trying to get her to leave, but Mrs. Polanski won't go. She's living in absolute squalor, doesn't bathe, doesn't wash her clothes anymore, and eats nothing but bananas and beans cold out of the can. Her daughter stops in and sees her every couple of days, and I drop in on her every day. Anyway, she's in bad shape and doesn't belong here, but her daughter's one of these people who's just *overwhelmed* by everything. But one of these days, she's going to have to get a court order or something and force her mom to move. And, Callahan, don't you know, has people meeting with her daughter trying to get her to do just that." Elinore sighed. "It's horrible when the mind goes before the body does."

DeMarco just nodded, but he was thinking she was right. He'd much rather have a heart attack at fifty-two like her late husband than end up with Alzheimer's.

"Then there's the Spieglemans down on the third floor," Elinore said. "They're in their late seventies. In fact, he might be eighty. He wants to move but Loretta—Mrs. Spiegleman—won't let him. She's on my side in this whole thing. The problem is Loretta's got health issues, and she's fading fast. As soon as she goes, Spiegleman—who doesn't have the guts God gave a chicken—will be out of here. Right now, he's afraid to leave their apartment because he's afraid he'll run into the McNultys.

"The last guy's a nut. He's down on the third floor, too. His name is Goodman and he's a young guy, only fifty-eight, but he's agoraphobic. He hasn't left his apartment in fifteen years. He just sits inside—he's got a gun like me—terrified. He has all his stuff delivered, although lots of times the McNultys will scare off the delivery guys. Callahan has a psychiatrist working on him—calls him on the phone every day—trying to get him over his phobia long enough to relocate."

Jesus, DeMarco thought. *What a band of misfits.*

Elinore laughed. "I'll bet you in a couple of months I'll be the only one still here."

"Maybe you should move," DeMarco said. Gesturing at the bottled water and the camp stove, he added, "This is no way to live. I mean, I know you're trying to make a statement about what people like Callahan are doing, but still. Callahan told Mahoney that he offered you two hundred grand. That's a lot of money."

"I'm not moving until my lease is up. And that's that," Elinore said. "As for the money he's offering, I don't need his money. I get a percentage of my husband's pension from the fire department, plus he had a life insurance policy I invested. I also get a small pension from the hospital where I used to work—back when I retired nurses still got pensions—and I get Social Security. So I got all the money I need. Plus, I like screwing with Callahan. I'm actually having a pretty good time taking him on."

DeMarco laughed but he was thinking in three years, when her lease expired, she'd be eighty-five—but he could see her still going strong until then. He could see Elinore Dobbs living to a hundred.

"So what are you doing here in Boston, Joe?"

"Mahoney sent me to check on you and to see if I could figure out some way to make Callahan stop harassing you. But I don't have a clue how to do that."

"Well, I appreciate you coming. You want another brew? I think, just to celebrate your arrival, I'll break my rule and have two today."

"Sure, why not. And maybe you can tell me more about the McNultys."

8

"He wants us to whack the old broad," Roy McNulty said. "He didn't say it, but that's what he wants."

"Yeah, I know," Ray said.

It was eleven in the morning and they were sitting in the Shamrock, drinking coffee spiked with Jameson's to kick-start their day. There were no customers in the bar. Doreen Vaughn, their bartender/manager/tenant, was behind the bar, reading the *Globe*. Doreen was short but broad—she probably weighed in at about 180—and her upper arms were bigger than the McMultys'. Her hair resembled a dark red Brillo pad and she had large brown freckles on her face. Right now, Doreen was pissed at them. She'd asked them to change out one of the beer kegs under the bar because her back was bothering her, but they'd told her to do it herself, as they were busy.

"Well, I ain't gonna do it," Ray said. "We kill her, we'll be suspects number one and two, and I'm not risking life in prison to get a new sign for the bar."

"He was talking about more than just a new sign," Roy said. "But I hear you. So, you got any ideas?"

"No. Maybe we oughta drive over there and just look around. Maybe something will come to us."

"Yeah, okay. Hey, Doreen," Roy called over to the bar. "We're going out for a while. "

Doreen flipped him the bird.

———————◆◆◆———————

They drove to the apartment building on Delaney in their old white Ford Econoline van. They had a sweet fire-engine-red Camaro that they got for practically nothing because they bought it directly from the guy who stole it, but they only drove it on special occasions. They sure as hell weren't going to drive it to a construction site where it would get all dirty.

On the way, some big mouth on WBZ started going on about Brady and the Patriots, and how they were going to crush everyone when the season started.

"Aw, Brady's washed up," Roy said. "The guy's damn near forty and . . ."

Roy had been speaking to the man on the radio, but Ray answered. "Washed up? Brady? You gotta be, without a doubt, the dumbest fuckin' white guy in Boston. Brady just won a Super Bowl and—"

"Brady didn't *win* the fucking Super Bowl. That idiot Seattle coach lost it, calling a pass on the one-yard line. And I'm telling you Brady . . ."

They argued about the Patriots quarterback until they reached the apartment building. As they entered the building, they saw the scrawny old guy, Spiegleman, who lived on the third floor with his wife, starting up the stairs holding a Walgreens bag.

"Hey! What have you got in that bag?" Roy said.

Spiegleman's head spun about and his eyes went wide with fear; he looked like a cornered rat. In fact, with his pointy nose, he looked exactly like a rat. For a minute Ray thought he might try to run up the stairs to get away from them—then Spiegleman apparently realized he could barely walk up the stairs, much less run. His voice quivered when he said, "It's my wife's medication, for her emphysema."

The McNultys walked over to him, standing close, looming over him as Spiegleman was only five foot four. "How do we know you don't have drugs in that bag," Roy said.

Spiegleman looked confused. "I *do* have drugs in the bag. I told you. My wife's medication."

"I don't mean those kind of drugs, you dumb shit. I mean real drugs, like heroin or something. This is a drug-free zone. Says so on that sign right down the street."

"What?" Spiegleman said.

Roy laughed. "Go on. Get out of here. I'm just fuckin' with you. Can't you take a joke?"

They watched Spiegleman start up the stairs, moving at the pace of an arthritic snail. When he turned once to see if the McNultys were still there, he tripped slightly and would have fallen if he hadn't been holding on to the handrail.

"So what do you want to do now that we're here?" Roy said.

Ray didn't answer. He was watching Spiegleman move up the stairs.

DeMarco was in the office of Superintendent Francis O'Rourke, the man in charge of BPD's Bureau of Field Services. O'Rourke was a slender, scholarly-looking man in his late fifties with wire-rimmed glasses and short gray hair. He was dressed in his uniform blues, not a suit. On the I-love-me wall behind his desk were photos of a young O'Rourke as a patrolman and one of him dressed in body armor with a SWAT team. In addition to a dozen plaques and framed certificates attesting to his service to the city of Boston, there was also a glass case holding a

folded American flag and the medals O'Rourke had received when he
was in the military. DeMarco noticed that one of O'Rourke's medals
was a Purple Heart.

The Bureau of Field Services, per the department's website, had "primary responsibility for the implementation of Community Policing
and the delivery of effective and efficient police services to the community"—among other things. Mahoney had given him O'Rourke's
name, saying that; O'Rourke was the senior cop in the department
responsible for protecting Elinore Dobbs.

And DeMarco got the impression that O'Rourke genuinely cared
about Elinore—although he may have been faking it to stay on Mahoney's good side. To reach his level in the bureaucracy, O'Rourke had
probably developed some acting skills.

"You have to understand, there's only so much we can do," O'Rourke
said. "I have patrol cars in the area and one of my men will stop in and
check on Elinore periodically. But unless Callahan or those two thugs
he's got working for him do something illegal—I mean something more
than turning off the power—I can't arrest them."

"Tell me about the thugs," DeMarco said.

O'Rourke shook his head. "They're a couple of rabid dogs. The older
one, Ray, did a year when he was seventeen for stealing a car. It was
actually the third time he'd been popped for grand theft auto but after
getting two free passes, the judge gave him a year at Westborough. After
that, he and his brother have been arrested multiple times, but haven't
actually spent all that much time in jail. The arrests were for drug possession, DUIs, shoplifting, stuff like that. One time when gasoline
prices were high, they ran around for six months siphoning gas from
all the cars in their neighborhood until they finally got caught.

"But mostly they've been arrested for assault, usually bar fights. Some
citizen would piss them off—and it doesn't take much to piss them
off—and they'd double-team the guy and pound him into hamburger.
The longest time they spent in jail was two years when they damn near

killed a guy who annoyed them at a Red Sox game. But their records don't tell the whole story. They got a bar in Revere . . ."

DeMarco knew Revere was a suburb five miles north of Boston.

". . . and after Mahoney called me, I talked to the chief who runs the department there. He told me the McNultys are hooked up with the mob down in Providence. They're like . . . You ever been to a Home Depot and seen those guys standing outside looking for work? You know, day laborers? That's what the McNultys are for the Providence mob. If they need a couple guys to drive a truck to pick up or deliver something, they'll call the McNultys if they don't have anyone else handy. The main thing they use them for is cigarettes."

"Cigarettes?"

"Yeah. Cigarette smuggling is a big deal. An article in the *Globe* said it's costing the state as much as two hundred and fifty million a year in lost revenue."

"I don't understand," DeMarco said.

"You know how much a pack of Marlboros costs in Boston? Almost nine bucks. It's even higher in New York. In Virginia, that same pack costs about five bucks, and it's because sin taxes on cigarettes in Massachusetts and New York are the highest in the nation. So you go down to Virginia, buy a truckload of cigarettes for five bucks a pack, and sell them here for seven bucks, which the smokers like, and you make a profit of two dollars on every pack. The cigarettes get sold under the table in all the bars and mom-and-pop stores, who know they're buying cigarettes without the state tax stamp, but they figure, hey, it's not like they're selling heroin.

"Anyway, if Providence needs a couple guys to make a run to Richmond and bring back a truckload of cigarettes, then distribute the cigarettes all over Boston, they might call the McNultys. The chief in Revere figures they probably made the Providence connection the last time they were in prison."

"So why haven't they been arrested?"

"Because they're the fleas on the dog, and the FBI and the organized crime guys in Providence are after the dog, not the fleas. They know the McNultys are there on the fringes but they're not worth the energy for surveillances and warrants and wiretaps and all that rigmarole. And like I said, we're talking cigarettes."

"What about their connection to Sean Callahan?"

O'Rourke shook his head. "Now that's weird. Callahan went to school with those mutts and as near as I can tell, they're still friends. But Callahan appears to be a standup citizen. He's big into charities and he's on Boston's A-list, but for whatever reason, he gives the McNultys work. He'll hire them for construction or demolition work but more often as haulers. Or, like he's doing now, as his so-called building superintendents in the building where Dobbs lives.

"So I don't know what else to tell you, DeMarco, except for this. Be careful with the McNultys. They're dangerous. They're the kind of guys who act first and think later. What I'm saying is, you make them mad, they're liable to pick up a two-by-four and beat you to death because it won't occur to them until later that killing you could land them in prison for life."

———— ◆◆◆ ————

DeMarco wasn't exactly sure what to do next, but thought he should go see a lawyer who specialized in property law. Although DeMarco may have been a lawyer, what he knew about property law could fit into a thimble. Or maybe half a thimble.

The lawyer he had in mind was a guy named Dooley who he'd gone to law school with, and who now lived in Boston. DeMarco occasionally had a beer with Dooley when he visited the city on Mahoney's behalf because he enjoyed Dooley's company and liked his wife. He pulled out his phone to call Dooley, but before he could punch in the number, his phone rang. It was Elinore.

"The McNultys are here," Elinore said, sounding out of breath.

"Are they bothering you?"

"No, they're just walking around the building. When I asked them what they were doing, they said they were doing their job, making sure everything's working okay."

"So is everything okay?"

"Yeah, for now. The power's on and the water's hot. The air-conditioning's still broke and when I asked about that, they said they had a guy coming out to look at the system, but I could tell they were lying."

"Huh," DeMarco said. "But they haven't threatened you or anything?"

"No, but they're up to something. I called because I thought you might want to have a word with them."

"I do," DeMarco said. "I'll be right over."

"Good," Elinore said.

DeMarco again had to park a couple blocks from Elinore's building because of all the construction work in the area. When he got to her place, he called her and asked if she knew where the McNultys were. She said she didn't, but suggested he go to the basement where all the equipment was—the electrical panels, the furnace, that sort of stuff.

He descended the staircase to the basement and because the landing lights weren't lit, kept his hand on the rail to keep from tripping and breaking his neck. He found the McNultys in a room that had a scarred workbench with a vise on one end and hand tools hanging on hooks attached to a pegboard. They were eating hoagies and drinking Budweisers and he heard one of them say, "So one thing we gotta do is put in a new bulb."

DeMarco didn't know what bulb they were talking about but later he would remember that one simple sentence.

At that moment, they saw him standing in the doorway and one of them graciously said, "Who the fuck are you?"

DeMarco smiled. "My name's DeMarco. And I just wanted to see you two and let you know that you're going to end up in jail if you keep harassing Elinore Dobbs."

Both men immediately stood up. They were wearing cargo shorts and tight white T-shirts and tennis shoes without socks. DeMarco knew their names were Roy and Ray, but didn't know which one was which. He did notice that one of them was missing a piece of his right ear. They were shorter than DeMarco by a couple of inches but powerfully built, with long muscular arms and big hands with knobby knuckles clenched into fists.

"What did you just say?" The one who spoke was the one with both ears intact.

And DeMarco thought: *Oh-oh.*

"Guys, I'm here to pass on a message. I work for Congressman John Mahoney and he sent me here to let you know that he's got Elinore's back. And I just finished talking to a superintendent in the BPD, and he's got her back, too. He's going to have his cops dropping in on her to make sure she's okay. If you guys harass her or threaten her, you're going to get arrested."

"Arrested for what? Talking to her?" the other one said.

DeMarco ignored the comment, because, for one reason, the guy had a point. They weren't likely to get arrested unless there was a witness.

"I've also got a lawyer looking into ways to sue you," DeMarco said. "And I mean you *personally*, not Sean Callahan. The lawyers are going to show that you turning off the power is putting the people who live here at risk. If one of these old people dies of heatstroke because it's a hundred degrees outside and you've intentionally disabled the air-conditioning system, they can put you in jail for manslaughter."

DeMarco didn't have any lawyers looking into anything and had no idea if he could make a manslaughter charge stick if someone died—but he figured the McNultys knew even less about the law than he did.

He'd expected that after his little speech the McNultys would deny that they were doing anything illegal—but that wasn't the response he got. Instead the one with two good ears said, "We're gonna kick your ass."

DeMarco realized at that moment that he should have listened to Superintendent O'Rourke. Like O'Rourke had said, these were two people with zero impulse control. They were very likely to beat him to a pulp and then, while he lay bleeding and broken on the floor, realize that they'd done something they shouldn't have. But, as O'Rourke had warned him, they wouldn't think about that until after they beat him half to death. It had been a mistake confronting them by himself, and even worse to do so down in the basement of the building.

DeMarco thought about running, but didn't. He had too much pride to run from these two. He did look to see if there was something he could use for a weapon and figured if he could make it over to the workbench there were a couple of big crescent wrenches that would do. The problem was that these long-armed apes were between him and the workbench.

Then the other one put his hand on the shoulder of the guy who had said they were going to kick his ass. "Not here, Roy," he said.

Ah, so Ray was the one with the mutilated ear—and in this case, Ray was his savior. DeMarco also later remembered the words "not here."

Then Ray McNulty, his savior, said, "But if you think some guy in a suit working for a politician scares us, you don't know where the fuck you're at."

※

After his friendly chat with the McNultys, DeMarco took the stairs to Elinore's fourth-floor apartment. It was stifling inside even with all the windows open and Elinore's two fans spinning. Elinore was in a good mood, however, and DeMarco suspected she was almost always in a good mood. She was listening to a radio playing rock music from the seventies and had just finished making some banana bread for the lady down the hall with Alzheimer's. He told her about his conversation with the McNultys, leaving out the part where he'd been worried about getting beaten to death.

She asked if he wanted a cup of coffee, which he declined. He told her he was going to talk to a lawyer to see if there was anything else that could be done about Callahan making her living conditions so miserable. Elinore said she appreciated that, but doubted a lawyer was going to do much good.

She left the apartment with him, her freshly baked banana bread wrapped in tinfoil. After she delivered the bread to Mrs. Polanski and checked on the Spieglemans downstairs, she said she was going to a movie in a theater with air-conditioning, a movie starring Brad Pitt. Brad, she said, was a hunk and a half.

DeMarco left the building and while standing on the sidewalk at the bottom of the steps, he called his old law school pal, Dooley, and suggested they meet for a drink. Dooley said how 'bout the Warren Tavern in Charlestown. Dooley now lived in a recently gentrified area of Charlestown, in a luxurious apartment constructed by a developer like Sean Callahan, and the apartment was within walking distance of the tavern.

As he was talking to Dooley, the McNulty brothers came out of the building and Roy McNulty pointed his finger at DeMarco, a gesture DeMarco interpreted as some sort of juvenile, I'll-be-seeing-you-later threat. DeMarco ignored the gesture and turned his back to them, and just as they were walking past him, he said into the phone, "Got it. The Warren Tavern at eight."

9

The Warren Tavern is in a white clapboard three-story building on Pleasant Street in Charlestown. It was established in 1780 and is supposedly the oldest tavern in Massachusetts; Paul Revere and George Washington had patronized the place. The wooden floor near the front door was made of twelve-inch-wide planks that were painted black—or maybe they were black from people walking on them for the last two centuries. The floor certainly looked old and worn enough that it was possible that George Washington's boots had trod upon it.

There was a painting of Old Ironsides—the USS *Constitution*—on one wall, and one of Paul Revere on another. In the Revere painting, the famous silversmith was holding a metal teapot, presumably one made by his own hands. Behind the bar—which was constructed of ancient-looking four-inch-wide planks polished to a high gloss—was a wide-screen television set showing a soccer game. DeMarco could never understand the appeal of soccer, a bunch of guys running around for an hour and a half and hardly ever scoring. He'd always thought that soccer would be a lot more entertaining if they reduced the number of players to six on a side so someone might score more than one or two goals a game. But, hey, more people on the planet liked the game than baseball and basketball combined, so what did he know?

DeMarco was dressed in shorts, a Nationals T-shirt, and topsiders without socks; it was too damn hot to wear anything more formal. Dooley and his wife were also wearing shorts, but instead of T-shirts they had on polo shirts with animals on the breast, a little alligator on hers, a little pony on his. Dooley's wife looked particularly good in shorts. She was tall and slender, and possibly possessed the best thighs in Boston. DeMarco had no idea how Dooley—who was short and tending toward pudginess—had managed to snag such a good-looking woman. DeMarco also had the impression—although maybe it was just his imagination—that Anna Dooley was coming on to him the way she looked into his eyes and patted him on his bare thigh every so often to emphasize whatever she was saying. They spent three hours drinking beer, munching on appetizers, and talking—but devoted no more than thirty minutes to Elinore's plight.

Dooley explained that the law was on Elinore's side—and damn near useless in aiding her. He said under Massachusetts's law, all landlords owe tenants something called a Warranty of Habitability.

"This means," Dooley said, "that a landlord is obligated to keep an apartment in good condition from the time you move in and until you leave." Furthermore, according to Lawyer Dooley, Sean Callahan was guilty of a "Breach of Quiet Enjoyment."

"What the hell's that?" DeMarco said. "Breach of quiet enjoyment" sounded like you were blocking someone's view of a sunset.

"It's a law," Dooley said, "that says a landlord can't interfere with your enjoyment of your apartment and requires him to furnish, among other things, utilities. In other words, the landlord has to provide electrical power and heat and hot water. And when the landlord fails to provide these things, the tenant can sue and ask that his lease be terminated or that the landlord pay back the rent the tenant's paid."

"Elinore doesn't want to terminate her lease," DeMarco said.

"I know," Dooley said. "So all the court can do is make Callahan pay restitution. That is, he can be forced to pay restitution if Elinore is able to place a value on Callahan's breach of her quiet enjoyment, which is tough to do. But the biggest problem Elinore has is that time is on Callahan's side.

"First, and as I'm sure Elinore has already done, she has to notify her landlord in writing of the ways he's failed to meet his obligations, then Callahan is allowed a reasonable amount of time to resolve Elinore's complaints, *reasonable* being weeks. Then when he fails to resolve her written complaints, Elinore can sue and the court sets a date to hear the case that's maybe six months later. Meanwhile, Elinore has to live without heat and power. Then the case finally goes to court after Callahan's lawyers have delayed as long as possible, and the court finds in favor of Elinore and orders Callahan to make restitution and fix the problems. Maybe the court orders him to give Elinore back whatever rent she's paid—which Callahan, of course, doesn't give a shit about— then he temporarily restores power and a few weeks later he shuts it off, and Elinore has to go back to court again. Usually what happens is the landlord wears the tenants down and they vacate, happy to accept any kind of settlement they can get.

"The real problem is that the judge is unlikely to do anything truly onerous to Callahan, such as throw his rich ass in jail. He'll be given citations that he ignores and fines imposed by the court that don't bother him one damn bit because once he forces Elinore out, he's going to make more than enough money to pay whatever fines he gets."

"But there must be something that—" DeMarco started to say but Dooley cut in.

"Let me tell you a story reported in the *Globe* a couple years ago. There's a landlord here in Boston who owns a bunch of run-down apartment buildings in Dorchester and Roxbury and he rents mostly to minorities who can't afford to live anywhere else. This guy—this slumlord—is a multimillionaire and he lives in a mansion in an exclusive area in Wellesley. Anyway, in the last ten years, he's been the defendant in over twenty lawsuits, has been taken to the Boston Housing

Court almost a hundred times, and has been cited for over five hundred safety and health code violations."

"What kind of violations?" DeMarco asked.

"Every kind you can think of," Dooley said. "There are rats and roaches in the apartments. The appliances don't work. The roofs leak. The wiring isn't up to code and it's lucky that none of his places have burned to the ground. And if you did have a fire, you can't open windows to get to the fire escapes. Anyway, like I said, he's been cited hundreds of times in a ten-year period and has been to Housing Court so often he should have a courtroom named after him. And do you want to know what the city has done to make this scumbag change his ways?"

"Yeah," DeMarco said.

"He's been given a grand total of forty thousand bucks in fines, of which he's paid less than ten percent because his lawyers have managed to get the fines dismissed. He hasn't spent a single day in jail. So if you think Elinore Dobbs can really cause Callahan a problem, you're dreaming."

"Well, shit," DeMarco said.

"Yeah, it's a shame," Dooley said. "On the other hand, those old buildings like hers don't have enough closet space and there often isn't room for washers and driers inside the units. They usually don't have more than a couple of electrical outlets in each room so you can't plug in all your electronics, and the kitchens are so small you can't even put in a dishwasher. Anna and I certainly don't want to live in a place like that, so if a landlord wants to attract renters with money, he needs to renovate."

"My God," Anna Dooley said. "Can you even imagine having to wash dishes by hand?"

The Dooleys were clearly grateful that some developer had remodeled their condo in Charlestown—and they weren't losing any sleep wondering where the people who used to live there had gone. As for those like Elinore not being able to afford to live in a place like theirs . . .

"Hey, what can you do?" Dooley said.

After that they just BS'd, Dooley and DeMarco recounting drunken escapades from law school that sounded better in the retelling than they'd actually been. DeMarco described life in D.C. surrounded by useless politicians, while avoiding talking exactly about what he did for Mahoney. Dooley, without being an ass about it, made it clear that he was a roaring success in his law firm.

As for Anna Dooley, she worked for a PR firm and it sounded as if she was a roaring success, too. She talked about a couple of her firm's celebrity clients who sounded like total goofballs. Anna was bright and witty and had a musical laugh—and DeMarco again wondered what could have possessed her to marry Dooley, other than the fact that Dooley was rich and getting richer. No, that wasn't fair. Dooley was a good guy; DeMarco was just jealous.

At eleven they parted company, and DeMarco, a bit high from all the Sam Adams Boston Ale he'd consumed, decided to walk around a bit rather than driving immediately back to his hotel. He wanted to get closer to the Breathalyzer legal limit before tackling the congested, confusing streets of Boston, which were hard even for the natives to navigate much less an outsider who was barely sober. He should have taken a taxi to meet the Dooleys, but since he'd paid for a rental car, he figured he'd use it. That was just one more mistake he made that night.

The temperature had dropped to a bearable number—maybe eighty—and it was pleasant on the streets of Charlestown, where it seemed all the women were young and good-looking. After half an hour of strolling and girl watching, he decided to head back to the garage where he'd parked.

The garage was on the waterfront, on Constitution Road, three blocks southeast of the Warren Tavern. Vehicles entered the garage via a ramp but there was a gray door to one side of the vehicle ramp with a blue sign that said PEDESTRIAN ENTRANCE. He opened the pedestrian door to find another concrete ramp, one that would accommodate wheelchairs, and started down it. Once he passed through the door he was no longer visible to people on the street or to anyone in the garage on the floor below who might be getting into or out of a car. At any rate, he'd just passed through the door and taken a couple of steps when he heard a sound behind him, like maybe a shoe scraping the concrete. Before he could turn to see who was there, the lights went out.

10

DeMarco woke up in the emergency room of a hospital, lying on a gurney, in a space closed off by a curtain. The back of his head had a large, tender knot on it; it felt like someone had hit him with a brick. In fact, his entire face hurt like it had been bricked, and when he tried to move, his ribs on the right side screamed that he should stay still. He thought about trying to stand, but decided not to, and a few minutes later the curtain was pulled back by a dark-complexioned woman wearing black-framed glasses and blue hospital scrubs.

"Ah, you're awake again," she said.

Again? He didn't remember being awake the first time. She stepped over to him, took his pulse and blood pressure, then said, "Follow my finger with your eyes." She moved a slim brown finger back and forth in front of his face to see if the muscles controlling his eyeballs still worked. "Good," she said. "But we need to get an MRI."

"Where am I?" DeMarco asked.

"Mass General. I'm Dr. Bhaduri. Do you know your name?"

"What?" DeMarco said.

"I asked if you know your name."

"Yeah, it's Joe DeMarco."

"And can you remember what happened to you?"

"No. I had drinks with a couple of friends at a place called the War-ren Tavern, but I can't remember anything after that."

"It appears you were mugged. Some college kids found you uncon-scious and were nice enough to call nine-one-one. You have a concus-sion, which is always a concern. You were also hit or kicked in the face several times, though none of those injuries are significant."

"My ribs hurt, too."

"We'll take X-rays," Dr. Bhaduri said.

The MRI showed that he had a short hairline crack in his skull that Dr. Bhaduri said would mend in time and wasn't anything for him to worry about. Easy for her to say since it wasn't her skull. The X-rays showed that two of his ribs were also cracked, but like the skull fracture, the ribs would mend. When he looked into a mirror, he saw that some-body had used his face for a punching bag. There was a large blue-black bruise on his right cheek and his nose was encrusted with dried blood. He touched his nose and it hurt, but it didn't appear to be broken. Thankfully, all his teeth were still in his mouth.

His wallet was missing but he still had his cell phone and his car keys—and it was the car keys that helped him remember: he'd walked into a garage to get his rental car and . . . He didn't remember what happened after that. It was apparent, however, that someone had hit him on the back of the head with something hard, and then kicked the shit out of him. Because it was a public garage and the streets of Charlestown were full of people at even eleven at night, whoever did it only had time to get in half a dozen kicks or punches before they took his wallet and fled.

So what happened? Had some opportunistic thief decided to relieve him of his wallet when he stepped into the parking garage? Or was it the McNulty brothers? He remembered the McNultys coming down the steps in front of Elinore's building as he was telling Dooley that he'd meet him at the Warren Tavern at eight. Did the McNultys go to the tavern, wait for him to come out, follow him to the garage, and beat him senseless? And if so, why?

He could come up with two answers to that question. A: it was a strategic move on the part of the McNultys. They didn't want him hanging around, protecting Elinore Dobbs, as his presence made it harder for them to drive her out of her apartment. Or B, the answer he liked better: beating the hell out of him wasn't at all strategic. The Mc-Nultys had just decided to tune him up because he'd threatened them and pissed them off, and because they were a couple of violent morons.

He called Dooley since he couldn't think of anyone else to call, and told him what had happened. "Oh, my God!" was Dooley's reaction. Dooley and his wife came to the emergency room, gave him a ride back to his hotel, and loaned him five hundred bucks since DeMarco didn't have any money or credit cards. In fact, he needed Dooley's help to convince the hotel clerk that the battered man standing before him in a bloodstained T-shirt was indeed a registered guest at the Park Plaza even though he didn't have any ID and had lost the key card to his room, which had been in his wallet. The first thing DeMarco did once inside his room was to cancel his Visa card and tell the Visa folks to express a new one to the hotel. Then he took a long, hot shower and collapsed into bed.

The next morning—his head throbbing and his ribs aching—he called Mahoney and told him what had happened. Mahoney's reaction was about what he'd expected.

"That son of a bitch Callahan," Mahoney said.

"I'm not sure Callahan had anything to do with this," DeMarco said.

"Sure he did. Those guys work for him. He's responsible."

Mahoney was angry that DeMarco had been attacked, and he was concerned for the health of his faithful employee—but there was something else. DeMarco had seen the movie *Gladiator,* the one with Russell Crowe, where the Roman emperor Marcus Aurelius sent an emissary to negotiate a peace treaty with some barbarian tribe—and the barbarians sent the emissary back to the emperor, tied to his horse, minus his head. And that was Mahoney's attitude: Mahoney, the emperor, had sent his emissary to Boston and Callahan had tried to send him back without a head. What Callahan had done was an insult to the emperor; DeMarco's head was a secondary issue.

After he spoke to Mahoney, DeMarco called Emma. She thought he was calling about Congressmen Sims's Purple Heart and immediately said, "I got call from a friend at the Pentagon yesterday and—"

"I almost got my head caved in last night," DeMarco said.

"What!"

"I'm okay," DeMarco said, and proceeded to tell her what was happening to Elinore Dobbs and what had happened to him.

"I'll catch the next plane up there," Emma said.

"No, no, that's not why I called," DeMarco hastily said. "I just want you to go to my place and get my passport and FedEx it to me so I'll have some ID to get on a plane when I'm ready to go home. Also my checkbook so I can get cash." Emma knew where he hid the spare key to his front door and the code to his security system. "Okay," she said. "But if you need some help . . . People like this Callahan character make me sick and I like that old lady even though I've never met her."

DeMarco figured that Callahan and the McNulty brothers should thank their lucky stars that he didn't ask Emma to come to Boston to help him.

"By the way, what did you find out about Sims?" DeMarco asked, although Sims was hardly a priority now, and the way he was feeling he really didn't care.

"There's no record of him receiving a Purple Heart," Emma said. "That doesn't necessarily mean he didn't get one, but the marines keep better records than the other services. I could ask my friend to dig some more, to see if there's a citation letter in some file or a recommendation written by whoever his CO was at the time, but if she does that she's going to have to talk to a bunch of people."

"Mahoney wouldn't want that," DeMarco said.

"I know. So I'm looking into another way to get more information."

"Great," DeMarco said. He didn't want to spend any more time talking about Sims. And the way his head was throbbing, he wondered if he qualified for a Purple Heart.

"Joe, you let me know if you need help up there."

"I don't. I've got everything under control." He didn't have anything under control but all he wanted to do was crawl back into bed and sleep some more.

An hour later, a phone call from Anna Dooley woke him. She wanted to see how he was feeling.

"I'm okay," he said, not wanting to sound like a wimp.

"Well, if you need any succor, let me know."

Succor? DeMarco thought he knew what the word meant—support, assistance, help—but there was something sexual about the way she'd said it. At any rate, he was in no condition to be succored in the way she seemed to be offering, so he went back to sleep.

———◆———

At noon, he decided he was hungry but was reluctant to leave his room. His head still ached, although it wasn't as bad as it had been when he first woke up, and when he pulled a polo shirt over his head his ribs protested, but he was able to walk okay. The bad part was his appearance: the right side of his face was now swollen and various shades of blue and purple. He didn't feel like subjecting himself to the stares he was going to get in the hotel restaurant, but was starving and didn't feel like sitting inside his room any longer.

He asked for a table for one and the hostess pretended to ignore the way he looked, then led him to a table at the rear of the restaurant so he wouldn't frighten the other customers. He ordered a Coke and a cheeseburger—glad that he still had teeth and could chew the cheeseburger.

Throughout lunch he thought about two things. The first of those was how to get back at the McNultys. There was no point running to the cops since he hadn't seen them and couldn't prove that they'd attacked him. But somehow, some way, he was going to get even with those two stumpy brutes. What he'd really like to do was find some way to separate them so he'd only have to deal with one of them at a time—and then give them a beating, like the beating they'd given him.

It occurred to him that he'd encountered thugs like the McNultys before and he didn't normally react this way. He normally tried to avoid violence—there was rarely an upside to violence—but he was willing to make an exception when it came to the McNultys. It had probably been a long time since they'd been given a good pounding and most likely because they double-teamed whomever they decided to fight. And a few months in jail for assault wasn't going to change the way they behaved—but a good beatdown might. Then he thought: *Who am I trying to fool?* He wasn't trying to change the McNultys' behavior. It was a matter of male pride: proving to them—and to himself—that he was just as hard as they were, and he wanted to repay them in a way they wouldn't soon forget.

The problem, however, was that he was currently in no shape to fight anyone bigger than a flyweight, and if he got hit in the head again, he could end up like some punch-drunk NFL lineman. Another problem was that he'd been sent to Boston to help Elinore Dobbs, and if he ended up in jail for assault, he wouldn't be much help to her.

So, for now, he would forestall the pleasure of getting even with the McNultys, but if the opportunity presented itself . . .

The second thing he thought about was how to help Elinore. He couldn't hang around Boston forever watching over her, and at some point the McNultys would recommence making her life miserable. He had no doubt that the old gal was stubborn enough and tough enough to hang in there until her lease expired, but he could just see her sitting in her apartment during the winter, her generator running, bundled up in a ski jacket and stocking cap after they cut off her heat. He needed to come up with some way to force Callahan to back off and leave her alone. And since his friend, Lawyer Dooley, hadn't shown him a way to use the law to protect her, he needed to come up with a different strategy.

And then a different strategy occurred to him.

He called Maggie Dolan, the lady who ran Mahoney's Boston office. Maggie knew everyone in the city of Boston who was anyone. She'd be able to get him a name. Half an hour later, she called him back and said the guy he wanted would meet him in front of Elinore's building at nine a.m. tomorrow.

11

---✦---

The man sitting on the front steps of Elinore's building was about seventy, a tall, lanky guy with short, bristly gray hair. When he shook DeMarco's hand, DeMarco could feel calluses. He was wearing khaki pants, a short-sleeved blue shirt, and steel-toed work boots. His name was Jim Boyer and he was a general contractor, now retired, and had spent all his adult life on construction sites.

When Boyer saw DeMarco's face he shot to his feet and said, "Whoa! What happened to you?"

"I got jumped by a couple of guys, which is one of the reasons you're here."

DeMarco explained the situation to Boyer. A developer named Callahan was renovating the entire neighborhood, as Boyer could plainly see, and a little old lady named Elinore Dobbs, who lived in the building they were standing in front of, was refusing to move out so Callahan was making her life a living hell—and DeMarco wanted Boyer's help to force Callahan to back off.

"Here's what I'm looking for," DeMarco said. "I want you to walk around with me and find safety and building code violations. The bigger, the better. Then you're going to call the right bureaucrat in OSHA or the EPA or whoever, and rat Callahan out. In other words, I want you to bring this project to a screeching halt, and if you can't do that, I want you to disrupt it as often as possible. Then, when the work is stopped, I'm going to sit down with Callahan and explain to him that for the next three years you're going to devote your life to fucking up this development."

"Oh," Boyer said, sounding uncertain. "I told Maggie I'd help you today but I don't know about three years."

"It's not going to take three years. I just want Callahan to *think* I have a guy who's willing to devote three years of his life to making him miserable if he doesn't leave Elinore alone."

Boyer looked skeptical.

"Hey, maybe it will work and maybe it won't," DeMarco said. "But in the meantime, Maggie Dolan will pay your hourly rate for whatever time you spend here. And if you know a couple of guys that have the kind of background you do, they can spell you if you're busy."

"Don't get me wrong," Boyer said. "I'd like to help the lady but you oughta know that most builders follow the rules and projects are inspected at various phases during construction, so it might not be as easy as you think to find problems."

"Tell you what," DeMarco said. "Let's just walk around and see what you can spot."

"Okay, but I need to get a couple things out of my truck first."

They walked a block to Boyer's truck—a Ford F-150 with a crew cab—and from the backseat, Boyer removed two hard hats, one white and one orange. "You wear the white one," he said, "since you're the guy in the suit. The bosses typically wear white hard hats." The other thing Boyer took from the truck was a rolled-up blueprint.

"The workers see a couple of guys walking around in hard hats, holding plans, they'll think we belong," Boyer said. "If anybody asks what we're doing, let me do the talking."

They started touring the development, walking first over to where the commercial buildings—the corporate headquarters for the solar energy company, the hotel, and the office buildings—were being erected and in various phases of construction. There'd apparently been no Elinore Dobbs to slow down the other parts of Callahan's project. Boyer was completely at ease walking around the construction site; DeMarco was worried about getting run over by a cement truck.

"You see those two guys up there, on the scaffolding?" Boyer said, pointing skyward.

"Yeah," DeMarco said.

"The most common safety violation you'll find on any construction site has to do with fall protection. You see that section of scaffolding there at the end? There's supposed to be a safety rail on it, but there isn't. And that one guy, he's got fall protection, that cable coming off the harness he's wearing. But the other guy should be wearing fall protection, too. OSHA makes it almost impossible to work these days as they require fall protection anytime you're more than about four inches off the ground, and you can come out here any day of the week and find a dozen fall protection violations. A month ago, a construction company over in Everett got a three-hundred-thousand-dollar fine for repeated violations."

DeMarco smiled. "That had to sting," he said.

"Well, yeah, but you gotta remember that that was the fine the company got. It doesn't mean they paid the fine after their lawyers got involved."

Boyer stopped again. "And all these cranes," he said, pointing upward at the yellow construction cranes looming over the site. "Two, three times a year, you'll hear about one of those things toppling over and killing someone because it wasn't assembled or operated correctly."

"A couple years ago," DeMarco said, "a crane working on the National Cathedral in Washington collapsed, and crushed a bunch of cars in a parking lot. But nobody got killed."

"*That* time, nobody got killed," Boyer said. "Which is why there are about a million rules these guys are supposed to follow when it comes to cranes, and about half the time they don't follow them. They're supposed to use load charts to figure out the crane's boom angle. The crane's not supposed to lift things greater than a certain percentage of its rated capacity. They're supposed to conduct trial lifts before hoisting people up in a box. And on and on and on. A company I used to work with over in Framingham got a seventy-thousand-dollar fine for operating a crane too close to energized power lines. If I was to spend a couple days out here just watching the cranes I know I'd come up with violations because experienced operators think they're too smart to have to follow all the nitpicky rules."

Boyer watched a crane swing a pallet loaded with bags of cement over a couple guys standing beneath it, then said, "Let's go back over to Elinore's building. I want to take a look at those three-deckers they haven't torn down yet."

On the way back to Elinore's, they walked past the sign that DeMarco had already seen that showed what the new high-end condos were going to look like. Boyer stopped, looked at the sign, and said, "This could be easier than I thought."

"What do you mean?" DeMarco said.

Boyer point at the sign and said, "Flannery."

The sign, in addition to showing an artist's rendition of the completed structure and photos of model apartments, listed the name of the architectural and engineering firm responsible for the design as well as the name of the general contractor, which was Flannery Construction.

"Flannery's a shitbag," Boyer said. "One of those guys who will cut every corner he can possibly cut, which is probably the reason Callahan hired him."

Boyer looked down at the footings for the new apartment complex for a moment, then started moving again, walking toward the four three-deckers that were waiting to be razed. But before they reached the houses, Boyer stopped again, this time near half a dozen industrial-sized Dumpsters where debris from the demolished buildings had been placed. He pointed at a chunk of six-inch carbon steel pipe lying on the ground near one of the Dumpsters. The pipe had a white, crusty film on it.

"Asbestos," Boyer said. "That's probably a steam pipe that came from one of the apartment buildings they already demolished. A lot of the buildings that used to be here were constructed before World War II and they used asbestos for insulation back in those days, on the pipes and in the walls. Linoleum and floor tiles contained asbestos, too. To remove asbestos, you basically have to shrink-wrap the building, the workers gotta be in space suits with respirators, you have to dispose of the stuff at a hazardous waste site, and a whole bunch of other things to make sure the workers don't end up breathing the shit.

"I'll bet you anything that Flannery, being the dirtbag he is, had his guys in the buildings at night when there was less chance of an OSHA inspector coming around, and they did the rip-out wearing nothing but those little paper filters over their mouths and noses. Flannery is required to have records showing what he did and how he disposed of the stuff, and knowing Flannery, he might not have 'em. Improper asbestos abatement is a showstopper."

"That's what I like to hear," DeMarco said.

"Let's go look at the triple-deckers. I was raised in a place in Southie just like the ones on this block. It's gone now, too."

The narrow three-story houses were nothing but shells, the exterior walls still standing, but the interiors gutted. Boyer pointed at one of the standing walls. "Bet you a nickel that's lead-based paint. Lead paint is like asbestos. There're a bunch of rules you gotta follow to remove it and dispose of it."

Boyer stopped abruptly. "Whoa! You see there, the soil around that hole in the ground, how oily and black it looks?" Boyer got down on one knee, pinched a bit of dirt between his fingers, and smelled it. "There used to be a fuel oil tank here and they yanked the tank out of the ground. But the tank leaked at one time and now the soil's contaminated. You can't just dump the dirt that's here and you can't leave it here. It's hazardous waste now. The soil all around this area has to be tested for oil contamination, and whatever's contaminated has to be properly disposed—which means, expensively disposed."

"Outstanding," DeMarco said.

"I've got enough right now to cause this guy some misery. And I know just who to call. There's this one young lady who works for Mass-DEP and—"

"Mass dep?"

"The Massachusetts Department of Environmental Protection. Anyway, this young gal is a bear when it comes to this kind of shit, especially asbestos violations. Her dad died of mesothelioma."

They were heading back toward where Boyer had parked his truck, DeMarco holding his borrowed hard hat in his hand, when his cell phone rang.

He didn't recognize the number.

"Hello," he said.

"This is Superintendent O'Rourke. Elinore Dobbs is in the hospital."

12

Elinore was in Mass General, the same place that had treated DeMarco. She was in a room with a woman who appeared to be on life support, judging by all the tubes going in and out of her. Elinore's right arm was encased in a cast from hand to elbow, and there was a bandage above her left eye. She didn't seem to be sleeping, but her eyes were closed and she was making little whimpering sounds as if she was in pain. She looked so small lying there in the big hospital bed.

DeMarco walked over to her and touched her gently on the shoulder and said, "Elinore."

She slowly opened her eyes. "Who are you?"

Aw, jeez.

DeMarco left her room and walked back to the nurses' station. "I need to talk to Ms. Dobbs's doctor," he said.

Elinore's doctor was a woman named Webster who looked like she should still be in college—or maybe high school. She was short—about the same height as Elinore—maybe five foot two. She had short blond hair, bright green eyes, and a button nose. She was cute—and just looking at her, you could tell she was smart as a whip.

"Do you have any idea what happened to her?" DeMarco asked.

"The EMTs who brought her in said she'd fallen down a flight of stairs," Dr. Webster said. "She has a broken arm. Her left ulna is cracked, which really shouldn't be a problem, and she'll make a full recovery from that injury. The big problem is she hit her head hard when she fell and she has a subdural hematoma, which means she has blood in the layers of tissue surrounding the brain. We may have to operate to relieve the pressure but I want to wait a while to see if the swelling subsides.

"The problem is her age. A younger person with the same injury would probably be okay in a couple of weeks without surgery or any other form of drastic intervention. But with the elderly it's different. As people age the tiny veins in the brain are more susceptible to tearing, and, as we age, the brain actually shrinks a little, creating more subdural space for the hematoma to expand into."

"She didn't recognize me," DeMarco said. "That lady was as sharp as a tack yesterday. There wasn't anything at all wrong with her memory."

"That's another symptom of subdural hematomas in the elderly: confusion and memory loss similar to what you see in people with dementia."

"Is she going to get better?"

"I don't know. I'm sorry. I wish I could tell you that she'll recover completely, but because of her age, she may not. We're going to keep her here for a couple more days, watch for swelling and internal bleeding, and maybe she'll recover. And maybe she won't. All I can tell you is that I'll do my best but you should pray for her."

DeMarco wasn't a big believer in the power of prayer.

He did, however, believe in the power of revenge.

When he stepped into Superintendent O'Rourke's office, the first thing O'Rourke said, when he saw DeMarco's face, was: "Jesus. What happened to you?"

The swelling on DeMarco's right cheek had gone down but the skin under his eye was various shades of purple, blue, and black. DeMarco told O'Rourke about the parking garage mugging.

"Did you report the attack?"

"No."

"But you think the McNultys did it?"

"I *know* they did, but I can't prove it. And what happened to me isn't important right now. Do you have somebody investigating what happened to Elinore? I don't believe for one fucking minute it was an accident."

"Calm down. And, yeah, I've got a guy on it. Normally, I wouldn't treat this as a criminal matter but considering what's been happening with Ms. Dobbs and because of Congressman Mahoney's interest . . ."

"Can I talk to your investigator?"

O'Rourke hesitated, then said, "Sure."

———◆———

The crack investigator O'Rourke had assigned to the case was a detective named Fitzgerald. He was in his fifties—most likely close to retiring—and a good fifty pounds overweight. He was wearing a white polo shirt with a small orange stain on the breast that DeMarco suspected was pasta sauce, wrinkled gray pants, and thick-soled, ankle-high boots, the kind he'd probably worn when he was a beat cop thirty years ago. He had a badge clipped to the front of his belt that you could barely see because of the gut flopping over the belt, and, on his right hip, in a pancake holster, a short-barreled revolver.

"So what do you think happened?" DeMarco asked after the introductions were made.

Fitzgerald shrugged. "I think she tripped at the top of the stairs and fell."

"Bullshit. I want to see the crime scene," DeMarco said.

"Crime scene?"

"That's right. This wasn't an accident. Elinore Dobbs was in better shape than you are, Fitz, a lot better shape. She moved like somebody half her age. And she would have been careful going down those stairs because the lights on the landings were out. When I walked down those stairs, I held on to the rail because the light was dim, and she would have done the same thing."

"The lights on the landings were on," Fitzgerald said. "At least they were when I was there."

"What?"

"But, hey, the boss said you were a guy with some juice so if you wanna drive over there, let's go."

Fitzgerald turned out to be right: the lights on the staircase landings were glowing; there were hundred-watt bulbs in the sockets. Those lights hadn't been on the last time DeMarco walked up the stairs.

When he saw Elinore in the hospital, DeMarco's first thought had been: *Lawsuit.* He was going to file a lawsuit on her behalf against Callahan for the poorly lighted stairs, which the suit would claim was the reason she fell. And he was going to hire a mean-mouthed barracuda for a lawyer to press the lawsuit, the kind of lawyer who could win a case against the Cub Scouts. But that plan just went out the window.

"When did she fall?" DeMarco asked.

"I don't know when she fell, but the medics were called at seven thirty this morning." At seven thirty, DeMarco had still been in bed, and by the time he met with Boyer at Elinore's building, she'd already been taken away by the medics.

"Who found her?" he asked Fitzgerald.

"Some wino. Since the front door to the building doesn't lock and most of the units are empty, winos sneak in here to sleep. Anyway, this guy was walking up the stairs and saw Elinore lying on the landing between the second and third floors. He said she was unconscious when he found her, and he went outside, found a woman with a cell phone, and she called nine-one-one."

"Huh," DeMarco said. He walked up and stood on the third-floor landing, looking at the stairs Elinore Dobbs had tumbled down. He tried to imagine her losing her balance, a hand reaching out, trying to grab the banister, the terror she must have felt before the impact. Then he noticed something: just a smidgen of sawdust on the top of the landing, which he was sure he wouldn't have seen if the landing lights hadn't been so bright. He knelt down and looked closer, then said to Fitzgerald, "Come here."

On one side of the landing was a wall and on the other side was the landing newel—a post with a round ball on top that the handrail attached to. He pointed at the hole in the base of the newel, a hole about one-eighth of an inch in diameter.

"You see that little hole?" DeMarco said.

"No," Fitzgerald said.

"Get down on your knees and look."

With a grunt and considerable effort, Fitzgerald knelt.

"Now do you see the hole?"

"Yeah."

"It's new," DeMarco said. "You can see the wood is white inside and you can see a bit of sawdust on the floor beneath the hole. I think someone drilled that hole recently. Now look at the wall on the other side of the staircase. There's a hole just like this one, about an inch off the floor." DeMarco paused, then said, "I think somebody strung a trip wire across here."

"Come on," Fitzgerald said.

"Get a CSI over here and have him check this out," DeMarco said.

"A CSI? You think this is television, DeMarco? What's a CSI going to do?"

"I want him to look at these holes. And take fingerprints, too."

DeMarco could tell Fitzgerald was about to give him an argument, then remembered the political muscle that DeMarco had. "I'll see if someone's available," Fitzgerald said. "But we may be waiting quite a while."

It turned out that they didn't have to wait even half an hour. It must have been a slow day for crime in Boston. A kid in his twenties with spiky dark hair, a grapevine tattoo on his neck, and a ring in one ear arrived carrying what looked like a tackle box. If he hadn't been wearing a blue Windbreaker with yellow letters that said POLICE on the back, DeMarco would have guessed the kid belonged to a not very successful rock band.

DeMarco told him to dust for prints and take a close look at the two small holes. The kid, not knowing who DeMarco was, looked over at Fitzgerald, and Fitzgerald nodded. "Why am I looking at the holes?" the CSI tech asked.

"Because I think someone rigged a trip wire across the landing and made an old lady fall," DeMarco said. "So just look and tell me what you think."

The technician applied fingerprint powder to the newel, the wall opposite the newel, and the handrail but didn't find any prints. DeMarco wasn't surprised there were no prints on the handrail because they'd be smeared by people holding on to the rail while coming down the steps. But he thought the tech might find something on the lower part of the newel, an area where you wouldn't expect people to touch. And if the tech found prints, they could lead to the McNultys, whose prints would be in the system. But no such luck.

"Dust the top of the steps near the post," DeMarco said, thinking maybe someone put a hand on the steps kneeling down to drill the holes, the way Fitzgerald had put his hand on the steps when he knelt down. But there was nothing, not even a print left by Fitzgerald, who'd probably smeared everything when he looked at the holes. Or maybe, if the McNultys had anything to do with this, they'd worn gloves. Whatever the case, there were no prints.

"Now take a close look at those holes," DeMarco said.

The CSI examined them first with his naked eye, then took a magnifying glass from his equipment box and lay down on the steps so he could put his head close to the holes. He examined the hole in the newel first, then the one in the wall.

He looked up at DeMarco and said, "You can see threads."

"Threads?" Fitzgerald said.

"Yeah, screw threads," the technician said. "I can't prove someone installed a wire, but if someone did, they might have drilled the holes, then screwed in an eyebolt or an eyehook like you use to hang pictures and then ran a wire, like picture-hanging wire, through the eyebolts. But that's the best I can tell you, and I'm just guessing."

"Well, I think that's exactly what happened," DeMarco said. Looking at Fitzgerald, he said, "Someone, most likely the McNultys, attached a wire to hooks like your technician said, then Elinore walked out here on this landing and headed down the steps and tripped. They were trying to kill her, figuring a woman her age would break her neck."

"I guess that could have happened," Fitzgerald said, although he didn't sound like a true believer. "But where's the wire? And with the lights on, if there had been a wire, she should have seen it."

"I'm telling you those lights weren't on yesterday," DeMarco said. Then, before Fitzgerald had a chance to debate the issue, he said, "What was the name of this wino who found her?"

"Greg Canyon, like Grand Canyon."

"Let's go talk to him. And let's go find out where the fucking McNultys were when this happened."

"What are you saying? That the wino rigged a wire, then took out the wire and the eyebolts before the medics got here?"

"Yeah, maybe. Or maybe the McNultys rigged it the night before and then got the wino to find her and remove the wire. And one other thing. I think they screwed in that hundred-watt bulb *after* the wino found her, while Elinore was unconscious and he was waiting for the medics to arrive. So I want to know where the McNultys were last night and this morning. Ditto for the wino. We'll go talk to the wino first."

"That might be kind of tough," Fitzgerald said. "I mean, he's a street person. He doesn't have an address."

"If the guy hangs out in this area, we should be able to spot him. We'll drive around and look. And I want you to do a record check on him. See if he's associated with the McNultys or Sean Callahan. See if he was in prison with the McNultys or went to school with them or if Callahan ever employed him."

DeMarco could tell he was annoying Fitzgerald, snapping orders at him—and he didn't give a shit.

Fitzgerald called somebody at the station and told whomever he talked to to e-mail him a summary of Canyon's record if he had one. Then he and DeMarco got into Fitzgerald's car and started cruising the streets near Delaney, trying to spot Canyon. According to Fitzgerald, Canyon was very tall—maybe six five or six six—and had wild black hair that went down to his shoulders and was wearing jeans and combat boots. "And he had on a ski jacket, a dirty blue one," Fitzgerald said. "Even though it was already about ninety when I talked to him."

DeMarco thought a ski jacket would be a good place to stash a few light bulbs and the wire that had been used.

Half an hour after they started their hunt, DeMarco was growing impatient and said, "Did you get that e-mail with his record yet?"

Fitzgerald pulled over to the curb and took out reading glasses and his cell phone. "Yeah, here it is." He squinted at the screen and said, "Just the usual shit you get with bums. Assaults for fighting with other bums. Peeing in some merchant's doorway. Being drunk in public." Fitzgerald laughed. "The only people ever charged with being drunk in public are homeless people. Half the guys who go to Fenway are drunk in public and a lot more violent than most bums, but we never charge them."

"Do they have a picture of him on file?" DeMarco asked, not caring about the inequitable ways the city of Boston dealt with drunkards.

"I guess. Probably."

"Have someone e-mail you his picture."

Five minutes later, after Fitzgerald and the guy he was talking to figured out how to e-mail Canyon's mug shot, Fitzgerald had it on his phone.

"I want to go to the places around here that sell booze, especially cheap booze," DeMarco said.

They stopped at three places, all of them three or four blocks from Elinore's apartment. None of the store owners recognized Canyon, and a guy as tall as him with a wild mane of black hair would have been noticeable. "Don't you find it strange," DeMarco said, "that this wino doesn't shop in any of the stores around here? Look at his arrest record and find out where most of his arrests occurred."

"The e-mail doesn't say. It's just a summary, like you asked for."

"So call the fuckin' guy that prepared the summary and ask him."

Fitzgerald did. "Almost all the busts were in Revere."

"Which is where the McNultys have a bar," DeMarco said. "The goddamn McNultys know this guy."

DeMarco was silent for a moment. "I want you to get Canyon's picture to every cop on patrol in Boston and Revere."

"You gotta be shittin' me," Fitzgerald said. "I mean, I know you're upset by what happened to that old lady—I am, too—but it's not like Canyon was one of the marathon bombers."

"Does it *look* like I'm shitting you, Fitzgerald?" DeMarco said.

Fitzgerald started to say something—then he recalled whatever O'Rourke had said to him about the necessity of keeping Congressman John Mahoney happy.

Fitzgerald made three or four phone calls and relayed DeMarco's order—and DeMarco could hear the people he was speaking to saying a variation of what Fitzgerald had said: *Are you shitting me?*

Happy that the cops were now on the hunt for Canyon—who DeMarco was a hundred percent sure was an accomplice to trying to kill Elinore Dobbs—DeMarco told Fitzgerald: "Let's go see the McNultys."

<hr>

An hour later—Fitzgerald had begged DeMarco to let him stop at a McDonald's before he collapsed from hunger—they parked near a bar named the Shamrock in Revere.

As they were walking toward the bar, DeMarco said, "You need to be careful with these guys. You might even consider calling for backup."

"Backup?" Fitzgerald said. "I don't think so."

DeMarco got the impression just then that Fitzgerald hadn't always been a fat cop waiting until he could draw a pension. In fact, he wouldn't have been surprised if Fitzgerald had a sap in his back pocket and would enjoy using it.

The tavern was a dump, which is what DeMarco had expected from the exterior. Dimly lit, broken-down furniture, smelling of spilt beer. There was a dartboard on one wall and the wall around the board was pockmarked from players too drunk to hit the target. The glass covering a picture of Larry Bird behind the bar was flyspecked.

Standing behind the bar, reading a paperback, was an ample-sized woman with frizzy red hair and arms like a stevedore. One unshaven old drunk who looked as if he'd forgotten where he put his dentures was the only customer in the place. The McNulty brothers were at a table, a bottle of Jameson's in front of them, watching Jerry Springer on the television over the bar. On the Springer show two large women were screaming at a scrawny, tattooed doofus, accusing him of cheating on them both. The doofus seemed very pleased with himself.

When the McNultys saw DeMarco, they smiled. Ray, the one with the bitten ear, said, "Hey, what happened to you? Looks like somebody cleaned your clock."

DeMarco almost lost it. He clenched his fists and took a step toward the table, then inhaled and stopped. He wasn't in good enough shape for a fight and, with his luck, and with Fitzgerald as a witness, he'd probably get arrested for assault.

"Where were you two shitheads last night?" DeMarco asked.

"Why you asking," Ray said.

"And you better watch your fuckin' mouth," Roy said.

"He's not asking," Fitzgerald said. "I'm Detective Mike Fitzgerald, BPD, and I'm the one who's asking. So where were you two shitheads last night?"

Elinore was an early riser and she'd been found by Canyon at seven thirty a.m., which was another thing that bothered DeMarco: a bum being up at that time of day. DeMarco figured that the trip wire had been installed the night before. He also figured that whoever installed it—the McNultys or Canyon—hadn't been worried about any of the other residents using the stairs late at night. Mrs. Polanski, the lady with dementia, didn't leave her apartment; Goodman, the agoraphobic, didn't leave his; and Mrs. Spiegleman was an invalid, and gutless Mr. Spiegleman would have been afraid to venture out at night. The trap had been set for Elinore because the McNultys knew that she'd be out and about early in the day.

"We ain't got nothin' to hide," Ray McNulty said to Fitzgerald. "We were here in the bar from, shit, I don't know, five until what?" he said, looking over at his brother. "Ten?"

"Yeah," Roy said. "It was probably about ten. The Sox game was almost over but they were so far behind we bailed before it ended."

"And what did you do after you left the bar?" Fitzgerald said.

"We had a couple girls over to our place."

"You two had *dates*?" DeMarco said, making it clear that he found it incredible than any woman would go out with them.

Ray laughed. "I guess you'd call it a date, but we had to pay them." He pulled out his wallet and handed Fitzgerald a card. Fitzgerald showed the card to DeMarco. It said Pinnacle Escort Services. "The two who came over were named Crystal and Terri," Ray said.

"No, her name was Sherrie," Roy said.

"Oh, yeah, Sherrie. Anyway, give 'em a call. They spent the whole night, didn't leave until eight this morning."

"That's your alibi?" DeMarco said. "Hookers?"

"We don't need an alibi," Ray said. "We didn't do anything."

"How come you didn't ask why we're asking where you were last night?" DeMarco said.

They shrugged simultaneously, like Siamese twins joined at the shoulder.

"We figured you just wanted to hassle us about something," Ray McNulty said. "So why are you asking?"

"Because someone tried to kill Elinore Dobbs this morning. Someone stretched a wire across the landing on the third floor, and she tripped over it and fell. She's got a concussion and a broken arm. And I think you two cocksuckers either did it or paid someone to do it."

Roy stood up. "I told you. You better watch your mouth."

Fitzgerald put his hand on his short revolver and said, "Sit your ass back down."

Roy did, but he was simmering, and DeMarco thought—actually, he *hoped*—that Roy would attack him.

"Where do you guys know Greg Canyon from?" Fitzgerald asked.

"Who?" they said in unison.

DeMarco looked over at the hefty barmaid standing behind the bar, listening to everything. "What's your bartender's name?" he asked Ray.

"Doreen. Why?"

DeMarco walked over to Doreen and said, "Were you here last night, Doreen?"

She scowled at him, making him think of a pit bull with freckles. "Yeah."

"And were the McNultys here the whole time you were here?"

"They were wherever they said they were."

DeMarco knew he was wasting his time. With people like Doreen loyalty to your friends always came first, plus the McNultys, since they owned the bar, employed her. Nonetheless, he said, "I know what they said, but I want to hear what you have to say. So were they in the bar last night and how long were they here?"

Doreen just crossed her arms over her broad chest and stared at him.

"They made an old lady fall down some stairs," DeMarco said. "They were trying to kill her." Doreen didn't even blink. "If she dies, Doreen, and you cover for them, you can be charged as an accessory."

"If you're not going to order a drink," Doreen said, "move along."

"Those goons did it," DeMarco said as he Fitzgerald drove back to Boston. "I'm absolutely positive."

"Yeah, maybe," Fitzgerald said.

"You gotta find Canyon, Fitzgerald. If you can find him, we can make him talk."

"I'll bet you my pension," Fitzgerald said, "that Canyon is long gone from here. But I think you're right about those guys being involved, for whatever good that does, but it's going to be impossible to prove."

———◆———

DeMarco stopped by the hospital to see Elinore again. When he walked into her room, she was eating orange Jell-O with little pineapple chunks and had dribbled several bites down the front of her gown.

"Elinore," DeMarco said softly. "How are you doing?"

"Pete? What are you doing here? You should be at work."

Aw, jeez. Pete was her fireman husband who'd been dead for thirty years.

DeMarco tracked down young Dr. Webster next. "How's she doing?"

Webster shook her head. "Physically, she's fine. She's mending. But mentally . . ."

"Yeah, I know. She didn't recognize me again."

"Do you know if she has any family?"

"I know she was married but her husband's dead. She didn't mention kids or anyone else. But I know a guy who's pretty high up in the government. I'll give him a call and see if he can find her next of kin."

"Good. She needs someone to look after her."

DeMarco didn't call the guy he knew that was high up in the government. Instead he called Maggie Dolan and told her to sic the interns on tracking down any relatives Elinore might have.

Two hours later he was informed that Elinore Dobbs had a daughter, which surprised DeMarco. He thought Elinore might have mentioned that, which made him wonder how close she was to her daughter. The daughter's name was Alice Silverman. She was sixty-two years old, divorced, and a retired college professor who lived in Portsmouth, New Hampshire. He passed on the information to Dr. Webster.

That turned out to be just one more mistake DeMarco made.

———◆———

As he was leaving the hospital, the retired contractor, Boyer, called him.

"Okay, I got MassDEP looking into what Flannery's doing. I'll bet by tomorrow they'll have stopped work on the project, or at least parts of it. Flannery might have records showing he removed and disposed of the asbestos the way he was supposed to, but I doubt it. Ditto with the contaminated soil. I'll go down there tomorrow to check on what's happening."

"Thanks, I appreciate that," DeMarco said.

But DeMarco was really thinking that slowing down work on Callahan's project was no longer good enough—at least not for him. And delaying Callahan wasn't going to affect the McNultys one damn bit.

The McNultys had to go—and DeMarco thought he knew a way to make that happen. As for Callahan, he hadn't figured out what he was going to do about him yet, but some slap-on-the-wrist fine for improper asbestos removal wasn't sufficient to pay for what had happened to Elinore Dobbs. Callahan and the McNultys hadn't killed the woman, but if she didn't recover mentally, they might as well have.

13

DeMarco had decided that if he couldn't use the law to get the McNultys, then he'd use outlaws.

Superintendent O'Rourke had given him the idea when he mentioned that the McNultys occasionally smuggled cigarettes for the Providence mob. But DeMarco wasn't going to screw around with a crime as benign as depriving the state of Massachusetts of its exorbitant tax on cigarettes. He wanted the brothers in jail until they were old and toothless. Or if not old, he'd be satisfied with toothless, a condition they were likely to achieve when they annoyed the wrong people in prison.

A couple years ago, Mahoney's middle daughter, Molly, had some trouble with an addiction to both booze and gambling. She was clean now, but as a result of the gambling she got into debt in a major way to a casino boss in Atlantic City, and to get out of debt, she conspired with the casino boss in an insider trading scheme. Then she was arrested. DeMarco was able to keep Molly from going to jail—even though she deserved to go to jail—by turning a mobster in Philly named Al Castiglia against the casino boss. As for the casino boss, well, he just disappeared.

The guy who did the disappearing was one of the scariest people DeMarco had ever met, a man named Delray. Delray—DeMarco didn't know if that was his first or his last name—was Al Castiglia's enforcer.

He was built like a linebacker, he rarely spoke, and his most distinctive feature was one milk-colored, blind eye; the eye had met the pointy end of a shank while Delray was in prison.

What all this meant was that DeMarco knew a mobster in Philadelphia "that he'd once helped," and the mobster might now be willing to help him. He checked flights departing Logan and four hours later found himself in the City of Brotherly Love, where he was hoping to launch a plan to destroy two brothers.

———◆◆◆———

DeMarco used a pay phone to call Delray, preferring that there not be a record of him calling a man in Delray's line of business. The first thing Delray said to him was: "How are your teeth doing?"

One of the odd things about his initial encounter with Delray was at the time he met the man, he was suffering from a cracked tooth, couldn't get in to see his regular dentist, and Delray had recommended a nephew who was just starting his practice in D.C. So Delray's nephew was now DeMarco's dentist. Talk about six degrees of separation.

"My teeth are fine," DeMarco said. "And I've recommended your nephew to all my friends."

"Yeah, my sister tells me his practice is really growing. So why'd you call?"

"I need to meet with you and your boss."

Delray picked DeMarco up at his hotel near the Philadelphia airport. Delray had a dark complexion—DeMarco wasn't sure of his ethnicity—and, as always, was wearing sunglasses. He rarely took the glasses off because of his disfigured right eye. He was dressed casually in lightweight gray slacks and a blue polo shirt. He didn't say a word to DeMarco during the thirty-minute drive to Al Castiglia's house; he hadn't become a chatterbox since DeMarco last saw him.

Castiglia's house was a sprawling older home in a working-class neighborhood of Philadelphia. The area had not yet been gentrified by greedy developers, and with Castiglia living there, it probably wouldn't be until he either moved or died. Al Castiglia was no Elinore Dobbs. When Delray rang the doorbell, Castiglia answered the door himself.

Castiglia was a big man and getting bigger as he aged; he was six foot four and weighed close to three hundred pounds. He'd gained weight since the last time DeMarco saw him. He was close to seventy and mostly bald, just a few wispy strands of gray hair remaining on his big head. Because Philadelphia was experiencing the same heat wave as Boston, he was wearing a sleeveless white T-shirt, baggy shorts that reached below his knees, and sandals showing off hairy toes.

"Let's go down to the basement," Castiglia said. "It's cooler down there. I'm starting to believe all that global warming bullshit might be real."

There was a billiard table in the basement and a seating area with two comfortable old couches positioned for viewing a seventy-inch television screen.

"You want a beer?" Castiglia asked DeMarco.

"Sure," DeMarco said.

"How 'bout you, Delray?"

Delray shook his head.

Castiglia took two bottles from a refrigerator near the billiard table, and used an opener attached to the refrigerator door to open the beers. He handed one to DeMarco, saying: "They make that right here in Philly."

The label on the bottle said Kenzinger, a brand DeMarco had never heard of. He took a sip and said, "It's good."

"So how's Mahoney doing?" Castiglia asked.

In order to keep his daughter from going to jail for insider trading, Mahoney had been forced to meet with Castiglia and, for whatever reason, the two men actually liked each other. Maybe that was because there wasn't that much difference between gangsters and politicians; they just belonged to different gangs.

"He's pissed that the Republicans still control the House," DeMarco said, "but other than that, he's doing fine. And he's pretty much the reason I'm here. You see, Mahoney met this tough little old lady in Boston."

DeMarco proceeded to tell Castiglia the tale of Elinore Dobbs, how Callahan and the McNulty brothers were trying to force her to move, and then, the last straw, had made her fall down the stairs.

"This old lady, who was sharper than a tack until this happened, can barely remember her own name now," DeMarco concluded.

"Those sons of bitches," Castiglia said. Delray didn't speak, but he shook his head to convey his opinion of the low-handed thing the McNultys had done—and DeMarco had been counting on this. It had been his experience that almost all men loved their mothers, even the most despicable men. And, by extension, most men tended to care about old ladies because old ladies reminded them of Mom.

"So what do you need from me?" Castiglia asked. "You want me to send someone to Boston to kneecap these assholes."

"No. I want them in jail, not a hospital or a morgue."

"Okay," Castiglia said. "But I'm not exactly in law enforcement."

No shit, DeMarco almost said. "Do you know anyone in Providence? I mean, someone in your line of business?"

Castiglia shrugged. "I might know a couple guys there."

"Here's what I want," DeMarco said, "and you can name your price as long as it's not too outrageous. Somebody in Providence uses the McNultys to smuggle cigarettes from Virginia into Boston. They're not part of the outfit in Providence. They're just guys they use when they want something transported and don't want to use their own people for whatever reason."

Castiglia nodded. "There's good money in cigarettes and the risk is fairly low. I mean, in terms of jail time."

"Yeah," DeMarco said. "But I'm not talking about cigarettes. I want you to buy a crate of automatic weapons. And I mean machine guns. M16s, AR-15s, something like that modified to fire on full automatic. I don't care if the guns are pieces of shit, but they have to be machine guns. Then I need you to contact whoever it is in Providence that uses the McNultys and . . ."

DeMarco concluded by saying, "The risk to you is almost zero. You won't have to go near the weapons. And I'll compensate you and Providence."

Castiglia finished his beer and said, "You want another one?"

"No, I'm fine," DeMarco said.

Castiglia opened another Kenzinger and took a long swallow. "You know, it'd probably be cheaper for you to just have these guys whacked. By the time you pay for the guns and me and Providence . . . Well, I'm just saying."

"I don't want anyone killed," DeMarco said. "What they did to that woman, I feel like killing them but . . . I'm just not going to go down that path, if for no other reason than I don't want to end up as an accomplice to murder. If we do this the way I want, nobody goes to jail but the McNultys. I'll be satisfied if they spend a long time inside, and when they get there, maybe you can reach out to someone and make their time in prison as uncomfortable as possible."

"You okay with this, Delray?" Castiglia said.

Delray nodded. "I mean, shit, an old lady. Yeah, I'm okay with this."

To DeMarco, Castiglia said, "Okay. I'll call you. It'll take a couple days to set all this up, and that's assuming the guy in Providence will go along with it. And then you're going to have to come up with the money."

That could be a problem: coming up with the money.

The first thing DeMarco did when he arrived back in Boston was to go see Elinore again. He was hoping to see that she'd improved. When he arrived at her hospital room he found a woman sitting in a chair next to her bed, talking on a cell phone. She frowned when she saw DeMarco.

The woman was in her sixties, thin as a rail, and had dark hair tied back in a severe bun. In fact, *severe* pretty much described the woman. She was wearing a black dress—something appropriate for a funeral and not the July heat—and with her sharp nose, thin lips, and a face that looked as if it was frozen into a permanent frown, she reminded him of a discontented crow. She ended her call, saying, "I'm not sure how much longer I'll be in this god-awful city. You're just going to have to deal with that while I'm gone."

"Who are you?" she said to DeMarco.

"My name's Joe DeMarco. Congressman John Mahoney sent me here to help Elinore with the problems she's having with a developer named Callahan. Who are you?"

"Alice Silverman. I'm Elinore's daughter."

DeMarco had given Elinore's doctor the daughter's name, and the hospital must have contacted her. He was thinking it was a good thing that Silverman was now in Boston to help her mother—that is, he thought it was a good thing for about two more minutes.

"My mother didn't tell me anything about some congressman helping her," Silverman said. "And right now she can't even remember who I am half the time. I knew she was fighting to stay in her apartment but now . . . Well, she no longer has that problem."

"What do you mean?" DeMarco said.

"Yesterday, Mr. Callahan offered my mother half a million dollars to vacate her apartment and I accepted his offer."

"What! Do you have the authority to do that?" DeMarco asked.

"Not that it's any of your business, but yes I do. My mother gave me power of attorney a long time ago in case she was incapacitated for any reason. So I'm accepting Mr. Callahan's offer on her behalf. I've also agreed that neither my mother nor I will file a lawsuit against Mr. Callahan for her accident since he's being so generous."

"Son of a bitch," DeMarco muttered.

"What did you say?"

"Nothing. So what's going to happen to her?"

"I'm taking her to live near me in Portsmouth. I'm placing her in an assisted-living facility there. Mr. Callahan said he'd help me relocate her, take care of her furniture and all that."

"Callahan's the reason she's in the hospital," DeMarco said. "She didn't have an accident. These two shitheads—"

"I don't like that sort of language."

"Like I was saying, these *shitheads* working for Callahan rigged a trip wire across the stairs, and that's why your mother fell. They were trying to kill her, and you should never have signed anything agreeing not to sue him. The last thing your mother would have wanted was you accepting his offer."

Silverman did not take kindly to DeMarco chastising her. "I won't tolerate you telling me what I should or shouldn't have signed, and I don't care who you work for. Now get out of here. My mother needs her rest."

Ignoring Silverman, DeMarco walked over to stand next to Elinore's bed. "Elinore, how are you doing?"

Elinore looked up at him, her eyes cloudy and unable to focus. "What did you do with Eli?" she said.

"What?" DeMarco said.

"Eli was her dog. He died fifteen years ago," Silverman said. "Now leave. Immediately."

DeMarco felt like punching his fist through a wall. While he'd been in Philadelphia, Callahan had somehow gotten to Elinore's dour daughter.

And although he didn't know for sure, he figured that Silverman was going to dump her mother into the cheapest assisted-living facility she could find. By the time Elinore recovered enough to manage her own affairs—assuming she ever recovered—Callahan would have cleaned out her apartment and started knocking down the walls so there would be no way that she'd be able to move back in.

He hated to do it, but he called Mahoney. Mahoney went ballistic, screaming so loud DeMarco had to hold the phone a foot from his ear.

When Mahoney finally stopped yelling, DeMarco said, "I'm going to get these guys, boss."

"How? How in the hell are you going to do that?"

"I'm not going to tell you how on a cell phone, but the McNultys are going to go to jail. Then I'll deal with Callahan."

"I'll believe it when I see it," Mahoney said. He paused, then added, "Goddamnit, Joe, I sent you up there to help that woman and the next thing you know, she not only loses her apartment, she's a fucking vegetable. How did you let this happen?"

DeMarco couldn't believe it: now it was *his* fault that Elinore had been hurt. But then he thought: *Maybe Mahoney is right.* Maybe he should have considered the consequences of threatening the McNultys before he threatened them. Whatever the case, he was going to set things right.

DeMarco didn't have anything useful he could think to do while he waited to hear back from Al Castiglia. He'd been planning to contact a lawyer to initiate a lawsuit against Callahan for Elinore's injuries—but that option was no longer on the table thanks to Elinore's daughter.

He called Emma, curious if she'd learned any more about Congressman Sims. She didn't answer her phone—which was typical of Emma—and he didn't bother to leave a message.

He called Fitzgerald, the BPD detective, to see if he'd had any luck in tracking down the bum Greg Canyon. He figured that if the cops could find Canyon, then maybe Canyon could be forced to testify that the McNultys had paid him to help injure Elinore or cover up the crime—which would be one more charge to file against the McNultys when the time came to file charges. Fitzgerald, however, said that Canyon was not to be found. DeMarco, who was not in the best of moods, said that Fitzgerald needed to get off his fat ass and find the man—which resulted in he and Fitzgerald getting into a screaming match. The call ended with Fitzgerald saying, "Hey, go fuck yourself." Then he hung up before DeMarco could say, "No, you go fuck *yourself.*"

He called Boyer next to see how things were going insofar as stopping work on Callahan's construction project. The last time he'd spoken to Boyer, he'd been in the process of ratting Callahan out to MassDEP for asbestos removal and soil contamination issues.

Boyer informed him that work on the three-deckers near where he found the steam pipe covered with asbestos residue had been stopped, at least temporarily. "And I haven't reported the oil tank soil contamination yet," Boyer said. "I thought I'd wait until Flannery is back to work after the asbestos thing, then I'll report that one.

"This is actually turning out to be kind of fun. I called two of my buddies, old retired farts like me with nothing better to do, and in the morning we all get together for coffee, then mosey down to the construction site. It's like a game now, seeing who can spot the most problems. Yesterday, we saw over a dozen fall protection violations and one of my buddies got a video of them on his cell phone. We'll send that off to OSHA in a day or two. All of us know Flannery, and we want that prick to suffer."

DeMarco almost told Boyer that Elinore Dobbs had lost her battle with Callahan. Thanks to the McNultys she could no longer live alone, and thanks to her daughter, she was vacating her apartment. But he didn't. Instead he said, "Good. Keep the heat on him."

"Uh, there's one more thing," Boyer said. "And this doesn't have anything to do with safety or environmental stuff."

"Oh, yeah. What's that?" DeMarco said.

"I noticed yesterday, the guys doing the actual construction work— you know, pouring cement, carpentry, stringing wire— they were mostly white or black. But the guys doing the grunt work, digging with shovels, loading up rubble from the demolition, they were mostly Hispanic."

"So what?" DeMarco said, then the penny dropped. "You think they might be illegals?"

"Maybe," Boyer said. "Flannery is supposed to be using union labor, and I doubt these guys are union. But maybe Flannery cut some kind of deal with the unions, or maybe the unions can't stop him. I don't know. But the thing is, I could call INS and suggest they might want to have somebody check these guys' papers."

DeMarco pondered Boyer's suggestion for a moment and said, "Leave this alone for now. We'll keep it in our back pocket." The truth was, he didn't want to see a bunch of Hispanic guys hassled just because they were Hispanic and maybe lose their jobs, or worse. But like he'd told Boyer, that was a card they could play later.

That night, DeMarco walked to Fenway a couple hours before the Sox were scheduled to play the Yankees. He paid a scalper an exorbitant amount for a ticket—kings have been ransomed for less—then paid similarly exorbitant amounts for two hot dogs and three beers. But he had the pleasure of watching the Sox whip the Yankees. Any day the Yankees lost was a good day, and there were worse ways to spend a hot summer night in Boston.

———————◆◆◆———————

Al Castiglia called the next morning as DeMarco was eating break-fast in the hotel restaurant. The bruise on his right cheek had faded somewhat—although it was still noticeable—but at least he wasn't forced to sit at a table where he wouldn't spoil the other diners' appetites.

"Okay," Castiglia said. "I got everything lined up if you still want to do this thing. I can get you ten of the items you wanted for eighteen hundred apiece. They're pieces of shit, but you said that didn't matter. So that would be eighteen grand, but why don't we round it up to an even twenty."

"Round it up?" DeMarco said.

"Yeah. I talked to Providence. The guy in charge doesn't know your Boston knuckleheads. He's never heard of them. He checked around and found out that one of his guys used them a couple of times just because they were handy and he had too much else going on. What I'm saying is, Providence doesn't give a shit about the McNultys, and for five, he's willing to do what you want."

"Five? For a phone call?"

"Yeah. This might come back on Providence in some way. You can never tell. So five seems reasonable to me."

"Jesus."

"And my end, I'm thinking ten."

"You gotta be—"

"Hey, my guy has to get the money to the guy who has the merchandise. There's risk in that."

By "my guy" Castiglia meant Delray. He didn't want to say his name on the phone.

"He doesn't have to go anywhere near the merchandise," DeMarco said. "I already told you that. He can FedEx the money."

Ignoring DeMarco's whining, Castiglia continued. "Then he's gotta fly to Boston and talk with these maniacs. I mean, you told me yourself they were dangerous."

"They're dangerous to old ladies, not guys like him. He could handle them if he was on crutches." And Delray probably could.

"Then there's my fee for, you know, consultation and coordinating with Providence. None of this could happen if I didn't have the right connections. Anyway, you add it all up, it comes to thirty-five, which sounds pretty reasonable to me."

"This is about payback for an old lady," DeMarco said. "I thought you cared about her?"

"I do care," Castiglia said. "But business is business."

DeMarco didn't say anything for a moment, then said, "Okay. I need to talk to my boss. How soon can the items be where they're supposed to be?"

"They'll be there twenty-four hours after you tell me you got the money."

14

Sean Callahan, at his home on Beacon Hill, was reclining on a lounge chair near the rooftop lap pool, sipping a mimosa, and admiring his wife's body. The third Mrs. Callahan was sunning herself topless, lying on her stomach, her skin slick with suntan oil. She was wearing a bikini bottom the size of a cocktail napkin. At twenty-five, her body was flawless and she just took his breath away.

Sean met his first wife, Connie, when they were both in community college. He'd been twenty-one and she was twenty. He divorced her four years later. She'd just been a youthful mistake, and he often thought of her as his "starter wife." In retrospect, he realized she'd brought nothing to the marriage other than her body. She had no money—although he didn't either at the time—no useful social connections, no head for business, and she wasn't particularly good at mingling with the kind of people he needed to mingle with in those early days to grow his company.

He married the second Mrs. Callahan, Adele, when he was twenty-seven and she was twenty-two. His first wife had been dark haired, short, and heavy breasted. His second and third wives were both blue-eyed, long-legged blondes with tiny waists and perfect, perky breasts; their facial features were so similar they could have been sisters.

Unlike Connie, Adele had brought a *lot* to the marriage: she came from money and she and her parents mixed with the class of people he needed to meet. Adele was also quite bright and he frequently took her advice. He divorced her the year she turned forty, and the primary reason was because she'd turned forty.

The year before he divorced her, he'd met Rachel in Savannah. Rachel was twenty-three at the time and she looked amazingly like Adele had looked when she was the same age. In other words, he basically traded Adele in for a newer version of the same model, like replacing a 1995 Jag with a 2015 Jag. Like his first wife, Rachel didn't bring much to the marriage—just her beauty and her considerable charm. She was a marvelous hostess—but at this stage of his life, Sean didn't need a wife for her financial portfolio or her connections.

The only problem with having such a young wife was that he had to really work hard not to look like her father. He'd had a bit of surgery done around the eyes and chin, worked out with a personal trainer three mornings a week, and was religious about his diet and the amount of alcohol he consumed.

Sean knew he should be feeling nothing but contentment. He was in good health. He had a gorgeous spouse. The stock market was booming, and Delaney Square, the biggest development he'd ever put together, was going to make him a fortune. Hell, the way things were going, he just might become a billionaire. Making his first million had been a watershed experience but that wouldn't even compare to making a billion.

The cherry topping the ice-cream sundae that was his life was that Elinore Dobbs was finally out of his hair. With her gone, he was confident that the other tenants in the building wouldn't last much longer. Yesterday, in fact, he'd talked to the psychiatrist who was trying to convince the agoraphobic guy on the third floor to vacate, and the psychiatrist had come up with a hilarious solution, which the nut had agreed to. The whacko would get into a big wooden box—fortunately he wasn't claustrophobic—and they'd carry the box to a windowless van, drive to a new apartment that was identical to his old apartment, then carry the box inside so the guy would never be exposed in any way to the big bad outside world. What a hoot!

The only fly in the ointment—the only thing keeping him from total bliss—was that spiteful bastard Mahoney. He could just kick himself for not having been more diplomatic with Mahoney, but Mahoney's attitude had just pissed him off. And although Mahoney couldn't really cause him any substantial damage, he was like a gadfly around a stallion, and the stallion was tired of getting stung.

He'd received word yesterday that the IRS was going to audit him again. He'd gone through an IRS audit five years ago and it was not only an enormous, time-consuming pain in the ass but the fees he ended up paying accountants and lawyers were mind-boggling. He'd probably have been better off just paying what the IRS claimed he owed them in the first place. He'd also been informed that the SEC was looking into stocks in a pharmaceutical company that he'd sold. There was some nonsense about the coincidence of him selling his shares three days after he had dinner with the company's CEO.

Then there was what was happening at Delaney Square. Some son of a bitch was calling OSHA daily reporting safety violations and now Flannery was tied up in some asbestos abatement bullshit that Sean didn't really understand. He certainly hadn't ordered Flannery to cut any corners when it came to asbestos. But the safety and the asbestos issues weren't showstoppers—any more than the IRS audit was a showstopper. They were just expensive annoyances. It was unbelievable how much a construction project could cost even when nobody was working.

There had to be some way to get Mahoney off his back. Or if he couldn't force him to back off, which he didn't think he could, maybe there was some way to make peace. Mahoney had already gotten all the favorable publicity he was going to get off Elinore Dobbs. What else did he expect to gain at this point by tormenting a man who'd been a substantial contributor in the past? Mahoney was just being a vindictive prick.

One other thing occurred to him. Right now, Mahoney was causing him problems with the IRS and the SEC and OSHA—but those problems were nothing compared to the problem Mahoney could cause him if he looked in a different direction.

What he needed to do was apologize to Mahoney, as much as he hated to do that. He'd call the damn guy up, say he was sorry for losing his temper and saying the things he'd said. He'd explain that he'd just been having a bad day, plus the heat hadn't helped. Then he'd point out that it wasn't his fault that Dobbs had tripped and fallen and, in the end, he did right by her, considering the amount of money he gave her to buy out her lease. He'd try to convince Mahoney that they both needed to quit being so emotional and that Dobbs was water under the bridge. They needed to look to the future, he'd say. He would continue to support Mahoney as a contributing constituent and, hopefully, Mahoney would continue to support his business ventures. One hand washing the other, as it had always been. Yeah, he needed to swallow his pride and call the old bastard.

He reached for his cell phone—and just at that moment, his wife rolled over on her back and her perfect breasts pointed upward, directly at the sky. At her age, nothing on her body sagged. It took all his willpower, but he picked up his phone, found Mahoney's cell phone number in the contacts list, and hit the DIAL button. The phone rang twice and went to voice mail, which meant that Mahoney probably saw who was calling and decided not to take the call.

He found Mahoney's office number next, called the number, and told Mahoney's secretary to pass on a message that Mr. Callahan would like to speak with him. "Tell him," he said to the secretary, "that I just thought we should, ah, clear the air. Write that down on the message slip, please."

His wife stood up and stretched—and thoughts of Mahoney disappeared. He could feel an enormous woody coming on. Thank God, he wasn't yet at the age where he needed Viagra to get it up. He said, "Hey, why don't you come over here."

"Okay," she said, smiling sweetly. Rachel was smart enough to understand the primary asset she'd brought to the marriage.

15

DeMarco flew back to D.C. to talk to Mahoney.

He hadn't liked talking to Al Castiglia on the phone about his plans for the McNultys. The FBI could have a warrant to eavesdrop on Castiglia's phones—Castiglia being who he was—or the NSA could be eavesdropping without a warrant. DeMarco didn't think that he and Castiglia had said anything on the phone that could cause either of them a legal problem, but he wasn't going to take that chance with Mahoney.

DeMarco met Mahoney at his condo in the Watergate complex. Instead of sitting inside his air-conditioned apartment, Mahoney was out on the balcony even though it was ninety degrees outside. The gin and tonic in his hand was his only protection against the temperature. He was wearing green-and-white-checkered Bermuda shorts and a crimson Harvard T-shirt. (Mahoney had not gone to Harvard.) He was barefoot, and his legs and big flat feet were the color of skim milk.

"How's Elinore?" were the first words out of Mahoney's mouth.

"Not good. She doesn't seem to be improving."

"Goddamnit," Mahoney muttered.

Before Mahoney could blame him again for Elinore's condition, DeMarco said, "But I'm working on something that'll put the McNultys in prison for a long time, boss. And it'll be hard time. Federal time. And not in a minimum security prison."

"So what's the plan?"

"You don't want to know. But it involves your old pal Al Castiglia and a guy just like him in Providence."

"Huh," Mahoney said. "How much time are we talking about for the McNultys?"

"Based on a recent case in Boston I'd say a minimum of six years, but more likely ten with their records."

"Good," Mahoney said. He was probably thinking the same thing DeMarco had thought when he developed his plan: if the McNultys were convicted for the attempted murder of Elinore Dobbs, ten years was probably about how much time they would spend in prison. However, no amount of time in prison would make up for what they had done to Elinore mentally.

"But there's a problem," DeMarco said. "I need thirty-five grand to pull this off."

"Thirty-five grand?"

"Yeah."

Mahoney wasn't a rich man—at least he wasn't rich to the point where he had thirty-five thousand dollars he could easily afford to lose. He made over two hundred thousand a year as a congressman, then made twice that amount in various and sundry ways, some of those ways being arguably illegal. The problem with Mahoney, however, was that he spent money as fast as he made it. He had a large home in Boston, the condo in the Watergate, and his wife had a sailboat that he never boarded. He dressed well, he ate well, and the never-ending campaigning was expensive. Money slipped through Mahoney's fingers like water.

DeMarco expected that Mahoney would now start screaming, asking why in the hell DeMarco was bringing him problems instead of solving them, but he didn't. Instead he said, "I think I know where we can get the money."

"Really?" DeMarco said. "Where's that?"

"Sean Callahan."

"Callahan?"

"That's right. He called today and left a message that it's time to clear the air between us. He wants to kiss and make up. I think some of the stuff you're doing up there in Boston to derail his project is one reason, and I think some of the stuff I'm doing, like siccing the IRS on him, is another. He figures, even being the rich son of a bitch he is, that having me for a friend is better than having me for an enemy. So I want you to go see him and tell him it'll cost him fifty grand to be my friend again. That's what he contributed to my last campaign, and I think it's only appropriate that he make another contribution."

DeMarco smiled. He loved it: using Callahan's money to put the McNultys behind bars.

<hr />

DeMarco flew back to Boston the following day and right after he checked back in to the Park Plaza, he called Callahan's office. He told Callahan's secretary he worked for Congressman John Mahoney and would like to meet with Mr. Callahan. "Tell Mr. Callahan that Congressman Mahoney got the message he left yesterday."

An hour later, Callahan's secretary called back and said that Mr. Callahan could meet with him at six p.m.

"Great," DeMarco said. "Where at?"

"Mr. Callahan would like you to come to his home for cocktails. He said to dress casually."

"What's the address?" DeMarco said.

"Seventy-four Beacon Street," the secretary said. Then she added, "The Benjamin Mansion."

She said "the Benjamin Mansion" like it was a name DeMarco should recognize. As he didn't, he resorted to Google, where he learned that Sean Callahan had paid fifteen million for his home, which was 8,450 square feet of historically significant elegance and luxury. It had six bedrooms, six bathrooms, and eight working fireplaces. There were two large decks, a media room, a library, a gym, and a rooftop infinity-edge heated lap pool that overlooked the Public Garden. The home was constructed in 1828 and its architect was a famous fellow named Asher Benjamin, although DeMarco had never heard of him. He was, however, suitably impressed.

A maid wearing a pristine white apron over a black dress answered when DeMarco rang the doorbell of Seventy-four Beacon Street. She led him to a beautifully appointed library where Sean Callahan and his wife were sitting. The library had comfortable brown leather chairs, a blue-and-white Oriental rug, and a fireplace large enough to roast a hog. DeMarco wondered briefly if Callahan and his wife actually read the books on the floor-to-ceiling shelves.

DeMarco hadn't met Callahan before. He was over six feet tall, slim, had thinning dark hair combed straight back from a high forehead, a longish nose, and thin lips. DeMarco's immediate impression, possibly prejudiced by what he knew of Callahan, was that he looked like an arrogant prick.

Callahan's secretary had said to dress casually for cocktails but DeMarco, not being sure what *casually* meant when visiting a Beacon Hill address, had opted to wear a navy-blue sport coat over a white polo shirt, lightweight gray slacks, and black loafers. The sport jacket was the last thing he needed considering the temperature. The Callahans, however, were indeed dressed casually, Callahan wearing topsiders without socks, white linen trousers, and a green golf shirt that said THE COUNTRY CLUB BROOKLINE, which DeMarco knew was one of the most expensive and exclusive golf clubs on the East Coast.

Mrs. Callahan, introduced as Rachel, was a willowy blonde who was two decades younger than her husband. She was wearing a yellow tank top, very short white shorts, and sandals. DeMarco had awarded the title of Best Thighs in Boston to Dooley's wife, but now concluded that Rachel Callahan might deserve to wear the crown. However, as lovely as she was to look at, DeMarco really needed to speak to Callahan alone. He didn't need a witness.

"Rachel and I are having mint juleps," Callahan said. "She was raised in Savannah and says it's the only thing to drink on a hot evening like this. Would you care for one, Mr. DeMarco?"

"Call me Joe, and sure, I'd love a julep," DeMarco said, although he couldn't remember ever having had a mint julep before and would have preferred a beer. Not knowing what to say next with Rachel present, he said, "You have a lovely home," to which Rachel basically said: *Oh, this old thing?* She then prattled on about the bother of living in such an old building and having to constantly call someone to fix this or that. DeMarco almost said: *You ought to try living like Elinore Dobbs for a while, having to haul a generator out on your balcony and firing it off every time your fuckin' husband shuts off the power.* However, since DeMarco's mission was to pretend that he was there to smooth things over between Callahan and Mahoney, he instead sympathized with Rachel, saying that older homes were indeed a pain. He should know, he said, as he lived in an eighty-year-old townhouse in Georgetown, although his home didn't have a swimming pool or a gym, and his media room was also his living room.

Fortunately, a few moments later, Rachel said, "I have to excuse myself, gentlemen. Sean and I are going to a fund-raiser later this evening for the Boston Symphony, and I need to make myself look presentable."

Rachel Callahan would have looked presentable wearing a black plastic garbage bag—and she knew it. Both Callahan and DeMarco enjoyed the sight of her perfect derrière as she sashayed from the room.

"So, what can I do for you, Joe?" Callahan said.

"Mahoney got your message, Sean, how you wanted to patch things up between you and him. I'm here to facilitate that."

"Facilitate? Exactly what do you do for Mahoney, Joe?"

"I'm a lawyer, but I'm really the guy Mahoney tends to use when he has problems that need to be solved, like the Elinore Dobbs problem." DeMarco figured that Sean Callahan already knew that he'd been sent to help Elinore; the McNultys would have told him.

"Why didn't John just call me?" Callahan said.

DeMarco shook his head. "You really made the congressman angry, Sean. You offended him deeply, the way you spoke to him. On the other hand, he knows you've been a good friend in the past."

"Well, you can tell John that I apologize for the way I acted the last time we met. I was having a bad day. Regarding Mrs. Dobbs, I don't believe there is anything else I can do. After she had that unfortunate accident, she vacated her apartment and I compensated her quite generously. In fact, I was incredibly generous. Is there something else John expects me to do for her?"

"No," DeMarco said. "At least not for Elinore." He pretended to hesitate, as if he was searching for the right words, then said, "I think at this point the congressman is wondering what you're going to do for *him*, Sean. He feels that in order to reestablish the relationship the two of you once had, he'd appreciate some tangible evidence of your support. I mean, this year with all the nonsense the Republicans have been pulling . . . Well, he's going to have a real fight on his hands and he needs all the help he can get."

For a moment Callahan looked puzzled and DeMarco felt like saying: *For Christ's sake, Sean, this is a shakedown! How much more specific do I have to be?* But then he got it, and DeMarco could see the man struggling to control his temper. He took a breath and said, "Exactly how much does Mahoney feel he needs for me to demonstrate my support?"

"He was thinking it would be appropriate if you matched the contribution you made for his last campaign."

"That son of a bitch!" Callahan said, slamming his fist into the arm of the chair where he was sitting. "It's like I told him. He can't stop me from completing that project. He doesn't have that kind of power."

"The congressman knows that, Sean. But as I'm sure you've already seen, it's much better to have him on your side than working against you."

"You're not a lawyer. You're a fucking bagman!"

DeMarco was surprised that Callahan was so angry. He figured that Callahan should have known that Mahoney would want him to make some sort of contribution to make things right. No, it wasn't the money that was bothering Callahan, even as much as it was. He was angry because he didn't like the way his arm was being twisted and DeMarco couldn't really blame him—not that he gave a shit.

DeMarco stood up. "I'll let myself out, Sean. But I was hoping—as was Congressman Mahoney—that we could reach an accommodation this evening." DeMarco turned to leave, then turned back to face Callahan. "By the way, someone pointed out to me that you appear to have a number of workers on Delaney Street who might not be American citizens. You might want to—"

"This is extortion!" Callahan said. "Are you telling me if I don't pay Mahoney's price he's going to sic Immigration on me next?"

"Of course not, Sean. And I'm not going to even mention to the congressman that you used a word like *extortion*. I was trying to do you a favor. I was about to suggest that you might want to have your builder . . . What's his name? Flannigan? Flannery? You might tell him to make sure he's using folks that have the right papers. He might have gotten careless about that, the same way he did when it came to removing asbestos. Anyway, thank you for your time, Sean, and I'll let the congressman know that you've decided, as is your right, not to support his campaign."

DeMarco was halfway to the door when Callahan said, "Goddamnit, hold on."

DeMarco figured that Callahan had probably calculated how much it was costing him every hour work was delayed on Delaney Square, and simple arithmetic was telling him that fifty grand was a bargain.

"Tell Mahoney," Callahan said, "we have a deal provided I have no more problems on the project and he gets the IRS to back off on the audit they're planning."

"I'm afraid it's too late to stop the audit, Sean. I mean, it would be inappropriate for Mahoney to even speak to the IRS about it. If he did, it would appear as if he was improperly using the power of his office to help a constituent."

"Are you shitting me! He's the one who told them to do the audit."

"I doubt that, Sean. As I understand it the IRS uses some sort of formula to decide when to audit. Other than that, it's just sort of random. But—"

"Random, my ass. Mahoney was the one—"

"Aside from the audit, Sean, Mahoney's on your side from this point forward. You have his word on that. But Sean, I'm going to need the money by tomorrow. In cash. I'm sure you understand."

"I'll call you. Now get out of my house."

16

A cheap briefcase in his right hand—the briefcase and its contents courtesy of Sean Callahan—DeMarco entered the Lansdowne Pub. The Lansdowne is directly across a narrow street from Fenway, about the same distance the pitcher's mound is from home plate. The place was jam-packed with boisterous Red Sox fans, most of them already drunk even though the game wouldn't start for another two hours.

The Lansdowne is the quintessential Irish pub with a long dark bar, cone-shaped stained glass lamps over the bar, Jameson Whiskey and Guinness signs on the walls. DeMarco knew from prior visits that the wood forming the shelves behind the bar had been imported directly from Ireland. For some reason he'd never understood, there was an elaborate mahogany-and-glass bookcase on one wall filled with old tomes and various other knickknacks. Sitting near the bookcase, alone at a table for four, was Delray drinking a draft beer. As full as the place was, it seemed as if there was an invisible barrier surrounding Delray's table; even Boston's most aggressive drunks sensed that Delray wasn't a guy whose space you wanted to invade.

Delray was dressed in khaki-colored Bermuda shorts and a sleeveless white T-shirt; crudely drawn blue-ink prison tats were visible on his upper arms. Maybe the prison tats were another reason the Lansdowne's patrons decided it wouldn't be smart to jostle Delray's table and spill the beer he was drinking. As always, Delray's Ray-Bans covered his eyes.

DeMarco took a seat across from him and said, "You couldn't think of a quieter place for this meeting?"

"I'm going to the game. I've never seen a game at Fenway before and I wanted to see one there before they tear it down and build another stadium."

"If you don't have a ticket already, it's going to cost you a fortune to buy one."

"I know a guy," Delray said.

That figured.

"Everything all set?" DeMarco asked.

"Yeah, just like you wanted. Provided you got the money."

DeMarco offered him the briefcase and Delray took it from him. "I didn't think we'd be meeting in a place like this," DeMarco said. "You might want to find someplace safe to put that briefcase before you go to the game."

Delray flashed one of his rare smiles. "You think somebody might try to take it from me, DeMarco?"

DeMarco ignored the rhetorical question. "How long will it take to get the goods?"

"We already got 'em. When you called yesterday and said you had the money, Al didn't think you'd stiff him, so he paid the guy to deliver what you wanted. They're in a rented storage unit in Greenfield."

"Can anyone trace who rented the storage unit?"

"Don't worry about that," Delray said. Meaning: don't try to teach your daddy to suck eggs.

"And they're in a big crate like I told you?" DeMarco said.

"Yeah. And the guy tossed a couple sandbags into the box to add weight. It'll take two men to move it."

"Good. And Providence is ready for the call?"

"Yeah. Stop worrying. Al's taken care of everything."

At that moment a lanky black kid, tall enough to play in the NBA, walked over to the table where Delray and DeMarco were sitting. "You Delray?" he asked Delray.

"Yeah."

The kid handed him an envelope. "Two tickets, two rows up, halfway between the plate and first base."

"Thanks, and tell your boss thanks," Delray said.

The kid walked away and DeMarco said, "Two tickets?" He was half hoping Delray might invite him to join him. And the location of those tickets . . . Hell, *movie stars* would have a hard time getting those seats in Fenway. Delray would probably be seated right behind Ben Affleck and Matt Damon.

"When do you want to meet with the McNultys?" DeMarco asked.

"How 'bout tomorrow around three? I'll call their bar first to make sure they're there. So you pick me up at my hotel at two thirty and after the meet, you can drop me off at Logan."

DeMarco had been reduced to playing chauffeur in this little drama. "Where are you staying?" he asked.

"The Ritz-Carlton, near the Common."

You gotta be shitting me! was DeMarco's reaction. A room at the Ritz was probably six hundred bucks a night. How much did Castiglia pay this guy?

"Now it's time for you to go," Delray said.

"What?" DeMarco said. He'd been distracted by a woman coming toward Delray's table. She was at least six feet tall in sandals and was wearing shorts displaying coffee-colored legs that seemed to go on forever. Two large unrestrained breasts were moving beneath a thin white tank top. She had the body of a Vegas showgirl or an NFL cheerleader—and every drunk in the Lansdowne Pub had his eyes glued to her.

"Hey, baby," she said to Delray in a voice coated with sugar. DeMarco stood up and said, "I was just leaving." Neither Delray nor the woman acknowledged him.

When DeMarco picked up Delray the next day he suspected Delray was in an excellent mood, having spent the night with a long-stemmed beauty. But with Delray it was impossible to tell since the man had the emotional range of cork. When DeMarco asked, "How was the game?" Delray just grunted. But it sounded like a positive grunt. They drove to Revere without speaking and DeMarco stopped half a block from the McNulty brothers' tavern.

DeMarco noticed the neon sign saying THE SHAMROCK was on the ground, leaning against the side of the tavern, and two guys in a cherry picker were in the process of putting up a new sign that said MCNULTY'S. The Shamrock—or McNulty's—was getting a makeover.

Delray opened the passenger-side door and left the car without a word to DeMarco.

Delray walked into the bar and stopped so his eyes could adjust to the dim light. There were two old boozehounds at one end of the bar bickering about politics. He heard one of them say, "I'm telling you, that fuckin' Obama—" Then he stopped abruptly when he saw Delray—or Delray's complexion. Delray didn't care; he hadn't voted for Obama.

At the other end of the bar was a hefty female bartender with frizzy red hair talking to an old lady who was drinking beer and wearing a black stocking cap even though it was almost a hundred degrees outside. The McNultys were sitting at a table—DeMarco had described them accurately—and as Delray got closer he could see they were looking at furniture in a bar supply catalog. They looked up when they saw

Delray standing there looking down at them and one of them said, "What the hell do you want?"

"I'm the guy who called earlier. Like I told you on the phone, Soriano's got a job for you," Delray said. "And you speak to me that way again, I'll knock your teeth out."

Thanks to the influence of their late parents, the McNulty brothers hated every race and religion on earth, whites and Catholics sometimes, but not always, being the exception. As their mother and father sat in front of the television, smoking and drinking beer—they went through a case of beer almost every night—Roy and Ray learned about the duplicitous natures of niggers and spics and chinks and kikes and ragheads. White people who had money were disparaged because they'd been born with a silver spoon stuck up their ass, and priests were all faggots, according to Mom and Dad.

So they didn't like Delray before he opened his mouth. They didn't know if he was black—it was hard to tell—but he was something other than white. Maybe a dark-skinned wop—maybe his ancestors had been Sicilians screwed by Moorish invaders—or maybe he was a spic or possibly even an Arab. Nah, he wouldn't be an Arab. No way would Soriano have anything to do with a Muslim; Soriano may have been a degenerate criminal but he was a patriot.

And when the guy said he was going to knock out Roy's teeth, their initial reaction was to jump up and pound the shit out of him. But then—and simultaneously—they realized that this guy was likely to whip them both and, on top of that, was probably packing a gun.

"Sorry," Ray said. "Didn't realize you were Soriano's guy. You want a beer?"

"No," Delray said. "I want to finish my business with you and get out of this dump."

"Hey!" Roy said, but Ray placed a restraining hand on his brother's forearm. Roy could really be an idiot at times.

"Well, maybe it's a dump now," Ray said. "But as you can see we're fixing it up."

"Yeah, it'll be the next Studio 54 when you're done," Delray said.

Ray didn't know what Studio 54 was. Some fancy bar in Providence?

"There's a crate in a storage unit in Greenfield," Delray said. "Soriano said you have a van, which you'll need to transport it. And the crate's heavy. It'll take two guys to move it but you won't need a forklift or anything like that. So you pick up the crate tomorrow and deliver it to Soriano in Providence."

"How much?"

"Two grand."

Ray did the math: Two hours to Greenfield, maybe half an hour to pick up the crate, two hours to Providence from Greenfield, then an hour from Providence back to Boston. Five and a half hours of driving for two grand.

"What's in the crate? Cigarettes?" Ray asked.

"Guns."

"Whoa!" Roy said. "You can do major time for guns."

Delray didn't respond.

"Why'd Soriano send you to us?" Ray said, now not so certain two grand was worth the risk.

"Because this thing came up fast. The guy with the guns called Soriano yesterday, said he needed to unload 'em to pay a lawyer, and he gave Soriano a good price. I just happened to be here in Boston on some other business, but I'm not driving a truck or a van, so Soriano told me to come see you. He said he's used you before."

"Two grand seems kind of low, considering the risk," Ray said.

"Hey, if you're not interested, I don't give a shit. I'm not going to sit here and dicker with you. You want the job or not?"

"How do we know Soriano sent you?" Roy said. "You could be FBI, for all we know."

Delray made a noise that might have been a laugh. "Do I look like FBI to you? Anyway, call Soriano if you want to be sure. You have his number."

Ray took a cell phone from his pocket and said, "I'll do that. What's your name?"

"You don't need my name. Just describe me to Soriano"—and then Delray removed his sunglasses.

When the McNultys saw his pure-white right eye, Ray just raised his eyebrows, but Roy said, "Jesus." Then he added, "Uh, sorry."

Delray put the glasses back over his eyes.

Ray punched a number into his phone and after a couple of rings, he said, "Mr. Soriano? It's Ray McNulty. There's a guy here in our bar, kind of a, a dark-skinned guy with one eye that's sort of, uh, fucked up. Anyway, he said you sent him."

Ray listened as Soriano talked, Soriano basically saying the same thing as the guy with the eye had said, how this deal came up just yesterday and he needed someone with a van to go to Greenfield right away.

"Why didn't you just call us?" Ray said.

"Because, unless you're an idiot," Soriano said, "you don't talk about shit like this on a phone."

"Two seems a little low," Ray said. He listened for another minute, then smiled. "Okay," Ray said and disconnected the call. To Delray, he said, "Soriano said we get twenty-five hundred."

Delray said, "That's between you and Soriano. He'll pay you when he's got the merchandise."

Ray started to say something but Delray cut him off. "Has Soriano ever stiffed you before?"

"No," Ray said.

"All right then," Delray said. "You just make sure those guns make it to Providence by tomorrow night. They don't make it, if you decide to find your own buyer . . . Believe me, you don't want me coming back here again."

"Hey!" Roy said, insulted that this nigger—or whatever he was—would say something like that to them. But before he could do anything, his brother pressed down on his forearm again, like yanking on a dog's collar.

Delray dropped a yellow Post-it sticker on the table. "That's the name of the storage place, the unit the crate's in, and the combination for the lock on the door."

Delray took one last look around the bar, shook his head, and left.

After Delray had passed through the door, Roy said to his brother, "We should have kicked his ass, talking to us like that."

"Yeah, we should have," Ray said. But Roy could tell that he didn't mean it. "The good news is we can use the money. Sean may be picking up the cost of the remodel but a little extra cash would be good, especially now that he isn't paying us to get that old lady out of that building."

"I wonder how she's doing," Roy said.

"Who gives a shit? She was a pain in the ass. Hey, Doreen, how 'bout bringing us a couple of beers?"

"Get your own damn beer," Doreen said.

"I just hope Greg doesn't make it back here anytime soon," Roy said.

"How's he gonna get back?" Ray said. "By now, he already drank the money we gave him."

The McNultys had given Greg Canyon, the bum who helped them with Elinore Dobbs, a hundred bucks, and two hours after Elinore was injured Roy put him on a bus with a one-way ticket to New York. They told him not to come back to Boston for a month, but they figured they might never see him again. Since Canyon spent every dime he panhandled on booze, he might not ever earn enough to afford a ticket back. The only problem was that Canyon had been raised in Boston and he didn't know anyplace else so it was possible he might make the effort to return. But then, so what if he did? The McNultys knew the cops were trying to find Canyon because cops had stopped by places near their bar that sold cheap booze looking for him, but it wasn't like he was number one on the FBI's Most Wanted list.

For an alkie, Canyon was actually a fairly bright guy. He'd even gone to college before he became a full-time drunk and lost everything he owned. The McNultys had used him a few times when he came around the bar looking for a handout and they had some shitty job that Doreen was too lazy to do, like cleaning the restrooms the time the sewer backed up.

But Canyon refused to rig the wire across the top of the landing, saying he'd help but he wasn't going to kill anyone. So the McNultys installed the small eyebolts and the trip wire the night before, knowing Elinore Dobbs always got up early and would be the first person down the stairs in the morning. They'd lied to DeMarco and the Boston detective about being in the bar that night, knowing Doreen would back them up. Canyon's job had been to be inside the building, down on the second floor, and when he heard Elinore fall, to figure out a way to get rid of the wire and the eyebolts; they even gave him a pair of pliers so he could snip the wire quickly. And that's what Canyon did: snipped the wire, removed the eyebolts, and put in a new bulb while Elinore was unconscious and before the medics got there.

Roy walked behind the bar—giving that lazy bitch Doreen a dirty look—and poured two Budweisers using the tap. When he returned to the table, his brother was back to looking at the catalog.

"You know," Ray said, "I think I like these black stools better than the red ones. They look, I don't know, classier or something."

DeMarco dropped Delray off at Logan after his meeting with the McNultys, then used a pay phone to call the Boston office for the Bureau of Alcohol, Tobacco, Firearms and Explosives. He told whoever answered the phone that he had information regarding a crate of machine guns about to be delivered to a gangster in Providence. The woman who took the call sounded bored—liked he was calling to report someone who hadn't paid his parking tickets—but she transferred him to a guy who had gravel in his voice box.

"Sometime tomorrow," DeMarco said, "two men driving a white Ford Econoline van, license number 534-PSV, are going to pick up a crate of machine guns from a rental storage place called Casey's in Greenfield, Massachusetts. After they get the guns, they're taking them to a mob guy in Providence."

"What's your name?" the ATF agent said.

"I'm not going to tell you," DeMarco said.

"So what's the name of the guy in Providence?"

"I'm not going to tell you that either."

"Okay, but can you tell me what kind of guns we're talking about here?"

"I don't know exactly. M16s, AR-15s, AK-47s, something like that, all illegally modified to fire on full automatic."

"Well, those aren't exactly machine guns. I thought you meant like M60s or something."

Jesus, what was with these people? "Whatever," DeMarco said. "I'm not talking about fucking BB guns. So are you interested or not?"

"Yeah, we're interested if you're telling the truth. How do you know about these guns and the people picking them up?"

"I just do. So if you have any desire to make sure a dozen assault rifles don't end up in the hands of gangsters, you might want to arrest these guys tomorrow."

"How do I know we won't send a dozen guys to Greenfield tomorrow, and they'll just sit on their ass all day? For that matter, how do

I know this isn't some kind of trap to get agents in a spot where they can be ambushed?"

DeMarco closed his eyes and put his head against the glass of the phone booth. *How hard could this possibly be?* "Look," he said. "You do what you want. But tomorrow, if you don't arrest these guys, I'm going to call the *Globe* and tell them you had a tip to get automatic weapons off the street and you chose not to act on the tip. And in case you think the *Globe* won't believe me, I've recorded this conversation."

He hadn't recorded anything, but what did gravel-voice know?

Thinking he was now being recorded, the ATF agent became more formal. "Well, sir," he said, "thank you for reporting this situation to the ATF. I'll advise my supervisor immediately."

"Thank you," DeMarco said.

17

The McNultys woke up early the following morning—*early* for them meaning about nine a.m.—wanting to get a jump on the day since they had about five hours of driving to do. They stopped at a McDonald's and bought Egg McMuffins, hash browns, and coffee, but instead of heading immediately toward Greenfield, they drove out of their way to go by their bar in Revere. They didn't go inside, but stopped across the street and admired the new sign over the door.

"Goddamn, that's just beautiful," Ray said.

"Man, you are right about that," Roy said.

On the way to Greenfield, Ray said, "Maybe we oughta be thinkin' bigger when it comes to the bar."

"What do you mean?" Roy said.

"I mean, getting the new sign and new furniture will make it look better, but we need to do something to attract more customers. Maybe we oughta have a wet T-shirt contest once a week, or maybe . . ."

"Where would we get the girls?"

"Or maybe happy hour, like on Fridays, sell beer for a buck a glass."

"We'd lose our shirts."

"Yeah, at first, but we'd grow the crowd. We need to get young guys into the bar, guys with jobs, guys who'll bring their girlfriends, instead of a bunch of old farts collecting Social Security. And we need young chicks for customers, chicks that'll attract guys. We could have like Ladies Night every Wednesday, any girl under thirty who isn't a complete dog gets drinks for half price.

"But what we really need," Ray said, unable to contain his excitement, "is to get someone besides Doreen behind the bar. We need a young broad with big tits. Goddamn Doreen, she's not exactly the friendliest woman on the planet, and the way she looks . . ."

"Yeah, I know what you mean," Roy said. "But if we hired a young gal, we'd have to pay her more than we're paying Doreen, and if we fire Doreen, who'd manage the bar?"

"Goddamnit! How come you come up with an argument for every idea I have? I'm just sayin' what's the point of fixing up the bar if we don't do something to increase business?"

They reached the storage place in Greenfield about noon; the guns were supposed to be in unit number sixteen. They found the unit, which had one of those roll-up metal garage doors, and could see the lock on the door. Ray pulled out the Post-it note with the combination for the lock, although the combination was easy to remember: 38R-24L-36R—like the figure he wished Doreen had.

The only thing inside the storage unit—which was hotter than an oven—was a single wooden crate with rope handles on each end. Roy went to one end of the crate, Ray to the other. "Use your legs, not your back," Roy said.

They picked up the crate and slid it into the back of the van.

"What do we do about the lock?" Roy said.

"Shit, I don't know," Ray said. "I guess we might as well take it with us. It's a good lock."

"Okey-dokey," Roy said.

Three miles from the storage unit, they stopped for a red light—and four huge black Suburban SUVs came out of nowhere, blocked them in on all sides, and about a dozen guys came out of the SUVs, all wearing body armor and helmets with visors, pointing M16s at them.

"Aw, fuck me," Ray said.

The arrest was reported in the *Globe* the following morning. It wasn't a big enough deal to warrant a press conference, but the ATF made sure they got the credit for taking ten assault rifles and two violent criminals off the street.

DeMarco called Mahoney first to let him know that the McNultys had been arrested. Mahoney's response was: "Good. But what about Callahan?"

"I don't know. I haven't figured out what to do about him yet."

"Well, figure it out," Mahoney said.

And DeMarco thought: *Would it have killed you, just once, to say, Great job, Joe.*

His next call was to Delray. "It's done. Thanks for your help and thank Al for me."

"They shouldn't have hurt that old lady," Delray said.

"Are you worried they might identify you or name Soriano? You told me you didn't give them your name but you're, uh, kind of distinctive-looking."

Delray made a sound that might have been a laugh. "No matter how much time they have to serve, those guys aren't going to say anything about Soriano or me. They know Soriano works for Gervasi and they know Gervasi can get to them in any prison in the country. And they think I work for Soriano. And even if they were dumb enough to say I told them to pick up the guns and deliver them to Soriano, I'd just deny it and so would Soriano. They're the ones who were arrested with the guns in their van, and they can't prove anyone else was involved."

At eleven a.m., not long after speaking with Delray, DeMarco attended the McNultys' arraignment. He made sure he got there early enough to get a seat right behind the defense table. When the McNultys were led out to stand next to a public defender they'd probably met fifteen minutes before the arraignment, they both saw DeMarco—and DeMarco smiled at them. Roy lost it. "You motherfucker," he screamed and started toward DeMarco, but a big bailiff grabbed his collar, jerked him backward, and told him to shut up and go stand next to his lawyer.

Naturally, they pled not guilty in spite of the evidence against them. Their lawyer requested bail, having the balls to say that although the McNultys' criminal records might indicate otherwise, they were respected local businessmen with deep ties to the community. Plus, neither brother had, or had ever had, a passport. The judge took about two seconds to set their bail at two hundred grand—a hundred per brother—and said they wouldn't be allowed to leave the state of Massachusetts without the permission of the court, and set a trial date for six months away.

It hadn't occurred to DeMarco that they'd be given bail. It *should* have occurred to him—he was a lawyer, after all—and he knew that with almost any crime less severe than murder even the most obviously guilty are allowed to roam the streets until their trial. But shit.

Six hours after their arraignment, Roy and Ray were back in McNulty's drinking. To scrape up the money they'd needed to pay the bondsman's fee, they had to give the bastard their second car, the red Camaro, which they were sure was worth at least ten grand. They also had to put up their bar for collateral; if they skipped before their trial, McNulty's would become the property of the bondsman, a Polack named Sandusky. They planned to get roaring drunk that night and, in the mood they were in, God help any dumb shit who pissed them off.

When they told Doreen to bring them a bottle of Jameson's—and not a bottle they'd watered down—she didn't tell them to get their own fuckin' bottle if they wanted one. The McNultys took a lot of lip off Doreen, but she knew this wasn't the time for lip. She also knew that this wasn't the time to ask what was going to happen to her if they went to jail.

The McNultys had spent the previous night in a cell pondering their fate and wondering how it was that they'd been arrested. They'd originally concluded that most likely the feds—FBI or ATF—had been monitoring Gervasi's or Soriano's phone calls, those guys being major hoods. But since they didn't say anything on the phone about picking up a crate of guns, the feds must have started following them after they talked to Soriano. Or maybe the feds had been following the guns, just waiting for someone to pick them up. Whatever the case, they were screwed.

They didn't see any way they wouldn't go to jail. Their defense was going to be that they'd been hired to pick up a box in Greenfield—hauling shit was the kind of thing they did to supplement their income, like hauling shit occasionally for Sean Callahan—and they had no idea what was in the box. Yeah right, a jury would say. But when they were asked who told them to pick up the box, well, that was going to be a problem.

They agreed it would not only be futile, but possibly suicidal, to point the finger at Soriano and that scary motherfucker with the white eye. For one thing, if they said that Soriano had hired them to pick up the weapons, Soriano would just deny it. When Ray had called Soriano to make sure the one-eyed guy really worked for him, he'd never even mentioned guns on the phone. Plus, Soriano hadn't even given them any money in advance. So the likelihood of them getting a reduced sentence by testifying against Soriano was almost zero since the cops wouldn't be able to build a case against Soriano using their testimony. But more importantly, they both knew—with absolute certainty—that if Soriano found out they were planning to testify against him, he'd have them whacked.

But when they saw DeMarco in the courtroom, they realized immediately that *he* was the guy who'd set them up. As soon as he smiled at them, they had no doubt. Somehow, some way, that slick son of a bitch had cut a deal with Soriano and he did it because of what they did to that old biddy. The bottom line, however, was still the same: they were going to jail.

When they'd asked their useless public defender how much time they could get for being caught with ten machine guns, he'd hemmed and hawed, and said it depended on this or that, but it was likely to be eight to ten years because of their records. Politicians didn't have the guts to change the gun control laws as that might keep them from getting reelected, so what they did instead was make sure that whenever some criminal committed a gun-related crime the sentencing judge came down on the criminal like a ton of bricks.

The McNultys knew they were screwed—and they knew it was DeMarco who'd screwed them.

"What are we going to do about the bar?" Roy said, and for a minute Ray thought his younger brother was going to cry. And he could understand why; he felt like crying himself. They'd just put up the new MCNULTY'S sign, telling the whole world that the bar was theirs, and now they might lose the place.

"I guess we could let Doreen manage it while we're inside," Ray said. "I mean, shit, she's the one who basically manages it now."

"Do you think she'll try to rip us off?" Roy said.

"Probably. But that's better than losing the bar. At least we'll have it to come back to when we get out."

It was funny, but neither McNulty really considered running. They'd never lived anywhere but Boston and had only traveled outside of the city a handful of times. And when they were away from Boston, they always felt out of place and always wanted to return home immediately. Furthermore, if they ran, how would they live? They could try to sell the bar before their trial and then run, but as the bar was the collateral they'd given the bondsman, he'd stop them from selling it if he could. Then even if they could sell it, they'd probably only get a hundred grand or two. How long could two men, who would have to pay for rent and food and booze, live off a hundred grand? Four, five years if they worried about every penny they spent? Whatever the case, they certainly wouldn't make enough from selling the bar to live on for the rest of their lives.

So, if they split before their trial, they'd have to find some shitty place to live that wouldn't cost them an arm and a leg—like fuckin' Penntucky—and eventually get jobs to support themselves. But as they'd never had real jobs before, what kind of jobs could they expect to get? Dishwashers in a restaurant? Washing cars? Their livelihood had always depended on the bar and knowing people—like that asshole Soriano—who could steer them toward petty crimes.

They also knew they could do the time. The longest stretch they'd done in prison was two years, but they knew they could do ten if they had to. They weren't going to go nuts or slash their wrists. They'd prob- ably end up having to join some white gang so the coloreds wouldn't kill them, but that was okay. Plus, they'd lift weights every day, and because they wouldn't be able to drink, they'd come out in great shape. And while they were in prison, they'd make connections that would be invaluable after they were free. Prison, for career criminals, was a great place to network.

Yeah, they'd survive—provided they could do the time in the same place. As long as they had each other's backs, they'd always be okay.

"What are we going to do about DeMarco?" Roy said.

"We're gonna kill him," Ray said.

18

What DeMarco wanted to do was skedaddle back to Washington.

He didn't like the idea of remaining in Boston with the McNultys on the loose, but he didn't have a choice. He wanted—and Mahoney wanted—Callahan to pay for what had happened to Elinore Dobbs. Callahan was the person really responsible for her condition; the McNulty brothers were just the tools he'd used.

He did have one idea for how to deal with Callahan, but he didn't want to play that card just yet. What he could do was offer the McNultys a deal: in exchange for a reduced sentence, they would agree to testify that Callahan had ordered them to kill or injure Elinore, and then the cops might be able to get Callahan as an accessory to attempted murder. Mahoney, of course, would have to lean on the right federal and state prosecutors to make this happen.

DeMarco didn't like this idea, however, because that would mean that the McNultys would spend less time in prison and he wanted them to spend a *lot* of time in prison to make up for Elinore. So he preferred to come up with something else when it came to Callahan.

Callahan, however, was a whole different animal than the McNultys. He wasn't a petty criminal, and he was rich. This meant that if he was committing crimes, they would be complicated, well-camouflaged crimes, crimes involving things like tax evasion or whatever laws developers stretch to maximize their profits. Callahan was not going to be maneuvered into doing something as stupid as picking up a crate of machine guns, and DeMarco figured he had a snowball's chance in hell insofar as proving Callahan was doing anything illegal. And even if he did learn that Callahan was breaking the law, thanks to his wealth, he would have a flock of well-paid lawyers helping to make sure he didn't spend a day in jail.

As for continuing to disrupt the project on Delaney Street, what would be the point? Elinore was no longer there and, in the end, no matter what problems DeMarco caused him, Callahan was going to complete the project and make a fortune.

So what was he going to do about Callahan? Ultimately, whether he liked it or not, he and Mahoney might have to be satisfied that they'd used Callahan's money to put the McNultys in jail, and Callahan was not only going to get away with what he'd done to Elinore he was going to become even richer.

As the old saying went: life sucked, and then you died. That is, life sucked for folks like Elinore, and it sucked for guys like the McNultys, but not so much for people like Callahan who lived in a mansion on Beacon Hill with a gorgeous young wife.

It occurred to DeMarco that he really didn't know all that much about Callahan and that he should do some research. Or maybe doing research was just a way of pretending he was doing something productive since he didn't know what else to do.

He went to the hotel restaurant—after a while a hotel room made him feel claustrophobic—plugged the power cord for his laptop into a convenient outlet, and ordered a pot of coffee. Callahan had been featured in a couple of Boston publications showing pictures of developments he'd completed, his historic home on Beacon Hill, and his two most recent wives. Five years ago, *Forbes* included Callahan in an article about up-and-comers in the real estate world, and he even had his own Wikipedia page. DeMarco was fairly sure he'd never have his own Wikipedia page unless he assassinated Mahoney.

DeMarco learned that Callahan hadn't been born with a silver spoon in his mouth, which surprised him. He hadn't been poor as a kid, but he hadn't been rich, either. He went to a community college, got a business degree, then hooked up with a guy named Carl Rosenberg. Rosenberg flipped houses, owned and managed a midsized apartment building in Chelsea, and was the brains behind a couple small developments: a strip mall near Medford and renovating some public housing in Dorchester. DeMarco wondered how Rosenberg felt about his protégé becoming such a huge success.

About the only other thing DeMarco learned was that Callahan wasn't the until-death-do-us-part type. He married his first wife, a lady named Connie, when he was twenty-one and then divorced her just four years later. With a little effort, DeMarco found Connie's Facebook page. At the age of forty-six—a year younger than Callahan was now—Connie was a dark-haired, attractive woman, the mother of three children by her second husband, and she liked gardening. In other words, to judge by her photo and profile, she as a nice forty-six-year-old mom who liked to putter in the garden—but certainly not a bombshell.

Callahan's second and third wives were bombshells—tall, long-legged, blue-eyed, curvaceous blondes. When he saw a photo of Callahan's second wife, he noticed that she looked enough like his third wife to be her sister—or, considering their age difference, her mother. But so what? The man liked young blondes. That hardly made him unique.

After an hour, DeMarco decided he hadn't learned anything online that would help him nail Callahan, and he was tired of sitting and pecking on a keyboard. He needed someone who could give him a better idea of the way developments were structured and financed, someone who might have some insight into how developers like Callahan bent the law to be so successful. It occurred to him that Callahan's old business partner, Carl Rosenberg, might be a good guy to talk to.

DeMarco called Rosenberg's office and Rosenberg answered the phone himself. DeMarco said he'd like to meet with him, and naturally Rosenberg asked why. DeMarco thought about lying, saying that he was interested in purchasing the apartment building Rosenberg owned in Chelsea, then decided not to.

"It's about Sean Callahan and his development on Delaney Street," DeMarco said. "I work for Congressman John Mahoney and he doesn't like the way Callahan has treated the tenants he's trying to force out of a building he wants to demolish."

"Yeah, I saw Mahoney's press conference with that old lady," Rosenberg said. "Sean can be a real . . . Let's just say he plays hardball."

"Well, that's what I wanted to talk to you about, Mr. Rosenberg, about the way Sean plays," DeMarco said.

"Sure, why not. I'll be here until three this afternoon. I'm located at . . ."

DeMarco thought about walking to Rosenberg's office—it was a little over a mile from the Park Plaza—but decided to take a cab. It was too hot and humid for walking, and he didn't want to drive his rental car because finding a parking space in Boston was like trying to find the Holy Grail. As he was waiting for a taxi to pull up to the hotel entrance, he glanced across the street—and saw the McNulty brothers, illegally parked in a loading zone, driving a ten-year-old blue Toyota Corolla.

"There he is," Ray said to Roy.

They were driving Doreen's car, which Doreen was not happy about—but they'd been forced to use her car since their van had been impounded by the ATF when they were arrested and they had to give the bondsman their Camaro.

The McNultys, like DeMarco, didn't have a plan. They weren't planners—they weren't strategic thinkers—they were opportunists, like vultures. In this case, they were hoping an opportunity to kill De-Marco would present itself as they considered him responsible for the many years they were about to spend in prison. And they wanted to kill him in such a fashion that they wouldn't be arrested for murder—but that's as far as their thinking had gone.

They'd found DeMarco by simply calling hotels in Boston, starting with five-star establishments and working their way down a list they found on the Internet. They figured a guy who wore a suit would stay at a nice hotel. They asked whoever answered the phone if they had a guest named Joe DeMarco registered, and an hour after they started calling, they struck gold at the Park Plaza. The clerk at the Park Plaza said, "Yes, we have a Mr. DeMarco staying here. Do you want me to ring his room?"

"Yeah," Ray said, and then hung up while the phone was ringing.

"So now what?" Roy said, after his brother told him that DeMarco was at the Park Plaza.

"I dunno," Ray said. "I guess we go over there and check the place out, see if we can spot him."

"Sounds like a plan to me," Roy said—even though it wasn't a plan at all.

And that's what the McNultys were doing when DeMarco stepped out of the Park Plaza to catch a cab.

Shit, DeMarco thought, when he saw the McNultys parked across the street. What were those two thugs doing?

DeMarco thought briefly about walking over to confront them, but at that moment a cab stopped in front of him and the hotel doorman opened the rear door of the cab.

DeMarco gave the cabbie Rosenberg's address, and as they were driving, he looked back to see if the McNultys were following. They were. Son of a bitch.

The first thought that crossed his mind was that they were planning to get even with him for their arrest, either kill him or beat him so badly he ended up in the hospital again. He could think of no other reason why they'd be following him. It wasn't like he was a witness to the crime they'd committed so they couldn't be planning to intimidate him into not testifying against them. It was possible that they wanted to understand how he'd gotten the Providence mob to cooperate with him and wanted to question him. Naw, these guys didn't want to talk to him or question him or intimidate him. They wanted to kill him.

The cab stopped at Rosenberg's address and when DeMarco stepped out of the cab, his initial impulse was to point at the McNultys when they drove by to let them know that he knew they were following him. Then he decided not to. Right now he knew they were tailing him, and they didn't know that he knew. Maybe there was some way he could use that to his advantage—but until then, he needed to be careful.

He wished he had a gun.

———◆———

"I wish we had a gun," Ray said.

"Yeah, me too," Roy said.

After they were arrested, the ATF not only searched their van and impounded it as so-called evidence, they also executed search warrants on their apartment and their bar looking for more weapons and any other evidence related to the assault weapons charge. At McNulty's, the ATF found a sawed-off shotgun they kept behind the bar in case some punk tried to rob them, and in their apartment they found an unregistered .45 automatic. The shotgun was illegal because it was sawed off, and the pistol was illegal because it was not only unregistered but the McNultys, being convicted felons, weren't allowed to possess firearms. These additional weapons charges were piled on top of the greater charge of being in possession of ten machine guns, but the bottom line was that they didn't have a gun.

"We could talk to Sheenan," Roy said. "He could hook us up with a piece."

"Yeah," Ray said. "But if we get caught with a gun on us, they'll revoke our bail and we'll end up sitting in a cell for six months before the trial."

"You got a point there," Roy said.

"Plus, shooting this fucker's too good for him," Ray said. "It'll be over too quick. I want to break every bone in his body before we kill him."

"We oughta get a couple of baseball bats," Roy said. "They can't revoke our bail if we got a bat in the car. We'll just say we were going to a batting cage to, you know, relieve the stress."

"Not baseball bats," Ray said. "They're too long. I think we should get those little bats they use to smack fish with. What the hell do they call those things?"

"Oh, I know what you mean," Roy said. "But I don't know what they call 'em. Little fish bats, I guess."

"Yeah, those would be perfect," Ray said. "We slip them inside our jackets and—"

"Our jackets! It's ninety-eight fuckin' degrees outside."

"You know, you say the dumbest things sometimes."

"I'm just saying . . ."

They sat in silence for a few minutes, Ray wishing they'd brought a cooler filled with beer and crushed ice.

"I wonder what he's doing inside that building," Roy said. "I wonder who he's seeing."

"I wonder what he's still doing in Boston," Ray said. "He came here to help that old broad, but she's out of the picture now. Then he stuck around to fuck us up with the ATF and hung around for the arraignment, but why's he still here?"

"I don't know," Roy said. "But you got a point. He could leave at any time and head back to D.C., although I suppose we could fly down there and get him if we have to."

"The judge said if we left the state, he'd revoke our bail."

"How would anyone know we left? It's not like we got those ankle monitors on."

"Because if we flew, there'd be a record of us flying. And we could even get stopped by those TSA guys if our names are on some kind of watch list."

"Why would our names be on a watch list? We're Americans, not fuckin' terrorists."

"You know, those watch lists aren't just used for . . . Aw, never mind. We can't afford to fly there anyway, and it'll take us eleven hours to drive there. We just need to work fast and take care of him before he splits."

19

Rosenberg's office was on Westland Avenue, about two blocks from Christian Science Plaza with its magnificent reflecting pool and a domed cathedral that looked like it belonged in Venice. The church was called the First Church of Christ, Scientist—making DeMarco think of Jesus holding up a test tube to see if He'd gotten the experiment right. If the experiment was the human race, He had some work to do.

Rosenberg's office was on the third floor of an older brick building, and as soon as DeMarco stepped inside, he could see that Rosenberg's office was also his home. He wondered if Rosenberg had fallen on hard times since he'd worked with Sean Callahan. In Rosenberg's living room, in addition to a small television set and a short sofa, were file cabinets and a desk with an ancient Dell computer on it. Behind the desk were black-and-white photos of historic Boston buildings: the Old North Church, Faneuil Hall, and the Old State House on Washington Street. DeMarco liked the photos.

Rosenberg was in his seventies, with wavy white hair that swept back over his ears and touched his collar and a neatly trimmed white goatee. He was dressed in a beige linen suit, a red bowtie, and brown-and-white saddle shoes. He looked spiffy, like a Jewish Colonel Sanders. His eyes crinkled into a smile when he saw DeMarco, and DeMarco got the impression that he was like Elinore Dobbs had been before she was injured: no matter what life tossed at him, he remained a perpetually cheerful, optimistic person.

Rosenberg pointed him to a chair and said, "So, Joe, what's on your mind?"

DeMarco again elected to tell Rosenberg the truth. He told him how Mahoney met Elinore, the sorts of things that Callahan had done to force the old woman to vacate the building, and how Callahan eventually won when Elinore took a convenient tumble down a flight of stairs.

"And you seriously think Sean was responsible for her getting hurt?"

"Yeah, I do," DeMarco said. "I think he told the McNultys to do whatever was necessary to get her out of the building, and those two morons rigged a trip wire across the stairs hoping to kill her. Now that poor woman can barely remember her own name."

"That's just terrible," Rosenberg said. "But what do you want from me?"

"To tell you the truth, I don't know. I'm just trying to get a handle on Callahan. Elinore can't sue him thanks to her daughter, so I'm trying to come up with some other angle to pursue. I figured since he used to be your partner, you might be able to help. How'd you meet him in the first place?"

"I used to be a guest speaker at a class that prepared folks to get their real estate licenses," Rosenberg said. "I'd tell the students about flipping houses and how you could get into serious trouble if you didn't do your homework and got too greedy. Anyway, Sean was in one of my classes, and after he got his license he asked me for a job.

"I've always worked alone, but at the time I had a lot going on and decided I could use his help. And it was a good decision. He was a go-getter, he learned fast, and he worked his *tuchus* off. The couple of years he worked for me, I made more money than I did in the previous decade.

"Anyway, one of the projects we worked on together was renovating some public housing in Dorchester, and Sean got smart on public housing, the federal and state agencies involved, the city council people who had some influence, and so on. Then he got wind of a plan to build some low-income housing in another part of Boston, and he pretty much went behind my back to get the contract. And he just took off from there."

"So he screwed you," DeMarco said.

"You could say that, but he didn't do anything illegal. We didn't have a formal partnership agreement—but a nicer guy would have included me in the deal since I'd been a mentor to him and gave him his first real job. Anyway, like I said, after that he took off like a rocket, using the money from that project to go after bigger things, and before he was thirty he was millionaire."

"Huh," DeMarco said. He didn't see how any of this could help, but then Rosenberg said something that did help.

"I'll tell you the person who really got screwed by him was Adele, his second wife. She was an only child and her family was worth ten, twenty million when she married Sean. Well, Adele's dad never liked Sean. Thought he wasn't good enough for his little girl and figured he'd never amount to anything. So her father forced Sean to sign a prenup to prevent him from getting his hands on the family money if they divorced."

Rosenberg laughed. "What Adele's old man never considered was that the prenup could work to Sean's advantage if he divorced Adele. You see, prenups often protect what's called nonmarital assets, and Adele's inheritance would be considered such an asset. But Sean's company was also a nonmarital asset since he formed the company before the marriage. What this meant was that Adele could get at income Sean made off his company while they were married, but she couldn't get to all the assets he had tied up in the company, like cash reserves and properties he owned for future development. And, as you might expect, almost all of Sean's wealth was in his company at the time of the divorce. So I don't know all the legal ins and outs. But by the time the lawyers got through fighting, Adele got the short end of the stick and only ended up with a condo in Boston, a house on the Cape, and a settlement of twenty or thirty million."

"I wouldn't call a house on Cape Cod, a city condo, and twenty million getting the short end of the stick," DeMarco said.

"No, but twenty million isn't two *hundred* million, which is what she might have gotten if she hadn't signed the prenup. But you're right: Adele's never going to have to apply for welfare. And the thing that really pissed her off wasn't the money. She was very prominent in the Boston social scene and Sean humiliated her when he dumped her for a twenty-something Georgia peach. Adele is one very bitter woman."

"Carl," DeMarco said. "Let me buy you lunch. I want to ask you a couple more questions."

"Sounds good to me," Rosenberg said. "A man's gotta eat."

They took the elevator to the lobby of Rosenberg's building and when they stepped outside, DeMarco looked around to see if the McNultys were parked nearby. They were. He still didn't want them to know that he'd spotted them tailing him, so he just glanced over at them once, then forced himself not to look again as he and Rosenberg walked to the restaurant. He needed to figure out some way to deal with those guys.

They ate at a place called Woody's Grill and Tap on Hemenway Street, half a block from Rosenberg's apartment/office. The waitress was a college-age kid with pink hair and a brilliant smile, and when she saw Rosenberg she said, "Carl! Where have you been? I thought you didn't love me anymore."

"I'll never stop loving you, darling," Rosenberg said, "but I'm just not ready to settle down with one woman yet."

"You're breakin' my heart, Carl," the waitress said.

Rosenberg ordered ice tea and a Reuben, and as that sounded good, DeMarco ordered the same. While waiting for their lunches to arrive, DeMarco said, "Tell me how a project like Delaney Square comes together."

What DeMarco was really wondering was how precarious Sean Callahan's financial position might be. If he was teetering on the edge financially, maybe DeMarco could devise a way to give him a wee nudge and over the edge he goes.

"Well, as you might guess, it's complicated," Rosenberg said. "A project, especially one as big as Delaney Square, starts five, six, seven years before they dig the first spadeful of dirt. The developer has to purchase the land or the properties he wants, and get some firm to design whatever he's building. He's got to do environmental impact studies and get a million permits from the city. And along the way there will be some neighborhood association or historical society fighting whatever he wants to do, and he's got to deal with them. Then, because he's going to have to tear up city streets and tie in to utilities like power, sewer, and water, he has to wrestle with the city to work all that out. So it isn't until after all the preliminary stuff is done and the design is complete and he's figured out a way to get around most of the roadblocks that he hires a construction firm and they start building. Then it takes however long it takes, depending on the problems he encounters during construction."

And DeMarco thought: *Someone like Elinore Dobbs being one of those problems.*

"But the first thing he has to do, before he completes the designs or buys all the land, is line up the money," Rosenberg said. "With Delaney Square, according to what I've read, you're talking five hundred million bucks. So Sean can't just walk into his local neighborhood bank and get a loan like he's buying a house. For a project that size, he'll have to convince one or more of the major banks to loan him the money, but they'll only loan him eighty percent of what he needs. He'll have to line up the other twenty percent from other sources or use his own money, which I imagine isn't all that liquid. So now we're talking about a hundred million that he has to come up with from private investors.

"The other thing is the bank doesn't give him the entire eighty percent up front. They dole it out in increments based on the project reaching certain milestones. For example, they give him twenty percent to buy the land, then, when that's done, they'll give him another ten percent to demolish existing buildings. What this means is that if Sean isn't making the progress he's supposed to make, the bank might not give him the money he needs to complete the project. They're not going to give him all the money up front, then get left holding the bag if he blows it and has nothing to show for it except a large hole in the ground."

"Why do they only give him eighty percent and not the entire amount he needs?" DeMarco asked.

"Because they want Sean and some other guys to have some skin in the game. More important, the bank wants to be able to force Sean to use his own assets or turn to these other investors when the project gets in trouble rather than running back to them with his hand out. Like I said it's complicated, but the bottom line is that Sean probably had to toss a lot of his own money into the pot and had to find some rich investors to cough up the twenty percent he needed.

"The thing you need to understand," Rosenberg said, "is that guys like Sean Callahan are walking a tightrope the whole time they're trying to complete a development and it doesn't take much to make 'em fall off the rope. They unearth a skeleton, and the project grinds to a complete halt until they can figure out if it's from an Indian burial ground or some guy from Southie that Whitey Bulger planted. Or the workers making the big components he needs for heating and ventilation go on strike, and Sean's screwed until they go back to work. I mean, if you've ever remodeled the kitchen in your house, you know how it can go. The contractor discovers dry rot when he's replacing the windows, the cabinets don't fit, the city inspector makes you rip out the wiring because it's not up to code. So if you think remodeling your kitchen is tough, imagine what it would be like to construct office buildings and a hotel on fourteen acres in downtown Boston.

"I've seen lots of guys go bankrupt," Rosenberg said. "They bite off more than they can chew, start having problems, and the next thing you know they're filing Chapter Eleven. I suspect Sean's leveraged up to his neck and if Delaney Square doesn't stay pretty much on schedule and close to budget, the bank will stop giving him money to complete the project. Then his investors will lose their money, and Sean goes under, loses his big house on Beacon Hill and maybe everything else he owns."

DeMarco really liked what he was hearing—and then Rosenberg burst his bubble.

"But also keep in mind that big developers anticipate having problems, and they budget for them. Like Elinore Dobbs. If she hadn't slowed him down, something else would have, and Sean most likely has more than enough money in his contingency fund to deal with somebody like her, so he's probably not in big trouble yet."

"Well, shit," DeMarco said.

The pink-haired waitress came by at that moment, refilled their ice tea glasses, and asked if they wanted some dessert.

"Not me, darling," Rosenberg said. "All my girlfriends like me slim and trim so I can dance the night away."

"How come you never take me dancing?" the waitress said.

"Darling, you'd never be able to keep up."

The waitress squealed and said, "Carl, you crack me up."

"Let me ask you one more thing," DeMarco said. "What kind of profit do you think Callahan will make on Delaney Square?"

"I have no idea," Rosenberg said. "Like I told you, big developments are a house of cards and he could lose his shirt. But Callahan's been in the game over twenty years and he's sharp, so I doubt that'll happen."

"But what's the normal profit margin on big developments?" DeMarco asked again.

"It depends," Rosenberg said. "If a developer makes ten percent after he pays off the interest on all the loans, and what he owes the builders and architects and lawyers, he's probably feeling pretty good."

"Ten percent on a five-hundred-million-dollar project would be fifty million," DeMarco said. "That'd make me feel pretty good."

"Yeah, but I'll bet Sean's going after a lot more than fifty. It depends on how he has things structured. He's probably getting a straight fee from the solar energy company for building their corporate headquarters, and he could be planning to sell the hotel to some chain like Hilton or Marriott for all I know. And the apartments he's building. Some of those are going to sell for more than a million, and I have no idea how much of a cut he'll get from them. When it's all said and done, Sean will lie about how much he made to keep the tax man from taking too big a bite, and he and the banks and his investors will probably all make a killing."

They finished their lunch and Rosenberg, after hugging the pink-haired waitress, headed back to his office. DeMarco didn't leave the restaurant, however. He walked over to a window, where he could see the McNultys still sitting in their car. What did those dummies have in mind? Were they hoping he'd walk into a deserted parking garage again? Whatever the case, he wanted them off his back—and then he realized there might be a simple way to accomplish that. He called Detective Fitzgerald of the Boston Police Department.

"The McNultys are following me," he told Fitzgerald.

"Oh, yeah? Why would they be doing that?"

"I think they think I had something to do with them being arrested for smuggling guns."

"Well, did you?" Fitzgerald said.

DeMarco couldn't tell Fitzgerald that he'd conspired with mobsters in Philadelphia and Providence to set up the McNultys, so he said, "No, of course not. But I went to their arraignment just to gloat about them getting arrested, and one of them accused me of setting them up. They're a couple of idiots, but they're violent idiots."

"Huh," Fitzgerald said. "It did seem odd to me that the ATF knew exactly when those guys would be hauling a van full of guns."

DeMarco ignored Fitzgerald's comment and said, "I'd like you to do me a favor."

"Like what?"

"I'm in a place called Woody's Grill and Tap on Hemenway. I want you to get a squad car over here and when I leave, I'm going to catch a cab and the McNultys are going to follow me. I want your cops to pull them over and search their car for weapons. If they have a gun in the car, their bail will be revoked and they'll get tossed into the can until their trial."

"What reason would our guys have for pulling them over? And what right would they have to execute a search of their vehicle?"

"Jesus Christ, Fitzgerald, tell them to use their brains. Invent a traffic infraction—failure to come to a complete stop, failure to signal when changing lanes. Whatever. Then when your guys check to see if they have outstanding warrants, they'll learn these clucks are currently on bail for transporting machine guns. That ought to be close enough to probable cause for a search."

Fitzgerald didn't respond.

"Fitzgerald," DeMarco said. "Do you really want the McNultys roaming around Boston for the next six months? Wouldn't you prefer they be inside a cage where they belong?"

"Yeah, okay. What kind of car are they driving?"

DeMarco ordered a piece of apple pie to give Fitzgerald enough time to send a squad car his direction, and saw one drive by while he was eating his pie. He hoped that the squad car he saw was the one

Fitzgerald had sent and not another cop randomly driving by. He paid his bill, stepped outside the restaurant, and flagged down a cab. On the way back to the Park Plaza, he checked to see if the McNultys were following. They were. Good.

About two blocks from his hotel, he saw a BPD squad car come through the traffic, get behind the McNultys' car, and the light rack on the police car light up like a Christmas tree. DeMarco had no idea what happened after that. He could only pray that the McNultys were packing a weapon or had some dope on them or had the smell of alcohol on their breath.

Fitzgerald called him fifteen minutes later. "Sorry, DeMarco, they were clean."

"Well, crap," DeMarco said.

Fitzgerald paused. "If you're really worried about these guys attacking you, you better take some precautions. I mean, I can't assign guys to protect you twenty-four hours a day, and I can't advise you to arm yourself but . . ."

"Yeah, I know," DeMarco said.

"Maybe you should head back to Washington. I don't understand why you're still here in Boston anyway."

"I just have something I need to wrap up here before I leave." There was no reason to tell Fitzgerald he was sticking around Boston to find some way to screw Sean Callahan.

———— ◆ ————

"Why the hell did they stop us?" Ray said.

"What do you mean?" Roy said. "You heard what that bull dyke cop said. She said we made an illegal lane change."

"Oh, that's bullshit. That was just an excuse to pull us over and search the car and hassle us. It's a damn good thing we didn't have anything in the car."

"How did they even spot us? Do you think they have us under surveillance?"

"Maybe. Maybe they think we got some big-time gun connection and they're hoping we'll lead them to that guy. Or maybe they know it was Soriano who hired us to get the guns."

"That motherfucker, Soriano. We shoulda known we couldn't trust a wop."

"Or maybe DeMarco spotted us and called the cops."

"He didn't act like he spotted us," Roy said.

"Then I don't know. But we better keep our eyes open to see if anyone's watching us. And we need to get a different car. We can't keep using Doreen's."

"Aw, screw Doreen."

DeMarco went to the Park Plaza bar and ordered a martini. While he drank, he thought about what he'd learned from Carl Rosenberg and concluded: not much. He'd found out that Callahan had a bitter ex-wife so maybe he'd drop in on her and see if she could tell him some dirty secret about Callahan that he could use. The only other thing he'd learned was that Callahan's financial situation was precarious, that he was probably leveraged up to his chin—but that this was almost always the case with developers trying to complete a project. It would take something a whole lot bigger than Jim Boyer identifying safety violations to cause Callahan a significant problem. It would be nice to know who was financing Delaney Square—the major banks and whoever else had invested—but even if he had that information, he wasn't sure what good it would do him.

Well, he'd worry about that next—after he'd figured out a way to deal with the McNultys. There was no way he was going to spend the next six months of his life looking over his shoulder for them. Since the first martini didn't inspire him, he had another—and the answer came to him. It wasn't going to be easy, and he might end up getting killed. On the other hand, if he didn't take care of the McNultys he might get killed anyway. He'd stay in the hotel for the rest of the day, then tomorrow, bright and early, he'd begin phase one of his plan for washing the McNultys out of his hair.

Two hours after DeMarco entered the Park Plaza, the McNultys were still parked near the hotel, and Ray and Roy, both being alcoholics, desperately needed a drink.

"How long are we going to keep this up?" Roy said.

"Until we get him," Ray said. "And it's not like we got anything better to do. If we could find out what room he's in, maybe we could knock on the door, say we're room service, and when he opens the door . . ."

"He's a pretty good-sized guy. I mean, the two of us can take him but he'd probably put up a fight and someone in the next room might hear. No, we have to get him alone someplace."

"Then maybe when he goes out to dinner. We wait until he comes out of the restaurant, get up on either side of him, stick a knife in his ribs, and force him into the car. Then we take him someplace and . . ."

"You think he's just going to let us walk up next to him? And at this time of the year, it's light out until after nine and there're people everywhere."

"Hey! Do you have any ideas of your own or you just going to keep shitting on my ideas?"

A couple hours later when DeMarco still hadn't left the hotel, they decided to call it a day and go back to their bar. They were going to die if they didn't get some alcohol into their bloodstreams soon. As they were driving toward Revere, Roy said, "We oughta call up a couple of broads. We're gonna be without pussy for a long time, so we better stock up now."

They didn't have girlfriends; the only women they could call to have sex with were hookers. But that was actually okay with them.

Ray had been married once for about a year. He met the woman while Roy was doing a six-month stretch. Maybe if Roy had been around, Ray never would have hooked up with her but Roy hated the woman the moment he met her. Her name was Colleen, and she was this chunky blonde who never stopped talking. At the wedding—Roy had been the best man, of course—Roy met the bride's mother, who was the size of a house, and he had no doubt Colleen would eventually be just as big.

Roy had hated living by himself—and hated that Ray was close to anyone other than him. Fortunately, for Roy that is, about eight months after the wedding—and by then Roy could tell that Ray was already getting tired of Colleen—she gave him a bunch of lip one night. Roy and Ray had gone to a Celtics game, done some serious drinking afterward, and Ray didn't get home until four in the morning—and Colleen jumped all over his ass about it. So Ray popped her in the mouth. She called the cops, they arrested Ray, he spent a little more time inside, and by the time he got out, Colleen had gone back to her fat mama and divorced Ray. Thank God.

Now, whenever they got the urge, they called an escort service. That night the service sent two gals over to their apartment, both ladies in their twenties, both sounding like they'd been raised in Southie. The hefty one—the one Ray got—said her name was Heather and the skinny one with bad teeth was Tiffany. Yeah, right. More likely they'd been baptized with names like Mary and Margaret, not that Ray or Roy cared. The brothers paid them, Heather and Tiffany serviced them professionally and efficiently, and left forty minutes after they arrived. Roy then opened a bottle of Jameson's, and he and his brother watched pro wrestling and drank until they passed out, side by side in their matching recliners, the kind that have a cup holder in the armrest sized for a can of beer.

20

DeMarco had set the radio alarm in his hotel room for five a.m. and when it went off, he jerked up in bed, totally disoriented, wondering where in the hell he was and who was yelling about tornadoes in Oklahoma. Whoever had used the radio alarm last must have been almost deaf, and had set the volume as high as it would go. DeMarco slapped blindly at the radio until he finally hit the right button, then just lay there, trying to force himself out of bed. He hated to get up anytime before eight, and he knew from past experience that he'd be dragging the entire day as a result of rising at such a god-awful hour.

Yesterday, sitting in the Park Plaza's bar, he came up with a way to get the McNultys' bail revoked and in such a way that it would add to the time they spent in prison. But he had only a rough idea of what he was going to do, and needed to flesh out the details. First, he needed to make sure the McNultys didn't follow him today—which was why he'd woken up at five. The McNultys didn't strike him as early risers. Second, he needed to find a location tailor-made for what he had in mind, and this spot needed to be outside the Commonwealth of Massachusetts. If the McNultys were caught out of state, their bail should be revoked; if they were caught doing something illegal out of state, their bail would definitely be revoked.

DeMarco finally, reluctantly, rolled out of bed and took a quick shower. He glanced in the mirror. The skin below his right eye was still discolored, but the bruise had faded considerably. He wasn't worried about how he looked, however. He was worried about being physically fit enough to do what he planned. He put on his boxers, but before he got completely dressed, he did some pushups. His ribs were still tender but he decided the pushups didn't hurt *that* much.

At five thirty he left the Park Plaza, and got his car from a valet who looked as sleepy as DeMarco felt. His first stop was a Dunkin' Donuts, and he drank his coffee as he drove through downtown Boston. He made the mistake of buying donuts with those little sprinkles on top, and half the sprinkles ended up in his lap.

He took I-95 south, then 295 south, and about forty minutes later, crossed the border into Rhode Island near the city of Pawtucket. He decided it was too congested near Pawtucket, so he arbitrarily took an exit and headed northwest on Highway 15 toward the town of Smithfield. He passed through Smithfield but still didn't see what he was looking for.

He started taking random turns, having no idea where he was going, and ended up near the town of Chepachet. At the edge of the town was a large abandoned factory that might do in a pinch, but he kept going. He ended up on a road called Putnam Pike—completely lost at this point—and again, arbitrarily turned onto a narrow, winding road called Pine Orchard. On Pine Orchard Road the houses were spaced farther apart and he saw signs for a couple of small farms. And then he rounded a curve and saw exactly what he was looking for. He pulled the car to the side of the road.

There was an abandoned building—actually more shed than building—that at one time might have been a fruit or fresh produce stand. It was constructed of warped gray wooden slats, with a tin roof and an opening that could be covered by a piece of plywood that folded down from the roof. The building was wide enough and tall enough that a man could hide behind it and not be seen from the road.

Looking directly at the shed from where he'd parked, he could see a small farmhouse to the left, up on a slight hill. There were no neighboring houses that he could see. The house appeared to be vacant—most of the windows had been broken by rock-slinging kids—and the front door was hanging on by a single hinge. To the right of the shed was at least an acre of small trees that DeMarco thought might be apple trees, but now looked too old and withered to bear fruit. He suspected the farm, the orchard, and the shed—he'd now concluded the shed was a roadside fruit stand—had all been part of the same piece of property, but for whatever reason had been abandoned. Farming was a tough business and foreclosures weren't uncommon.

DeMarco got out of his car and walked behind the fruit stand and found what he wanted: a fork in the road. That is, when he stood behind the fruit stand there was a gravel road going left to the abandoned house and a beaten-down trail in the weeds heading right, toward the orchard. During daylight hours, if DeMarco took either fork—the one to the house or the one to the orchard—he would be clearly visible from the highway. But at night, he'd be hard to spot. Out here in the countryside, it would be darker than the inside of the devil's bunghole when the sun went down.

DeMarco took out his iPhone. It informed him there was no moon that night and the weather was supposed to be cloudy. It appeared as if God had decided to help out with his plan. Well, okay, maybe He wasn't *helping*, but at least He wasn't interfering.

He spent the next half hour studying the area. Or maybe, considering what he was planning, *reconnoitering* would be a better word. The abandoned farmhouse was about a quarter mile away from the fruit stand. He figured if he ran as fast as he could—considering his age and the fact that he'd be running uphill—it would take him at least a minute and a half to reach the house, which was way too long. Then he noticed, about halfway up the road to the farmhouse, there was another small wooden structure that was only about five feet high and surrounded by weeds. He suspected it might be a well house, or maybe a toolshed. DeMarco figured he could run from the fruit stand to the toolshed in under a minute.

Next he walked toward the orchard. The beginning of the orchard was only about fifty yards from the fruit stand, but the only thing to use for cover inside the orchard was a bunch of spindly, gnarled trees, the trunks less than eight inches in diameter. A guy his size wasn't going to be able to hide behind an apple tree trunk. He walked deeper into the orchard, looking for a better place, and about a quarter mile later came to a pile of old wooden crates. The crates were made of thin slats of wood, about two feet square and six inches deep; they had probably been used for transporting the apples after they'd been picked. All the crates—there were at least two hundred of them—had been tossed into a stack that would make an impressive bonfire. DeMarco studied the pile of crates for a moment and decided they would do—but not located where they were.

It took him almost an hour to lug about a hundred of the apple crates closer to the fruit stand. He then arranged the crates into another disorganized pile similar to the one he'd seen deeper in the orchard. By the time he finished, he had constructed a barrier that was about six feet high and six feet long—in other words, a little wall that didn't look like a wall that he could hide behind.

Lastly, he looked around for something he could use for a weapon. Up near the abandoned farmhouse, he found a rusty rake that someone had discarded or forgotten. He broke the rake off the handle, leaving himself with a wooden pole about four feet long. He hoped he didn't have to use the rake handle—he was planning to obtain another weapon—but in case that one didn't do the job, the handle would do. He hoped. He placed the rake handle behind the apple crates he'd moved.

He walked back to his car and took one more look at the place he'd selected. It was perfect: it was remote, it would be dark at night, and it wasn't in the state of Massachusetts. He consulted the GPS in his rental car, and although he'd spent more than two hours driving around, he was only an hour and twenty minutes from Boston.

———◆◆◆———

He drove back to Smithfield and found a diner. He was starving and needed a real breakfast. After he washed his hands, which were grimy from moving the apple crates, he ordered eggs, sausage links, and hash browns. As he was waiting for his breakfast to arrive, it occurred to him that because he'd risen at such an early hour, it wasn't that late; it was only ten thirty. Maybe he could accomplish one other thing today, and still have time to deal with the McNultys that night.

He called Maggie Dolan and asked her to use the Harvard interns to find him an address for the second Mrs. Callahan, first name Adele. He told Maggie that according to Carl Rosenberg, Adele had a condo in Boston and a place on Cape Cod, but that's all he knew. By the time he finished his lunch, a young lady called him—at least she sounded young—and gave him Adele's phone number, her address on Cape Cod, and said that Adele now used her maiden name, which was Tomlin.

"I called her house on the Cape and asked for her," the girl said. "Said I was doing a poll, and she hung up on me. So that's where she is, or at least where she was five minutes ago."

DeMarco didn't bother to ask how the intern had obtained Adele's phone number; he was just grateful that Maggie only hired kids who had IQs that were bigger than his and Mahoney's combined. He also wondered what sort of hours the interns put in working for Mahoney and why anyone would want such a job. He certainly wouldn't have worked for Mahoney if he wasn't getting paid.

On the way to Cape Cod, he pulled into a shopping mall outside of Pawtucket to get the other items he would need for the night to come.

At a JCPenney, he bought a pair of black jeans, a black T-shirt, and black tennis shoes. He would be one with the night. His next stop was a hardware store where he bought a small pocketknife and a package of eighteen-inch-long zip ties, like cops sometimes use for makeshift handcuffs. His final stop was a supermarket where he bought the biggest Idaho potato he could find. He didn't care if it was organically grown or not.

Now ready for combat, he continued on his way to the Cape.

◆◆◆

Around noon, about the time DeMarco left the Pawtucket shopping mall, the McNultys were just getting out of bed. They were hungover and depressed. The only food they had in their apartment was a box of Cheerios—but they had no milk—and a frozen pepperoni pizza. Ray put the pizza in the oven, then sat down across the kitchen table from his red-eyed, unshaven, stubbly-headed brother. He thought Roy looked like death warmed over—and imagined he looked the same way. They were both wearing white wifebeater T-shirts and boxer shorts.

"Maybe we outta go to Mexico," Roy said.

"Mexico? What would we do in Mexico?" Ray said. "We don't speak Spanish and even spics can't get work in Mexico. Why do you think they sneak into the U.S. to steal American jobs?"

The McNultys were adamantly opposed to illegal immigrants coming across the border and taking jobs from Americans. It didn't matter if the Mexicans were doing work like mowing lawns and picking fruit, jobs they wouldn't have done if they'd been starving. It also pissed them off that American tax dollars were being used in one way or another to support the illegals, like when they sent their kids to American schools. The fact that the McNultys didn't pay taxes because they lied on their tax returns was irrelevant. It was the principle that mattered.

Roy, however, looked confused. So Ray said, "Roy, I'm saying, how would we live down there? We wouldn't be able to find work, and I doubt they got some kind of food stamp program for Americans. We're going to jail, Roy. You might as well get used to the idea. But we're going to settle the score with that prick DeMarco first."

"You want to head over to his hotel after we eat?" Roy said. Ray could tell his brother wasn't enthused by the idea, and neither was he.

"Nah, there's no point in going over there during the day. Let's wait until this evening, like around six or so. Maybe he'll head out to dinner and after it gets dark, go someplace where we can get him."

They finished the pizza, thought about taking showers, then said screw the showers, put on cargo shorts and tennis shoes, and headed over to their bar. They were overdue for an alcoholic eye-opener.

As they were having their first drink of the day, hoping the booze would make their hangovers less painful, Doreen walked up to the table where they were sitting.

Doreen, like them, was wearing a sleeveless T-shirt—the front wet from sweat—baggy shorts, and high-top tennis shoes without socks. Ray was always amazed at how big her flabby upper arms were. One of these days he was going to get one of those cloth tape measures like tailors use, and see how much bigger her arms were than his.

"I need to find out what's going to happen if you guys go to jail," she said. "I mean, if you sell the bar, I'm—"

"We ain't selling the bar," Ray said.

"But if you do, I mean if you're forced to, I have to find a job and another place to live."

"I'm telling you, we ain't sellin' the fuckin' bar," Ray said. "You're gonna run it for us until we get paroled." Then something occurred to him. "You go get a lawyer to draw up some papers that says you got power of attorney or whatever it's called."

"Are you going to pay for the lawyer?"

"Hell, no," Roy said. "We're doing you a favor letting you live here and run the place for us while we're gone. Now quit bugging us. We got things to figure out."

"And we'll need your car again later," Ray said. "In fact, we're gonna need it until they release our van."

"But what if I need my car?"

"You don't need your car. And if you do need a car, call your mom and borrow hers. Your mom's too old to be driving anyway. Now get back behind the bar and do your job. That old broad with the stocking cap is waving at you to get her another beer."

After they had three beers apiece—and a couple of those ham and cheese sandwiches that could be heated up in the microwave—they drove to a Dick's Sporting Goods in Saugus.

"We want a couple of those little bats you use for smacking fish," Ray said to the clerk. "What do you call those things?"

"I don't know," the clerk said. "Fish bats, I guess. They're on that wall over there."

They discovered they had a choice of bats made out of wood or polypropylene. One of the bats had a label on it calling it a Fish Tamer, like if you whacked the fish you could make it sit up and beg. They chose two wooden ones, about twelve inches long with a good grip on the handle and a leather lanyard you could loop over your wrist. Walking back to their car, Roy smacked his palm a couple of times with his new fish bat. "Yep, this'll do the trick."

They decided to go back to their apartment and take a nap until six and then head on over to the Park Plaza.

"Pray to God," Ray said, "that son of a bitch goes someplace tonight where we can get him."

21

Adele Tomlin's place on Cape Cod was near the town of Truro. It was on the waterfront, nestled among sandy dunes covered with beach heather, and it overlooked the bay in the direction of Boston. The siding was painted white, it had hurricane shutters and a weathered cedar shake roof with two chimneys, and DeMarco figured the house was about three thousand square feet—a rich man's definition of a "cottage." It probably cost two or three million. DeMarco could imagine himself sitting inside in the winter, snug and warm in front of a roaring fire, sipping brandy while reading a book, as a cold wind blew off the Atlantic. Since he'd never be able to afford a place like this all he could do was imagine.

DeMarco walked up to the door, rang the bell, and a moment later a squat Hispanic woman wearing a white apron over a T-shirt and shorts opened the door. "Yes?" she said, sounding irritated that her work had been interrupted.

"I'm here to see Ms. Tomlin. My name's Joe DeMarco, and I work for Congressman John Mahoney."

"You wait here. I'll see if she wants to talk to you."

Nobody, it seemed, was impressed by politicians these days, not even domestic help.

The surly Hispanic maid, housekeeper, cook, whatever she was, led DeMarco through the house and to a large gray-painted deck in back. The deck was about a thousand square feet and there was a long staircase going from it down to the beach. Adele was on a lounge chair, under a beach umbrella to keep the sun from damaging her fair skin. Next to the lounge chair was a glass half filled with ice cubes and what looked like club soda. Adele was wearing large sunglasses and a small white bikini, and DeMarco thought she was a gorgeous-looking woman at the age of forty-two.

"Pull over one of those chairs," she said, pointing to a pair of faded green Adirondack chairs on the other side of the deck. DeMarco did.

"Sonya said John sent you here."

"He didn't send me but I work for him," DeMarco said.

"And how is the old lecher doing?"

Being on Boston's A-list while she was married to Callahan, and Callahan being a Mahoney contributor, Adele had probably encountered Mahoney several times at fund-raisers and parties. Considering the way she looked, she no doubt had firsthand experience with his lecherousness.

"Still lecherous," DeMarco said, and Adele laughed.

"I always get a kick out of him. So why are you here, Joe?"

"Did you see the press conference Mahoney held regarding your ex-husband's development on Delaney Street?"

"No, I didn't see it. I don't watch the news all that much."

"Well, let me tell you about a lady named Elinore Dobbs and what your ex did to her."

DeMarco recounted the tale of Callahan's attempts to drive Elinore out of her apartment, her tumble down a flight of stairs, and her current medical condition. While he was talking Adele polished off the drink on the table next to her.

"My God! That's just awful," Adele said when DeMarco finished speaking—although the way she said it, she didn't sound as if she thought it was *that* awful. DeMarco got the impression that Adele would have a hard time imagining herself in Elinore's situation and that empathy was a rare emotion for her. He was also willing to bet that if she'd still been married to Callahan, she would have defended the things he did to get Elinore out of her building.

"But I don't understand why you're here, Joe," she said. "Is there something you expect me to do for that poor woman?"

"No. I'm here because I heard that Sean really took advantage of you when you divorced, and—"

"Took advantage of me! That son of a bitch bushwhacked me. He started seeing that little tramp a year before we split up, making all these trips to Georgia on some deal he claimed he was working on. Well, during that year, in addition to screwing Miss Georgia, he screwed me, too. He started moving money around, burying it in places I couldn't get to, and his lawyer rolled right over the idiot I hired. I was lucky to come away with anything."

DeMarco didn't bother to point out that he'd learned from Carl Rosenberg that she'd ended up with eight figures. Instead he said, "Well, you're a beautiful woman and I think he was a fool to divorce you." He figured flattery couldn't hurt.

"But you still haven't said why you're here, Joe. What exactly do you want from me?"

Considering her attitude toward Callahan, DeMarco figured there was no point beating around the bush. "To be completely frank, Adele, I'm hoping you can help me figure out some way to screw Sean for what he did to Elinore Dobbs."

Adele just sat for a moment looking at him, then she laughed. The idea of getting back at her ex-husband clearly had some appeal. DeMarco also got the impression that Adele was a bit drunk and that the drink on the table next to her wasn't club soda. She turned her head and yelled, "Sonya!"

The stocky maid came out of the house, a frown on her wide brown face, and said, "Yes, ma'am?"

"Make me another vodka tonic and make one for Joe, too." After the maid departed, Adele said, "Well, I'd love to help you, Joe. I really would, after what that bastard did to me, but I don't see how I can."

"Maybe you can't," DeMarco said. "But what I'd like to do is find some way to stop his project on Delaney Street. According to Carl Rosenberg . . ."

"He's such a lovely man," Adele said, "and Sean treated him so shabbily."

"Yes, he did. Anyway, Carl said Sean is most likely leveraged to the hilt, and if there were some way to shut down the work on Delaney Square for a long time or get his investors to call in their loans, he'd take a bath. But I don't know how to make that happen. So I was hoping maybe you'd know something else I could use to cause your ex some pain."

At that moment, the maid came back bearing the vodka tonics. Adele started to say something, then instead took a couple sips of her drink, and DeMarco got the impression she was trying to make up her mind about something.

"Did you look into where Sean got the investment money for Delaney Square?" she finally said.

"No," DeMarco said. "Should I?"

Adele hesitated again. "About eight years ago, Sean and I took a vacation to celebrate our wedding anniversary. We stayed at a resort in Los Cabos, near the Sea of Cortez. It was an absolutely gorgeous place, and the service there was just incredible.

"While we were there we met a marvelous Mexican couple, Javier and Danielle Castro. Danielle is the same age as me, and very beautiful. Javier is about ten years older than Sean and so handsome, like a telenovela star. And he has the most marvelous manners, courtly I guess you'd say. When you talk to him, he makes you feel like you're the most important person in the universe, unlike Sean, who didn't even listen half the time when I was talking. I just love him and Danielle."

"Okay," DeMarco said, wondering where she was going with this.

"Well, we noticed right away that Javier had his own security team, like a politician might have. You know, hard-looking guys in suits with those ear things who talk into microphones on their wrists. Like the Secret Service."

And DeMarco thought: *Oh-oh*. But now he could see where this was going.

"We didn't think too much about his security," Adele said. "It was Mexico and with all the drug violence and kidnappings and such, we figured a lot of wealthy Mexicans hired private security. Anyway, we became quite good friends in the ten days we were there. Sean and Javier played golf together and went fishing, while Danielle and I shopped and went horseback riding. It was actually very comforting having Javier's security people with us while we shopped. I certainly felt safer with them around. The men, of course, discussed business, Sean telling Javier about projects he was working on at the time.

"When we asked Javier what he did for a living, he said he was involved in a number of businesses. Telecommunications, a large cement plant in Mexico, real estate, and so forth. One night while we were having drinks, Sean started talking to Javier about a project that was just in the preliminary planning stage. It was Delaney Square. At that point, Sean was still looking into financing for the project and had an architect working on some sketches, and Javier said he might be interested in investing.

"Three months later, after Javier did whatever due diligence investors do, he invested with Sean. Back then, we still talked about his business, but I don't know how much of a stake Javier has in the project. I do know that Sean was impressed and grateful. But Sean had done his due diligence on Javier, too, and he learned that Javier wasn't your ordinary investor. He was the leader of one of the largest drug cartels in Mexico."

"Whoa!" DeMarco said—although that's what he'd been expecting to hear.

"Yes. Whoa. What Sean learned—I don't know who his sources were—was that at the time we met Javier and Danielle, Javier was slowly backing away from the cartel, turning it over to a cousin of his, and by the time Sean and I divorced, he was supposedly out of the drug business entirely. Now he's just another successful Mexican businessman."

"Are you saying that Javier is laundering drug money through Sean's development?" DeMarco said.

Adele shrugged. "I'm not sure that he's *laundering* anything. I know he didn't send boxes filled with cash to Sean. And when I asked Sean basically the same question—back then I didn't want my husband to go to jail for being involved with a drug dealer—he said the money was clean as far as he knew and that it came from a consortium in the Caymans, like a venture capital company or real estate investment company. But I don't know if the money was clean or dirty. I just know that it originated from a guy who used to sell drugs for a living."

"Huh," DeMarco said. He sipped his drink, mulling over everything she'd told him. He had an idea for how he might use what she'd told him, but he wasn't sure he wanted to go there. As for Adele, she just sat there looking pleased with herself.

"Do you still keep in touch with Danielle?" DeMarco asked.

"Oh, yes. And with Javier. Javier, unlike Sean Callahan, is the type who will never divorce his wife. I enjoy their company very much, and right after my divorce Danielle knew I was feeling low and invited me to their place in Mexico City. They have a gorgeous home there, and I stayed for a week and had a marvelous time. I go shopping with Danielle when she comes to New York, which she does several times a year. Her daughter is a student at Columbia. The girl's beautiful enough to be an actress but she wants to direct movies and write screenplays. Anyway, the Castros have an apartment in the city and when Danielle comes to see her, sometimes I'll meet her."

"Does Javier come with his wife when she comes to see their daughter?" DeMarco asked.

"No. Or I should say, the times I've met her in New York, she always came by herself and he stayed in Mexico. Why are you asking?"

"Just curious," DeMarco said, but he was wondering if Javier Castro was afraid to travel to the United States. He may not have been in the drug business now, but that didn't mean all his past sins had been forgotten by the DEA.

Adele, now a bit tipsy from the alcohol she'd consumed, and maybe wanting to prove to herself how desirable she still was, asked if DeMarco would like to stay for dinner—and he got the impression that if he did, Adele would be the dessert. But as lovely as she was, he didn't really want anything to do with the woman. Trying to sound regretful that he couldn't stay, he said that lecherous slave driver, Mahoney, was forcing him to meet with someone later, but the next time he was on the Cape . . .

22

By the time DeMarco returned to Boston from Cape Cod it was about eight p.m.—which was perfect timing—but he had a long night ahead of him. He stopped in front of the hotel entrance, stepped out of his car, and looked around casually for the McNultys. This time he was hoping he would see them, and he immediately saw the same dusty blue Corolla they'd used the last time they tailed him, but the McNultys weren't in the car. Then he spotted them. They were standing in a doorway on Arlington, about half a block from their car drinking something out of king-sized cups—and they were watching him.

The valet came out to take DeMarco's car but he told the valet to leave the car parked where it was, saying he'd be right back down. DeMarco knew the McNultys had seen him but he lingered outside a little longer, pretending to ask the doorman for directions he didn't need, and the doorman helpfully pointed down the street.

When the McNultys saw DeMarco pull up in front of the hotel, Roy said, "I hope he's not in for the night." He was just dying to try out his new fish bat on DeMarco's skull.

"No, look," Ray said. "The valet's not moving his car. And he just asked for directions. He's going someplace. Come on. Let's get in the car. And pray to Jesus he goes someplace where we can get him." When he said this, Roy made the sign of the cross. Ray just shook his head.

———————◆◆◆———————

Back in his room, DeMarco quickly changed into his ninja outfit—the all-black clothes he'd purchased at JCPenney earlier in the day. He put the pocketknife in one pocket of his new jeans and several zip ties in another. He then shoved the big baking potato into a sock and gave the bed a couple of hard whacks. It would do. He hoped.

The biggest problem was that he didn't know what sort of weapons the McNultys might be carrying. He didn't think they'd have guns because he didn't think they would take the risk of being caught with a firearm in their possession, which would automatically land them in jail. On the other hand, the McNultys were idiots. All he knew was they would be armed in some way: knives, saps, brass knuckles, a chunk of lead pipe. If he was wrong about them not having guns, he was going to feel pretty stupid bringing a potato to a gunfight.

Before he left the hotel, he peeked through a window to see where the McNultys were, and saw them sitting in their car. He wondered how many parking tickets they'd been issued while they parked there waiting for him. He suspected that two men about to serve a decade in prison weren't all that concerned about parking tickets.

DeMarco walked out of the hotel, tipped the valet who held the door open for him, and got into his car. He had to time this just right. He wanted it to be light enough outside that they could easily follow him—and at eight p.m. it was—but he wanted to reach the abandoned fruit stand in Rhode Island when it was dark.

Traffic leaving Boston was heavy and DeMarco did everything he could not to lose the McNultys: he stopped at every orange light, signaled long before every turn, and when the McNultys were stopped by a red light, DeMarco crept along like an octogenarian on the way to church to give them time to catch up. As he and the McNultys crossed the border separating Rhode Island from Massachusetts, he smiled. The McNultys had now violated the judge's order not to leave the state.

"Where the hell's he going?" Roy said.

"It looks like Providence," Ray said. "It's a good thing we filled the tank earlier."

"You think he's going to see Soriano?"

"How the hell would I know?"

When DeMarco turned off 295, heading in the direction of Chepachet, Roy said, "Now what's he doing? He's heading into the fuckin' sticks."

"This could be good," Ray said. "Wherever he's going, there'll be less people around than if he's in Providence or Boston."

They drove in silence for a while before Roy said, "I've been thinking about that thing with Doreen, that power of attorney thing to let her run the bar while we're inside."

"Yeah?" Ray said.

"What if we just transferred the title to her?"

"Why in the hell would we do that?"

"What if the judge gives us a fine and we get forced to sell the bar to pay the fine? What if there's some law out there that says guys in jail can't have a liquor license? What if the cops ever find Canyon, and they make him tell that we paid him to help with the old broad? She could sue us and maybe take the bar."

"Huh," Ray said. His younger brother was actually making sense for once. "You think we could trust Doreen that much? If we transferred the title to her, she could sell the place and take the money and run."

"Doreen knows if she did that we'd track her down and beat her ugly hide. Plus, Doreen's like us. She doesn't know anyplace but Boston, and her mom still lives here. But I'll tell you one thing we'll make clear to her. She better not change the name of the bar."

The sun had disappeared from the sky but DeMarco could see the headlights of the McNultys' car behind him. When he was about a mile from the abandoned fruit stand, he asked himself: *Are you sure you want to do this?*

There were three potential problems with his plan, the first and biggest of those being that the McNultys might have guns. The second problem was not knowing for sure what the McNultys would do when they came to the fork in the road behind the fruit stand. If they didn't behave as he expected them to, he might also end up dead because he didn't think he could fight them both at the same time and win. The third thing was that he might be overestimating his ability to take them even if he was fighting them one at a time. He was strong enough and motivated enough to beat them, but they were a couple of guys used to brawling, and he wasn't.

So should he head back to Boston or do what he'd planned? Screw it. He was going to do what he'd planned. If he didn't, they'd just come after him again, and in some spot where he wouldn't have the advantage. Plus, the simple truth was he was looking forward to fighting them. He was going to get even with them for the beating they gave him.

When DeMarco reached the fruit stand, he stopped the car, and then started moving quickly. He pulled on the lever under the dash-board that released the hood latch, grabbed his potato-filled sock, and got out of the car. He went immediately to the front of the car and raised the hood, then stood to the side of the car where he'd be visible to approaching vehicles. He was ready to run—and the car containing the McNultys was coming toward him rapidly.

"Look!" Roy said. "His car broke down!"

"We got the fucker," Ray said. "There's no one within miles of this place."

Ray stepped on the gas.

Both McNultys were grinning, looking like feral dogs when they did.

DeMarco saw the car coming toward him accelerate, and when it was about a hundred yards away, he ran. It would take him only seconds to reach the back of the fruit stand. And in the dark, with the black clothes he was wearing, he'd barely be visible; he'd be like a moving shadow.

"Son of a bitch! He saw us," Roy said.

"We'll get him," Ray said, and slammed on the brakes. The Corolla skidded to a stop, almost hitting the rear bumper of DeMarco's rental car. They grabbed the fish bats and took off in the direction DeMarco had taken. Running with the small clubs in their hands, wearing shorts and high-top tennis shoes without socks, the McNultys looked like a couple of cavemen chasing down a meal.

When they reached the back of the fruit stand, they stopped. "Shit, where'd he go?" Ray said. "He couldn't have gone far, not unless he's some kind of goddamn Olympic sprinter. He's hiding close by."

"Yeah, but it's so fuckin' dark out here," Roy said, "he's going to be hard to spot. I wonder if Doreen has a flashlight in her car."

"We don't have time to get a flashlight. If he's got a cell phone, he's probably calling the cops. We need to find him fast."

Ray pointed to his left. "See that little shed up there?"

"Yeah," Roy said. He could just make out the shape of the shed in the darkness.

"He either went that way," Ray said, then pointed to his right. "Or he went that way, into those trees. I'll look in the shed. That's most likely where he is, either in it or hiding behind it. You go see if you can spot him in the trees."

"I don't think we should split up," Roy said.

"If we don't split up, and if I'm wrong about him being behind the shed, he's going to go through those trees and circle back to the road, and then he'll start running down the road, hoping a car will spot him. And like I told you, if he's got a phone, he'll call the cops. The good news is way the fuck out here in the middle of nowhere it'll take the cops a while to get here. But we gotta move.

"If you spot him, yell, then start beating on him, and I'll be there in two minutes to help. If I spot him, I'll do the same thing. But if you find him, don't go killing him all by yourself. I want some of him, too."

"Okay," Roy said. With the fish bat held in his big right hand, he started jogging toward the orchard. He was really worried about the darkness, thinking he could run right past the guy and not see him. They really should have looked for a flashlight in Doreen's car, but knowing Doreen, if she had one, the batteries would be dead.

DeMarco watched the brothers as they stood behind the fruit stand, and saw one of them raise a hand and point at the toolshed, then point in the other direction, toward the orchard. He couldn't see their features in the darkness; all he could see were the shapes of their short, muscular bodies. What were they going to do? Both go the same way or split up? He smiled when he saw one man run toward the toolshed and the other start jogging toward the orchard—the direction DeMarco had taken.

DeMarco was standing behind the pile of apple crates he'd constructed near the edge of the trail leading into the orchard. He figured the man coming toward him would either walk past the crates, in which case he'd step out and hit him from behind with his potato-filled sock, or he'd look to see if DeMarco was hiding behind the stack of crates. And if he did that, as soon as his head appeared, DeMarco would swing his homemade sap.

He could hear the man approach the apple crates, and then heard him stop. The guy was trying to decide if he should keep going or see if DeMarco was hiding behind the crates. The sock was ready in DeMarco's hand—and when Roy McNulty took a peek to see if DeMarco was there, DeMarco swung the sock as hard as he could. He put every ounce of strength he had into that swing; he hit Roy McNulty hard enough that he turned his baking potato into a mashed potato. The reason he'd filled the sock with a potato as opposed to pennies or a rock was that he didn't want to kill the McNultys; he just wanted to hurt them badly.

But as hard as he swung, the thickheaded son of a bitch didn't go down. He was clearly stunned, but still standing. So DeMarco dropped the sock and hit him with a right-hand uppercut—right on the point of his chin—and this time he went down. Roy McNulty was unconscious.

DeMarco quickly flipped him over onto his stomach, then used a zip tie to bind his hands behind his back. He used a second zip tie to bind his feet. It had taken him less than a minute to deal with one McNulty—and now it was time to deal with the other one.

DeMarco started to pick up the rake handle he'd placed behind the crates earlier in the day to use for a weapon, then noticed the small club that Roy McNulty had been carrying in his hand: a little bat about twelve inches long, like a cop's nightstick. He'd known the McNultys would be armed, and he bet that Ray McNulty had an identical bat. Unlike with DeMarco's potato-filled sock, if the McNultys had started whaling on him with the little bats they would have killed him, which was most certainly their intention. DeMarco thought about it for a moment, then decided to use Roy's bat instead of the rake handle. If he used a weapon belonging to one of his attackers, that would add to the impression that he hadn't known in advance that he'd be attacked. He hoped.

He stepped out from behind the pile of apple crates. Due to the darkness, he couldn't see Ray McNulty, but suspected he was near the toolshed. But DeMarco didn't have any intention of sneaking around and hunting for Ray. Instead he yelled, "McNulty! McNulty! I just killed your brother." He paused, then said, "I slit his fuckin' throat."

Sound carried well out there in the country with no cars passing by or any other urban noises. DeMarco heard Ray yell, "You motherfucker, I'm gonna kill you." Unlike DeMarco, who was dressed in black, Ray McNulty was wearing a white T-shirt, and although DeMarco couldn't see his features clearly, he could see his blocky form running rapidly toward him—and that's what he wanted: Ray's head filled with rage and the desire for revenge and not thinking about anything else.

DeMarco didn't run toward Ray. He just waited where he was, holding the fish bat in his right hand. He didn't realize it, but he was smiling.

DeMarco had thought that Ray would stop a few feet away—but he didn't. Ray believed that DeMarco had killed his brother, and the *only* thing he was thinking about was killing DeMarco. He ran toward DeMarco at full speed, no hesitation at all, the fish bat in his right hand, raised in the air, ready to bring it down on DeMarco's skull. Ray didn't notice that DeMarco was armed with the same weapon.

DeMarco waited until Ray was about ten yards from him and unable to stop his forward motion—and he threw the fish bat directly at Ray's head. And just like when he'd brought the potato sap down on Roy's head, he threw the bat as hard as he could—and he didn't miss. The short club pinwheeled in the air and the blunt end of the bat hit Ray right between his eyes.

Ray staggered backward from the blow and before he could react, DeMarco was on him. His first punch broke Ray's nose—and then DeMarco just kept throwing punches. Right, left, right, left—until he beat Ray to the ground, where he continued to hit him until he wasn't moving.

It took all his willpower to stop hitting Ray. He didn't want to kill the man, or more to the point, he didn't want to face the legal consequences of killing him. He got up off Ray, his chest heaving from the exertion of pounding on him.

Now what DeMarco needed to do was stage the scene to match the story he planned to tell the cops. The first thing he did was take the shoestrings out of Ray's tennis shoes and use them—instead of his handy-dandy zip ties—to bind Ray's hands behind his back. Then he walked back to Roy McNulty, who was still unconscious; this was beginning to worry DeMarco. He used his newly acquired pocketknife to cut the zip ties binding Roy's hands and feet, then used Roy's shoestrings to bind his hands because he couldn't leave the zip ties in place. He threw the remnants of the zip ties into the stack of apple crates, then took the sock containing the potato and flung it far into the apple orchard. He didn't want there to be any evidence lying around that his encounter with the McNultys had been premeditated.

He returned to his car and called 911. He told the dispatcher that his car broke down and he'd been attacked by two men with clubs. He said he barely managed to fight them off, and that both men were injured and needed medical attention. When she asked for his location, DeMarco said he didn't know where he was exactly, just that he was on Pine Orchard Road, near the town of Chepachet. He added that he was parked by an abandoned fruit stand and his hood was up.

"Are you hurt?" the dispatcher asked him.

"No. Fortunately. But I was lucky they didn't kill me." He wanted that statement on tape.

His next call was to Detective Fitzgerald, BPD. "I'm going to need some help. I was just attacked by Roy and Ray McNulty. They followed me out to a place in Rhode Island—"

"Rhode Island?"

"Yeah. Anyway, my rental car broke down—the engine stopped running—and they attacked me. With clubs. I was able to, ah, overpower them, and now they're both tied up."

"Both of them?"

"Yeah. I already called nine-one-one to report the attack and the cops are on their way. But I don't know who has jurisdiction. I'm near a town called Chepachet. Anyway, I need you to talk to the right cop here in Rhode Island to back up my story that the McNultys were following me in Boston and about their history with Elinore Dobbs and the weapons charge against them."

"How were you able to beat both of them if they had clubs? Are you some kind of karate guy?"

"I just got lucky. And what difference does it make? I'm the victim here."

It turned out that the cops in Glocester, Rhode Island, had jurisdiction for Pine Orchard Road. A Glocester patrol car showed up about fifteen minutes after DeMarco called 911, its light bar flashing blue and red. Five minutes later an ambulance belonging to the Glocester fire department arrived at the scene.

The Glocester cop, a young guy no more than twenty-five, took DeMarco's statement as the medics attended to the McNultys.

"I was just driving along and my car died and—"

"What's wrong with it," the cop asked.

"I don't know. It just died on me. What difference does it make? Anyway, I'd just raised the hood to take a look when the McNultys pulled up behind me, so I took off running."

"You knew your attackers?"

"Yeah. They're bad guys from Boston."

DeMarco gave the cop the backstory on the McNultys: how they had been hired to harass Elinore Dobbs, how they rigged a wire to cause her to fall down a flight of stairs, then how they were later arrested by the ATF for transporting machine guns with the intention of selling them.

"For some reason," DeMarco said, "these guys, who by the way are connected to the Providence mob, got it into their heads that I was responsible for their arrest. After they got out on bail, they started following me around Boston. You can verify that with Detective Fitzgerald of the BPD. So tonight, when I drove out here to see a guy—"

"Who did you drive out here to see?" the cop asked.

"You don't need to know his name," DeMarco said. DeMarco had anticipated this question. Why was he driving around in the sticks of Rhode Island late at night? But he couldn't give the cop the name of a man who didn't exist, a man the cop might want to call to verify DeMarco's story.

"Look," DeMarco said. "My boss is Congressman John Mahoney." He figured that tossing out Mahoney's name couldn't hurt. "And he just wanted me to talk to a guy who lives out here. It has to do with a congressional hearing that's coming up. But I can't tell you his name. It's confidential, at least until after the hearing. And what difference does his name make anyway? I was just going to see this guy and my car broke down, and the McNultys attacked me with those clubs you saw."

The cop looked skeptical. But then skeptical was the way cops usually looked.

"How were you able to beat them both?" the cop asked.

"Well, you see, when I first ran, I hid behind the fruit stand, then I saw that pile of crates, so I ran up and hid behind them. When the McNultys got to the fruit stand, they didn't know which way I'd gone, so one of them went that way, to see if I was hiding by that little shed up there, and the other one ran toward those trees to see if I'd gone that way. Anyway, when the one guy got to the pile of crates, he looked to see if that's where I was hiding, and when he stuck his head around the corner, I hit him."

"Hit him with what?"

"My fist. What else? I hit him a good one, stunned him, then I hit him again and knocked him out."

"Huh," the cop said. Like: *Huh, I'm impressed.* Or maybe it was: *Huh, sounds like bullshit to me.*

"Then I started to run back to my car—"

"But you said your car wasn't working."

"It isn't, but I'd left my cell phone in the cup holder. I was going to grab it and call nine-one-one and then start running down the road to get away, but that's when the other one saw me. He came charging at me with that club he was holding, and we sort of crashed into each other, and when he took a swing at me and missed, I hit him. Hard. Then, well, I guess I just kind of went crazy and started throwing punches and knocked him out. I tied their hands so they couldn't attack me again, and called you guys. I was lucky they didn't kill me."

"Yeah, I guess," the cop said. "You're going to have to come back to the station with me."

"What?" DeMarco said. Like: *How could you possibly doubt my story?*

———◆———

An hour later, DeMarco was still at the Glocester police department.

He was placed in an interrogation room and an older cop, one with sergeant's chevrons on his sleeves, came in and asked him to repeat the story of how he'd been attacked. When the cop asked him if he wanted a lawyer, DeMarco said, "A lawyer? First of all, I am a lawyer, but second, why would I need one? Those assholes attacked me and I just defended myself."

"It's kind of amazing how your car happened to break down where it did," the cop said. "I mean, in a spot where you could find a place to hide. The other thing that's kind of amazing is we sent a guy to tow your car back here, and when he tried to start it, it started right up."

"Well, I don't know what to tell you about that," DeMarco said. "I was just driving along and it died, like it had run out of gas, but there was plenty of gas in the tank. Maybe the fuel line got plugged up or something. How the hell would I know? I'm not a mechanic. All I know is the car died, and I was just lucky I was able to hide behind those crates. I mean, how was I supposed to know there'd be a bunch of crates there?"

A female cop stuck her head inside the room and said to the sergeant, "Pat, there's a detective from Boston here to see you."

"Boston?" Pat said.

Twenty minutes later, Fitzgerald came into the interrogation room. He didn't look particularly like a member of law enforcement wearing grape-colored Bermuda shorts and a lime-green polo shirt stretched over his considerable gut. Fitzgerald had been at home when DeMarco called him and he obviously hadn't taken the time to change clothes before driving to Rhode Island.

Fitzgerald didn't say anything for a moment as he stared at DeMarco, then he pointed at a camera mounted high on one wall. "I told them to shut that off."

"Okay," DeMarco said.

Fitzgerald paused again before saying, "The cops here know you're not telling them the whole story, but I convinced them that the McNultys are bad guys so they're going to arrest them for assaulting you."

"Good," DeMarco said.

"Yeah, but I think you set them up, DeMarco. I think you . . . you *lured* them here. I also think you set them up so they'd get caught with those assault rifles in their van."

For a moment DeMarco thought about going all Al Pacino on Fitzgerald—an Oscar-winning performance, his face first displaying bewilderment, followed by shock, and finally outrage at Fitzgerald's ridiculous and offensive allegation. But he didn't do that. Instead, he looked into Fitzgerald's bloodshot eyes and said, "So what if I did?"

Fitzgerald started to snap something back, and then he, too, reconsidered his response. He just nodded and said, "Tomorrow I'll call the federal prosecutor who handled their arraignment, tell her they were following you in Boston and then they followed you out of state and attacked you. She'll go talk to the judge, he'll revoke their bail, then a couple of federal marshals will escort them back to Boston."

"Sounds good to me," DeMarco said. "How are the McNultys doing, by the way?"

"I don't know. I just know they're not dead or this could be a whole lot worse for you." Fitzgerald stood up. "You're an operator, DeMarco, and I don't like operators. I'm sorry about what happened to that old lady, but I'll be glad when your ass is out of Boston."

Roy and Ray McNulty were in the same room, lying in hospital beds with rails on the sides. Their left ankles were handcuffed to the rails. A cop was standing outside their door, flirting with one of the nurses.

They were both awake, and both had headaches. Roy had a concussion and Ray had a bandage across his broken nose and half a dozen stitches over his left eye. Both his eyes were black.

Roy McNulty couldn't remember what had happened to him. His last clear memory was walking toward a stack of old wooden boxes looking for DeMarco, but after that *nothing* until he came to in the emergency room. For the third time—he apparently couldn't remember the first two times—he said to his brother: "What the fuck happened, Ray?"

By the time DeMarco retrieved his car from the Glocester cops and drove back to Boston, it was after one a.m. He tossed his car keys to the valet, handed him a ten-buck tip because he was in an excellent mood, and immediately went to the bar for a celebratory nightcap. Tomorrow it would be time to work on the Sean Callahan problem, which he suspected was going to be a lot more dangerous than dealing with the McNulty brothers.

23

The next morning DeMarco woke up at nine. His ribs were sore from the exertion of beating on the McNultys, but otherwise he felt good. In fact, he felt great. He went to the hotel restaurant and had a big breakfast of bacon, toast, and a vegetable-filled omelet. It occurred to him that about the only time he ate vegetables was when they were in omelets and pizzas—and he wasn't sure that counted.

While waiting for his breakfast to arrive, he decided to check on Elinore to see if her condition had improved. He figured by now that Elinore's daughter would have moved her from Mass General to an assisted-living facility in Portsmouth as she'd said she was going to do. But since he didn't know which facility she might be in, he called Maggie Dolan and asked her to use the interns to find Elinore.

"You're a pain in the ass, DeMarco," Maggie said.

"And you're an angel, Maggie," DeMarco said.

He ate his breakfast and read the *Globe* as he waited to hear back from Maggie. He skipped over all the misery on the front page and flipped to the sports section. The Nationals were three games out of first place in the National League East, still in a good position to win the division. The Wizards were getting a seven-foot-two Ukrainian to replace their aging big man, also good.

His phone rang. It was one of Maggie's hotshots, this time a boy. The kid informed him that Elinore was currently in a facility called Glendale in Portsmouth. DeMarco called Glendale and told the woman who answered that he was Ms. Dobbs's nephew. He said that since he lived in Texas, he couldn't just drive over and see her, but his mom had said that Aunt Elinore wasn't doing so good, and he was just calling to check on her.

Whoever answered the phone said she didn't know who Elinore Dobbs was but to give her a moment. Five minutes later a different woman came on the line and said she was the nurse on duty. "I'm just calling to see how Elinore's doing," DeMarco said, and again explained his fictitious relationship to Elinore, figuring the staff would be more likely to talk to a relative about her medical condition.

"Well, you know," the nurse said.

Jesus. "No, I don't know. That's why I'm calling. I know she had a subdural hematoma and it affected her memory but the doctor said she might improve with time."

"I'm sorry, but she hasn't. She spends most of the day sitting in a chair looking out the window. She's afraid to go outside and when we try to get her to go out, she gets agitated. She's easily confused by simple things like what dessert she would like or what to wear. Her short-term memory is not good at all. She can't remember my name and the other day she didn't remember her daughter's name when her daughter came to visit. All I can tell you is she presents with dementia and so far we don't see any sign of improvement."

"Aw, jeez," DeMarco said.

"But it hasn't been that long since her injury, so there's hope," the nurse said, although to DeMarco it didn't sound as if the nurse was all that hopeful.

DeMarco thanked the nurse and hung up. He now had all the motivation he needed when it came to Sean Callahan.

DeMarco hadn't yet told Mahoney what he'd learned about Sean Callahan's relationship to the former leader of a Mexican drug cartel. He also needed to learn more about Javier Castro, and Mahoney could help in this regard. Naturally when he called Mahoney, Mahoney wasn't available, so he told Mahoney's secretary to have the great man call him as soon as possible.

He returned to his room to wait for Mahoney's call. As he waited, he thought about Castro. A guy like him probably didn't send two morons with fish bats to kill you if you pissed him off. He remembered this one episode of the television show *Breaking Bad,* the show about a high school chemistry teacher who became a meth dealer working for a drug cartel. In the episode, Javier Castro's fictional counterpart cut the head off a DEA informant named Tortuga then glued Tortuga's head to a turtle's shell. The next scene showed the head moving, low to the ground, through desert foliage, as the turtle walked slowly toward the U.S. border, where a passel of confused DEA agents were waiting.

DeMarco did *not* want to end up with his head glued to a turtle's shell.

His cell phone rang. It was Mahoney, and the first words out of his mouth were: "How's Elinore doing?"

"Not good," DeMarco said, and relayed to Mahoney what the nurse at the assisted-living place had said.

Mahoney's response was: "Son of a bitch." After a brief pause, he said, "You figure this out, Joe. I'm not going to let Callahan walk away with a smile on his face, and the fifty grand you forced him to cough up to get the McNultys is the equivalent of a parking ticket for a guy like him. A parking ticket isn't good enough. Not for me."

DeMarco almost told Mahoney then about what had transpired with the McNultys the night before, how the last time he'd seen them they were being carried to an ambulance and would soon be back in jail awaiting trial. Then he decided that wasn't a conversation he wanted to have on a cell phone.

"The reason I called, boss, was to tell you what I learned about Callahan from his ex-wife." He paused. "One of the investors in Delaney Square is a guy named Javier Castro who ran, or maybe still runs, a Mexican drug cartel."

"You're shittin' me!" Mahoney said.

"Nope," DeMarco said, and he relayed the story of how Callahan had met Castro when Callahan and his ex took a vacation to Mexico.

"So what are you thinking?" Mahoney said. "We get Treasury or the DEA involved and use them to prove that Callahan's laundering money for this cartel?"

"No, I think that'll be way too complicated and time consuming, and maybe even futile. I'm guessing Javier Castro is no virgin when it comes to money laundering."

"So what do you want to do?"

"I don't know. Yet. But there has to be some way to use this information."

"Well, you figure it out."

"I will," DeMarco said. "But I need to know more about Castro." The only thing that Adele Tomlin had told him was that Castro was handsome and had lovely manners. DeMarco suspected that you didn't become a kingpin in the drug business by saying please and thank you. "I was hoping you could get someone in the DEA to talk to me about him."

"Aw, for crying out loud," Mahoney said, like making a couple of phone calls was going to kill him.

Another hour passed while DeMarco watched morning television talk shows in his room because he couldn't find anything better to watch. How in the hell can people watch this drivel every day, he wondered. His cell phone rang again.

"This is Bill Wilson, San Diego DEA. I was told to give you a call."

"Thanks. I need some background on Javier Castro."

"Yeah, that's what I was told. But why?"

"Did the guy who told you to call me tell you to ask questions, or did he tell you to help me because I work for a big shot who can be a major pain in the ass?"

Wilson hesitated. "He told me to help you."

"Okay, then. What can you tell me about Castro?"

"Right now, as far as we know, Castro's an upstanding citizen. He probably made about a billion dollars dealing drugs—"

"A billion?" DeMarco said. "Really?"

"Last year the Mexican cartels made over twenty-two billion. So do I know for sure that Javier Castro's a billionaire? The answer's no. It's not like his books are open to the public. But I do know that he made a hell of a lot of money and a billion wouldn't be out of line. Anyway, about five years ago, Castro turned his operation over to a cousin, a guy who's a total psycho, and now Castro's completely legit."

"Yeah, but what kind of guy is he?"

"He ran a drug cartel. What kind of guy do you think he is? He got into the business when he was about seventeen like most of these guys do because his family was poor and he didn't have any education. He probably figured he could either be a drug dealer in Mexico or a strawberry picker in California. So he went to work for a guy named Guerrero, and he did what all the young guys do. He snuck drugs across the border, collected money, protected Guerrero from other cartels, and killed people Guerrero wanted killed. By the time he was twenty-five, he was one of Guerrero's top guys, Guerrero obviously recognizing that he was smarter than most of the mutts who worked for him. Then, when he was thirty-four, he whacked Guerrero and became the guy in charge. We figured in four or five years, someone would come along and whack him, either one of his own people or another cartel. But that's when we learned he was different."

"Different how?" DeMarco asked.

"Castro is one of those rare drug dealers who asks the question: When is enough enough? He didn't try to expand his empire. He just protected what he had because he figured out that he was making more money than he was ever going to be able to spend. So he formed alliances with the other cartels when he could to avoid turf wars. He didn't allow his guys to massacre people in tourist spots because he knew that would just piss the government off, plus he had investments in the tourist spots. The other thing he did was educate himself. It was too late for him to go back to school so he brought in tutors, learned to speak English, and basically earned an MBA so he could figure out what to do with all his money. Then, very gradually, he backed away from the cartel. He put his cousin in charge, paid off the right politicians so the federales would leave him alone, and became just another wealthy Mexican living off his investments. You asked me what kind of guy he is. Well, I guess I'd say the main thing about him is that he's analytical."

"Analytical?"

"Yeah. He *thinks* before he does things. He doesn't get emotional. He'll kill somebody if he has to, but only if he has to. He's got an ego but he doesn't allow his ego to make him do stupid things. But I'll tell you one thing. He might not run the cartel anymore, but if you piss him off, he'll cut your heart out."

"I guess that's better than getting my head glued to a turtle," DeMarco said.

"What?" Wilson said.

———◆———

DeMarco called Adele Tomlin, the second Mrs. Callahan. "I need to talk to Javier Castro. Do you have any idea where he might be right now?"

"He could be in any number of places. He spends most of his time in Mexico City but he also has property in Veracruz and Oaxaca. And the last time I saw Danielle, she said he was buying a place in Switzerland. But if I had to guess, I'd say he's most likely in Mexico City."

DeMarco did *not* want to go to Mexico to talk to Javier Castro.

"I was thinking," DeMarco said. "Since you're such good friends with Danielle, maybe you could call her up and chat with her, see how she's doing, that sort of thing, and find out where her husband is."

Adele hesitated. "When I told you Javier had invested money in Delaney Square, I'd had a few drinks. Plus, I was pissed at Sean—I'm always pissed at Sean—and wanted to help you find a way to hurt him. But I don't want Javier to know that I talked to you about him. Javier and Danielle are my friends but—"

"Yeah, I understand. Javier's not a guy you'd want to irritate. And Javier will never find out you talked to me. I have connections in the government, Adele, and those people have also talked to me. In fact, I just got off the phone with a DEA agent in San Diego. So do you think you can find out where Javier is right now?"

"Why don't you use your government connections to find him?"

"I could, but that will take time. It'll be easier and faster if you just call his wife." When Adele didn't respond immediately, DeMarco tried to think of some way to diplomatically say: *Hey, Adele, your ex dropped you for a younger woman and if you want to get back at him, give me a hand here.*

But before he could think of a way to phrase that sentiment differently, Adele said, "Okay, I'll give Danielle a call."

Forty minutes later Adele called back.

"Javier's in Mexico City, like I thought," she said. "But guess what? Danielle is coming to New York next week to see her daughter. She just finished some student film project and Danielle's coming to see the show, the screening, whatever you call it. Anyway, she'll be staying with her daughter next week, and I just might go down to see her. I'm glad you asked me to call her."

DeMarco didn't care where Danielle Castro was going to be next week. It was Javier he needed to talk to.

"Thanks, Adele. Oh, do you happen to have Castro's address in Mexico City?"

"Sure. I send them a Christmas card every year. Hang on a minute. I'll get it. By the way, do you think you might be coming out to the Cape again soon?"

DeMarco now had Javier Castro's address but he really didn't want to travel to Mexico to talk to the man; that would be like walking into a lion's den and poking the lion with a stick. So since he had another card to play with the McNultys, he decided to play it. If the McNultys refused to cooperate, then he'd go see Castro. Maybe.

He called his pal Detective Fitzgerald and like a true pal, Fitzgerald said, "What the hell do you want now?"

"I want to talk to the McNultys. Where are they?"

"The Essex County jail up in Middleton, the same place they put the marathon bomber before his trial."

"How far is the jail from Boston?"

"Forty minutes."

"Good. I want to talk to them. Can you arrange that?"

"Why?"

"I want them to testify against Sean Callahan. I want them to admit that he paid them to kill Elinore Dobbs."

"Why would they do that?" Fitzgerald said. "Right now they're in jail for possessing guns, not attempted murder."

"But if I can guarantee they'll serve less time on the gun charge, that they'll get immunity for hurting Elinore, and that I'll refuse to testify that they assaulted me in Rhode Island, then maybe they'll be willing to testify against Callahan."

"Do you have the authority to make that kind of deal? I mean, did I miss the part where you became a federal prosecutor?"

"No, you didn't miss that part. But I know a guy who might be able to get the Justice Department to cooperate."

"Yeah, I know you do. The only reason I'm even talking to you is because of the guy you know."

"So can you set it up so I can meet with them?"

"Yeah, all right, I'll make a call," Fitzgerald said, sounding just like Mahoney, like a phone call was going to break his back.

———◆◆◆———

DeMarco met with the McNultys in an interview room at the Essex County jail. They were wearing white T-shirts, blue jeans, and flip-flops. To his delight, they looked like somebody had beaten the shit out of them, Ray looking much worse than Roy, and much worse than DeMarco had looked after they stomped him in the parking garage. Both of his eyes were black, and he had a bandage over his nose and stitches on his forehead. With the two black eyes, he looked like an angry, not-too-bright raccoon. Roy didn't have any visible marks on him—DeMarco had hit him on top of the head and on the chin—but his eyes looked glazed and he seemed to be having a hard time focusing. To DeMarco's relief, they were handcuffed and the handcuffs were attached to big eyebolts in the center of a table and the table was anchored to the floor with more bolts.

"What do you want?" Ray McNulty said. "If we didn't have these cuffs on we'd beat you to death."

"You saw how well that worked out for you last time," DeMarco said.

"Fuck you," Roy said.

"What do you want?" Ray said again.

"I got a deal for you," DeMarco said. "I want you to testify that Sean Callahan paid you to kill Elinore Dobbs."

"We didn't have anything to do with that old broad getting hurt."

"Ray, you're going to get at least ten years in prison for the assault weapons charge. Then you're also going to be convicted for trying to kill me in Rhode Island, which means even more time. Do you think Sean Callahan would do that kind of time for you?"

"We ain't rats," Roy said.

"If we admitted we had anything to do with that old bitch," Ray said, "the government will pile an attempted murder charge on top of the weapons charge. And as for us assaulting you, it's just your word against ours. You think we're stupid?"

"Yeah, I do think you're stupid because you're not listening to me. If you'll agree to testify against Callahan, I'll work out a deal for you so you get immunity for what you did to Elinore, I won't testify against you for assaulting me in Rhode Island, and you'll get less time for the weapons charge. You're not going to get off scot-free but instead of doing ten years, maybe you'll do five."

"We ain't rats," Roy said again, which so far had been his only contribution to the conversation. DeMarco may have hit Roy too hard with his potato sap.

"Are you shitting me?" DeMarco said. "You think you're Mafia guys who took some kind of omertà oath? Well, I got news for you. Even Mafia guys don't believe in omertà. They all rat each other out."

"We ain't rattin' anyone out," Roy said. "And we don't trust your slick ass."

DeMarco certainly couldn't blame them for not trusting him.

"We're going to do our time," Ray said, "and when we get out, we're going to hunt you down and kill you."

This was hopeless.

DeMarco drove back to Boston, still unable to believe that the McNultys wouldn't take the deal. They were stubborn, stupid fools but for God knows what reason loyal to Callahan. Or maybe it wasn't loyalty. Maybe they just didn't trust him like Roy had said, and thought he was playing them in some way. Whatever the case, he was now going to have to go to Mexico to meet with Javier Castro. He could call the guy, but he didn't think a phone call would have the same impact as a face-to-face meeting. But going to Mexico . . .

DeMarco's impression of Mexico was that the country was lawless. The police were either corrupt or incompetent, and the drug cartels appeared to act with total impunity. He didn't know how many articles he'd read about cartels slaughtering anyone who opposed them, no matter who they were. The last major atrocity he'd read about concerned forty-three college students who'd disappeared, and it took the Mexican cops months to figure out that their bodies had been incinerated by one of the cartels for reasons that never made any sense. How hard would it be to make one American disappear?

❖

DeMarco made a reservation on Delta that left Boston at six the next morning and would arrive in Mexico City about noon. To find a hotel, he looked up the address Adele Tomlin had given him for Castro on Google Maps, and made a reservation at a nearby Marriott. The helpful elves at Google also informed him that Castro lived in an upscale area of Mexico City called Polanco in the Miguel Hidalgo borough, and that some of the wealthiest families in the city lived there.

Travel arrangements complete, he went to the lobby, copied down the number of one of the pay phones there, then called Mahoney. He was surprised when Mahoney answered his cell phone. He expected he'd need to leave a message and then have to wait around until Mahoney called him back.

"You need to go find a pay phone," DeMarco said, not knowing how long that would take. The disappearance of pay phones in the last few years made this sort of skullduggery more difficult. "I need to tell you something and I don't want to do it over a cell phone. Call me at this number," he said, and read him off the number of the hotel pay phone. He thought it pretty unlikely that anyone would be monitoring Mahoney's phones, but he didn't want to take the chance. Mahoney, with a minimal amount of complaining, agreed and fifteen minutes later called DeMarco back.

"I'm planning to fly to Mexico tomorrow to meet with Javier Castro."

"Why would you do that?" Mahoney said.

"I'm going to threaten him with the fearsome might of the U.S. government if he doesn't help me screw Sean Callahan." Then DeMarco explained what he had in mind and when he was finished, Mahoney said, "You think it's a good idea, blackmailing a guy who used to run a drug cartel?"

"No, I think it's a really bad idea but you're the one who said that forcing fifty grand out of Callahan to set up the McNultys wasn't good enough. You said, and I quote, that it was like giving him a parking ticket. So if Castro does what I want, Callahan's not getting a parking ticket. He's going to go bankrupt."

"Yeah, but still," Mahoney said. "You remember, just a year ago, some cartel kidnapped a DEA undercover down there? They flayed all the skin off him before they killed him. Those people are nuts."

That was *just* what he needed to hear. "So what do you want me to do?" DeMarco said. "Give Callahan a pass for what he did to Elinore and let him make however many millions he's going to make off Delaney Square?"

"No," Mahoney said. "I'm just saying you better be careful down there."

Ya think?

"I will, but I doubt Castro's going to do anything to a guy who works for an American congressman," DeMarco said, although he wasn't really sure that was true. "But that's one of the reasons I called you. If you don't hear from me in a couple of days . . . Well, call somebody."

———◆———

After talking to Mahoney, he decided to go have an expensive steak dinner in the hotel dining room. He couldn't help but think of it as the last meal for a condemned man. Following dinner, which was excellent, he headed over to the bar to have a nightcap or two. Or three. He took a seat at the bar and looked around, and lo and behold, there was a woman there who looked like the actress Amy Adams.

DeMarco would never have admitted it to anyone, but he had a thing for Amy Adams. She had one of those sweet, virginal faces and early in her career she'd played the enchanted princess and the plucky but pure girl next door. But as Amy grew older—she was about forty now—she started taking parts that showed off her edgy sexy side, which DeMarco liked.

There was a romance writers' convention taking place at the hotel. He'd seen a sign in the lobby when he got back from visiting the McNultys, and on the sign were photos of a couple of authors he'd never heard of. DeMarco had never read a romance novel in his life, but he'd seen the ripped-bodice book jackets and figured a romance writer's head would be filled with sexual fantasies. Or maybe better than fantasies, actual hands-on experience the writer could draw upon.

The woman he was looking at had long red hair, like Amy's hair in that movie where she played a con man's hot mistress. She was sitting at a table with three other women and DeMarco assumed they were all romance writers. The other women were frumpy-looking, overweight, and in their fifties or sixties, and DeMarco was fairly sure they all relied on strong imaginations when it came to their books rather than recent sexual experience. But the Amy look-alike . . . She was cute—short and curvy. She'd noticed DeMarco looking at her, made eye contact with him, and flashed him a smile—which made DeMarco think here was this writer, far from home, in a setting where she could go a little wild, and maybe do some hands-on research on him.

As DeMarco was trying to devise a way to separate Amy from her friends, she again looked over at him, then nudged the woman sitting next to her, a hefty lady in her fifties with long gray hair and no makeup. The other woman looked at DeMarco, said something to Amy, then both women rose from the table where they were sitting and walked toward him.

"Hi, my name is Madeline Cummings," Amy said. "And this is my writing partner, Janice Brooks. We wondered if you'd allow us to take your picture."

"My picture?" DeMarco said.

"Yes. I know this is going to sound odd, but there's this villain in the book we're currently writing and when I saw your face, I said to myself: That's Bruno! Our villain! You see, it really helps us capture the characters in our books, particularly the main ones, if we have an actual person in mind. So would you mind, terribly, if I took your picture?"

"I've got the face of your villain?" DeMarco said.

"Well, yes. I mean, you're sort of hard-looking," Madeline said.

"Sort of gangster-looking," Janice said.

"Sort of menacing," Madeline said.

"Sort of brutal," Janice said.

"Brutal?" DeMarco said.

"No offense intended," Madeline said. "I'm sure you're a very nice man but you have this face that . . . Well, you're our Bruno."

Come to think of it, up close, she didn't look so much like Amy Adams. In fact, she didn't look at all like Amy Adams. Her eyes were too close together and her nose was kind of fat.

"Uh, sure, snap away," DeMarco said.

Madeline—definitely not Amy—framed DeMarco's face in her smart phone, took a picture. Then she said, "Just one more," and took another.

"Thank you so, so much," Madeline said.

"No problem," DeMarco said.

They went back to their table and DeMarco looked at his reflection in the mirror behind the bar. What a bunch of bullshit. He didn't look "menacing," whatever the hell that meant, and he sure as hell didn't look brutal. He decided to go find another bar to drink in, someplace not filled with a bunch of screwball writers. Then tomorrow he'd fly to Mexico and threaten a guy who used to run a drug cartel.

24

---◆---

As the plane descended for landing at Benito Juárez International Airport, DeMarco could see the sprawl of the great city. Mexico City proper was home to about nine million people but the population of the entire metropolitan area was closer to twenty million. It seemed to go forever.

DeMarco had only been to Mexico once and it had been years ago, before the drug violence got so bad that he had no desire to visit again. But the one trip he'd taken had been marvelous and memorable. He and a woman he was dating at the time—the lady worked for the State Department and was proud of her high school Spanish—had stayed at a resort in Puerto Vallarta on the Pacific Coast. There were two things DeMarco remembered most about the place.

The first thing—and similar to what Adele Tomlin had said about the Los Cabos resort where she and Sean Callahan met the Castros—was that the service had been incredible. He remembered one dinner at the resort's main restaurant where four waiters hovered over them while they ate.

But the other thing he remembered, and this stuck in his mind more than the magnificence of the resort, was the poverty. DeMarco and his lady friend had spent most of the week in Mexico inside the gated compound of the resort, near the beach and the bars and the swimming pool, but one day they decided to rent a car and tour the area. And that's when DeMarco saw how the poor in Mexico lived. The most vivid memory he had was driving through a village where a brown stream that looked like an open sewer ran down the middle of a road between small shacks with tin roofs—hovels appropriate for a third world country— and a naked little girl of about three was playing in the stream. It was as if the resort was a feudal castle and if you stayed inside its walls, you were spared the reality of the way the serfs lived. Maybe the country had changed for the better in the years since he'd visited; he hoped so.

There was no sign of abject poverty, however, in the part of Mexico City where the Marriott was located and where Javier Castro lived. It looked no different than the prosperous sections of American cities, and the twenty-two-story Marriott was about ten steps up from the Park Plaza in Boston where he'd been staying. The lobby was breath-taking, with marble floors and flowers in tall vases and modern art-work. There was a dark paneled library off the lobby if a guest desired a quiet space, a restaurant that specialized in French cuisine, and a bistro for more casual dining on a terrace looking out at Chapultepec Park. Nearby was the Museum of Anthropology, showcasing Aztec and Mayan artifacts, as well as Masaryk Avenue, Mexico City's version of Rodeo Drive in L.A., with high-priced shops, nightclubs, and trendy restaurants—none of which DeMarco was likely to see as he planned to be in town for as little time as possible.

He didn't have Javier Castro's phone number. He could have asked Adele Tomlin for it, but had decided not to, and since he had Castro's address, he didn't really need the phone number. He took a shower, and put on a suit, a white shirt, and a tie. It wasn't as hot in Mexico City as it had been in Boston and he imagined that was due to the city's elevation, but it was still a warm afternoon, in the eighties. Nonetheless, he figured he needed to dress appropriately for a man representing a United States congressman.

He took a cab to Javier Castro's house. The cabdriver—like everyone he'd met so far since arriving in Mexico City—spoke English. Javier lived on a street named Retorno de Julieta, in a neighborhood of large, luxurious homes. As for Castro's home, all DeMarco could see from the cab was a white stucco wall that was about ten feet high with red and purple bougainvillea growing along the top, a twelve-foot-wide wrought iron gate, and a winding tree-lined driveway.

He told the cabbie to wait for him and walked up to an intercom panel near the gate. He punched the button and while waiting for someone to answer, he noticed a security camera looking down at him. Then he noticed a couple of other cameras almost hidden in the bougainvillea. A moment later a voice said something in Spanish.

"I'm here to see Mr. Castro," DeMarco said.

"Who are you?"

"My name is DeMarco. I'm here on behalf of United States congressman John Mahoney."

There was a long pause, then whoever was speaking said, "Mr. Castro isn't here right now."

DeMarco had expected that this might happen. He reached into a pocket and held up a small white envelope. "I have a note for Mr. Castro. Could you please see that he gets it?"

Again a long pause, followed by: "Wait where you are."

A moment later, a dark-haired guy wearing a floral-patterned shirt and jeans came down the driveway. He was about forty, appeared to be in excellent shape, and tucked into the front of his jeans, plainly visible, was an automatic pistol.

DeMarco handed the envelope through the bars of the gate, saying, "My phone number is on the note."

The guy—a security guard, DeMarco assumed—didn't say anything. He just took the envelope and walked back up the driveway.

DeMarco told the cabdriver to take him back to the Marriott. All he could do now was wait to hear from Castro. On the note to Castro he'd written: "Mr. Castro, I represent United States congressman John Mahoney and wish to discuss Sean Callahan's Delaney Square development in Boston. Congressman Mahoney has no desire to cause you any sort of legal or financial problem, but there is an issue with regard to Mr. Callahan that needs to be resolved. It would be in your best interest not to speak to Mr. Callahan until you've spoken to me. Please call me at your earliest convenience, although this is a matter of some urgency." He signed the note "Joseph DeMarco" and wrote his cell phone number below his name.

———◆◆◆———

By the time DeMarco got back to the Marriott, it was almost five. He didn't know if he'd hear back from Castro that night—he didn't know if he'd hear back from Castro period—but he decided to stick close to the hotel so he could catch a cab if he needed to. The other reason he decided to stay inside the hotel was that he'd be safe. He hadn't told Castro's guy where he was staying, but he didn't feel like taking chances.

As he'd told Mahoney, he didn't think Castro would be foolish enough to harm a man representing a United States congressman, but he could envision himself walking down some street, a vehicle pulling up, and a guy pointing a gun at his face and telling him to get in the car. The next morning the body of an American missing his wallet would be found in some neighborhood where people getting mugged wasn't all that unusual, and the American Embassy would conclude that DeMarco had been foolish enough to venture into the wrong part of Mexico City. Or maybe a body would never be found. He figured he was being paranoid—but sometimes it's not a bad thing to be paranoid.

He went to the bar off the main lobby and ordered a margarita instead of his usual vodka martini. When in Rome. The bar was practically empty. Nearby were two very tall, shapely blondes who were speaking German and a silver-haired older couple who sounded like they might be from the American South. He checked his cell phone to make sure he was getting a signal; yep, he had four bars. As he was sipping his drink and wondering what he'd do if Castro decided not to meet with him, two guys—both blond, both tall, both handsome—walked up to the table where the two blond German women were sitting. They all left the bar together, a striking group that made him think of the Hitler Youth, an organization only perfect Aryans were allowed to join. A moment later, the older American couple left, too, leaving DeMarco sitting alone in the bar except for a bartender who was as silent as stone.

DeMarco thought: *This is dumb, hiding inside the hotel.* It was a beautiful evening, and it wouldn't be dark for another couple of hours. He was going to go for a walk and eat at some swanky place on Masaryk Avenue. He wasn't concerned about the money he was spending on a five-star hotel and what he planned to spend for dinner; he figured a portion of the extra fifteen grand that Mahoney had made off Sean Callahan could finance his Mexico adventure. He asked the concierge to recommend a restaurant and got directions to a place called Biko. According to the concierge, Biko was one of the best restaurants in all of Latin America, not just Mexico City, and specialized in Basque cuisine. And DeMarco thought: *Why not?* He hadn't been planning to have tacos.

He strolled over to the restaurant, was greeted effusively by a lovely young hostess, and was seated at a table holding what seemed like an excessive number of wine glasses. His waiter, a dignified Mexican gentleman in his sixties, patiently discussed the menu with him, and DeMarco decided to go for the priciest options. He ordered foie gras with mustard seeds and green onions for an appetizer, to be followed by duck breast simmered in amontillado sherry and Manzanilla olives; a different wine would accompany each course. Fifteen minutes later, his first glass of wine half consumed, the waiter placed the foie gras in front of him, the plate looking like a work of art. He took a moment to appreciate what he was about to eat, raised a fork to begin—and that's when two men walked up to his table.

"Mr. DeMarco," one of them said, "we'd like you to come with us. Mr. Castro wishes to speak with you."

And DeMarco thought: *Whoa!*

Both men were Hispanic, in their early thirties, and wearing suits, white shirts, and ties. They were tall, lean, and muscular; they reminded DeMarco of greyhounds. He was willing to bet that their suit jackets concealed weapons.

Castro was sending him a message—and DeMarco was impressed. The only way these guys could have found him so fast was by using his cell phone to locate him. Which meant that in the two hours since he'd asked the guy at Castro's gate to deliver his note to Castro, Castro had contacted someone and told that person to locate DeMarco using his phone. Castro had also found DeMarco's picture somewhere so his guys would recognize him, and that too was impressive. DeMarco didn't have a Facebook page, and he'd never been photographed by the media, so how did Castro get his photo? DMV? His congressional ID? He didn't know, but somehow Castro had gotten a photo. He imagined that Castro had also done other research on him. Whatever the case, Castro's message was: *I can find you anytime I want.*

"Can I finish my dinner first?" DeMarco said, gesturing at the foie gras.

The guy who'd spoken to him just stared at him.

"Well, okay then," DeMarco said. Shit. He got up, dropped a hundred bucks on the table—hoping that would be enough to cover the wine and an appetizer he hadn't touched—and followed the two guys to an SUV with tinted windows parked outside the restaurant.

One of the men drove. The other sat in the backseat with DeMarco.

"Where are we going?" he asked.

The guy in the back with him didn't answer his question. Instead he said, "I need to frisk you to make sure you're not armed."

"I'm not armed," DeMarco said.

The man didn't say anything. Just like he'd done in the restaurant when DeMarco had asked if he could finish his dinner, the guy just stared at him.

"Frisk away," DeMarco said, raising his arms above his head.

The bodyguard patted him down; he was very thorough. Embarrassingly thorough. When he finished, DeMarco asked again, "Where are we going?"

The man didn't answer.

DeMarco's imagination kicked into overdrive. He could see himself, kneeling in front of a shallow grave, a gun pressed to the back of his head. Then he thought: *Get a grip on yourself!* Castro isn't going to do anything until after you've talked to him—which wasn't particularly comforting. It had been a bad idea coming to Mexico.

Twenty minutes later, the SUV pulled up to the gate in front of Castro's house. The gate opened when the driver used a remote, then he drove up the long tree-lined driveway and parked near an oversized redwood door with elaborate black wrought iron hinges. The bodyguards didn't take DeMarco into the house, however. Instead they led him around the house to an outdoor courtyard paved with colorful ceramic tiles. The courtyard contained a burbling stone fountain and was surrounded by green and red broad-leaved plants; purple and pink fuchsia overflowed pots hanging from support posts. In the background, music was playing, some classical piano number, which DeMarco could barely hear. It was an incredibly tranquil place although he wasn't feeling all that tranquil.

Javier Castro was seated at a patio table, drinking a glass of wine. The bodyguards took up positions, standing a few feet away, far enough not to be able to hear a conversation but close enough to shoot him.

Adele Tomlin had told him that Javier Castro looked like a telenovela star, and DeMarco supposed he did. Unlike DeMarco and his bodyguards, Castro was dressed casually in a white guayabera shirt, gray slacks, and tan dress sandals. DeMarco knew he was close to sixty as Adele had said that he was about ten years older than Callahan, but he looked younger than sixty and appeared to be in excellent shape. He wasn't as tall as his bodyguards—he was about DeMarco's height— but like his guards he was lean and muscular. He had curly dark hair streaked with gray, a strong square chin, and a thin mustache. He was a handsome man.

He gestured for DeMarco to sit. He didn't offer him a glass of wine but got right to the point.

"What can I do for you, Mr. DeMarco?" he said. He had just a trace of a Hispanic accent. Whoever taught him English had done a good job.

"As I'm sure you know," DeMarco said, "Sean Callahan is spearheading a large development in Boston called Delaney Square. Building the project required knocking down an apartment building where an old lady named Elinore Dobbs lived, but Elinore refused to vacate. When Callahan couldn't buy her out, he tried to force her to move by shutting off her power and water and air-conditioning, and doing anything else he could think of to make her life miserable. So she went to my boss for help and he sent me to help her, but before I could make Callahan leave her alone, Callahan had two thugs make her fall down a flight of stairs. She hit her head hard and is now suffering from dementia."

"Why are you telling me all this, Mr. DeMarco?" Castro said. "I know Sean Callahan socially, but I have nothing to do with his business."

Now DeMarco had to figure out a way to call Javier Castro a liar without calling him a liar.

"Mr. Castro, my boss is determined to make Callahan pay for what he did to Elinore Dobbs. So one of the things I did was look into the financing associated with Delaney Square. I was frankly hoping to find something that could cause Callahan a legal problem, and that was when I learned that you're a substantial investor in the development. Specifically, I discovered that money originating from you passed through an investment company in the Caymans and was loaned to Callahan."

At least that was what Adele Tomlin had told him, and he could only hope she'd gotten the facts right.

Castro's only reaction to DeMarco's statement was to take a sip of wine. Then he said, very calmly, "Assuming what you say is true, I still don't understand why you're talking to me."

The good news was that Castro was no longer denying being invested in Delaney Square.

"Mr. Castro, Congressman Mahoney doesn't want Sean Callahan to profit from Delaney Square, and he wants you to make sure that he doesn't. And the congressman doesn't care how you do it."

"I don't know what you're talking about," Castro said.

"For example," DeMarco said, "you could have the Cayman company that invested in Delaney Square call in the loans they made to Callahan, and when he can't repay the loans, you can use that as an excuse to force him out and put your own man in charge."

"Even if I wanted to do such a thing," Castro said, "I don't know that I could. A *company* with many investors invested in Delaney Square, not me personally, and I don't know that they can arbitrarily call in their loans."

"I'm sure you can convince them to do whatever you want," DeMarco said. The Cayman company laundered money for drug lords, so DeMarco figured the drug lords were in charge. He also figured that if the money flow could be disrupted in any way, then Callahan wouldn't be able to pay his builders and architects and the suppliers who provided materials. And when he couldn't pay these people, construction would grind to a halt, the U.S. investment bank wouldn't give him the money he needed for the next phase of the project, and eventually the bankers would force Callahan into bankruptcy so they could get some of their money back.

"There's another solution," DeMarco said, and this was the solution he really liked. "Callahan can simply walk away from Delaney Square."

"Walk away?" Castro said.

"Yes. Callahan has a company that manages his developments. So Callahan resigns from his company and his general manager, or whoever is his second in command, completes Delaney Square without him."

"But how would I make Sean walk away?" Castro said.

Come on, Javier! You make him an offer he can't refuse. You hold a gun to his fucking head!

"That would be up to you, Mr. Castro," DeMarco said. "But I'm sure you could find a way."

"And if I don't do what you want?" Castro said.

DeMarco shook his head, as if he hated to be the bearer of bad news. "Then, Mr. Castro, I'm afraid you could end up with some serious problems. As I'm sure you know, the United States government has some rather extraordinary powers when it comes to freezing assets and seizing property belonging to criminal or terrorist organizations. So if you elect not to force Callahan out of Delaney Square, then Congressman Mahoney starts the wheels of the U.S. government spinning. The Treasury Department, the Justice Department, and the DEA will form up a task force, and by the time they're done, I imagine you'll lose a lot of money.

"So, it's up to you, sir. Congressman Mahoney doesn't care what you do or how you do it, provided Sean Callahan doesn't profit from what he did to Elinore Dobbs."

As he was speaking, DeMarco had been watching Castro's face and when he started talking about seizing assets, Castro's eyes became chips of ice and the expression on his face became harder and crueler. De-Marco was no longer talking to some benign middle-aged guy who hobnobbed with Mexican politicians and movie stars. He was now talking to a man who used to kill people when they got in his way.

"Before you say anything, Mr. Castro, let me explain something. Congressman Mahoney doesn't care about you. Furthermore, he knows you're no longer engaged in your former business and he has no objection to you investing in American enterprises.

"You see, Mr. Castro, this whole thing is about egos and it's gotten way out of hand. John Mahoney's ego was bruised when Callahan disrespected him and refused to leave Elinore Dobbs alone. Then Callahan let his ego get the best of him when he thought he was too rich to have to bend to Mahoney's will.

"Well, sir, you don't want your ego to cause you legal and financial problems you don't need. I asked a DEA agent about you, and he told me that you're an analytical man. A man who acts rationally and not emotionally. I'd suggest, Mr. Castro, that this is a time for you to be analytical. If Delaney Square is completed and you make a handsome return, John Mahoney doesn't have a problem with that. All Mahoney wants is for Sean Callahan to pay for what he did to Elinore Dobbs."

DeMarco stood up.

"With your permission, sir, I'll be leaving now. Why don't you think about all I've told you and let me know what you plan to do. Soon. I'll be heading back to Washington tomorrow."

Castro fixed his dark eyes on DeMarco's face for what seemed an eternity, then he said something in rapid-fire Spanish to his bodyguards.

DeMarco followed the two bodyguards back to the SUV that had taken him to Castro's home. When the driver opened the door for him, without thinking about it, DeMarco got into the car and sat in the front passenger seat. The other bodyguard sat in the rear seat behind DeMarco—and that's when DeMarco's imagination went wild again. He could see the guy in the backseat slipping a garrote around his throat, and him thrashing in the front seat, kicking out the windshield, as he was strangled to death. Or maybe the guy sitting behind him would simply take out a gun and shoot him in the back of the head. The drive back to the Marriott was the longest ride of his life.

When they dropped him off at the hotel—it occurred to him later that he'd never told them he was staying at the Marriott—he went straight to the bar.

25

After DeMarco left, Castro closed his eyes and took in several deep breaths to calm himself. When he was a young man first starting out in his chosen profession, he'd had a violent temper and he reacted to any sort of threat or disrespect with violence. When he was eighteen, if DeMarco had threatened him the way he had today, he would have pulled out a gun and shot him without thinking twice about it. Fortunately—for DeMarco—those days had passed and he'd learned to control his temper. More important, he'd learned that violence was a tool that should only to be used to accomplish some specific objective, and not for personal gratification.

He poured himself another glass of wine and considered his options.

What Mahoney's lackey didn't realize—and that's all DeMarco was: a lackey—was that he wasn't the only investor in Delaney Square. DeMarco was not just threatening him; he was threatening a number of very serious people.

When he first met Sean Callahan and his second wife at the Los Cabos resort, he was already backing out of the cartel and turning it over to his cousin Paulo. He didn't need to make more money from drugs, nor did he need to take the risks associated with drug trafficking. He didn't need to remain a target for the American or Mexican police, or rival cartels, or the ambitious people who worked for him—like crazy Paulo. He'd made enough money to last not only his lifetime, but also the lifetimes of his family for generations to come.

So at the time he met Callahan, he already had money invested in other legitimate businesses and was looking for other opportunities. Although he didn't need to make more money, if he could do so safely, he would. When Callahan told him about the Boston project, he'd been intrigued and had his financial people research Callahan. They concluded that Callahan was an astute businessman, had been successful many times in the past, and Delaney Square would likely generate a substantial return.

Callahan had also been very honest with him, and maybe that was because of who he was. Callahan had warned him that real estate development could be very profitable for key investors, but at the same time, it was an extremely risky business in that unexpected events, completely out of his control, could cause a project like Delaney Square to fail.

Callahan had said that he needed a hundred million from private investors, and once he had those investors in place, he would get the remainder he needed from American banks. Castro, however, had no intention of putting a hundred million into a single project. That would be too many eggs in one basket. What he did instead was talk to several men in Mexico to see if they wanted to invest. Some of those men—like his cousin—were still involved in drug trafficking. Others were men like himself, men no longer in the business but looking for opportunities. In the end, he and six other men invested in Delaney Square, each putting up approximately fifteen million.

The problem with these other investors was that they would not react well if Delaney Square failed to show a profit—and they'd blame him. A man like his cousin would have the most violent reaction and, blood ties aside, was likely to take his anger out on him in an irrational way—such as kidnapping his wife and daughter for ransom to recoup his fifteen million. Paulo now controlled the army he used to control.

The other problem—and it was really the larger of the two problems—was that none of these men wanted the Americans looking into their finances. As DeMarco had said, if the Americans discovered that drug money had been used to finance Delaney Square, they might freeze assets and seize properties. The fact was he didn't really know what might happen if the Americans started looking closely into the financing of Callahan's project. All he knew for sure was that he didn't want them looking.

His long-range plan had always been to move away from Mexico, most likely to Europe. Mexico, thanks largely to men like himself and his cousin, was simply too dangerous a place to live. He wanted to become a *simple* rich man. An anonymous rich man. He wanted to protect the money he had and make money in the future in a legitimate way for his family, and the last thing he needed was this nonsense with Mahoney and Callahan.

The other thing he realized was that DeMarco would have to be some sort of financial genius to have uncovered his investment in Delaney Square—and he doubted that DeMarco was a genius. The cartel used people with MBAs from Stanford who worked with experienced international bankers to launder money through multiple shell corporations. It would be hard, if not impossible, for experienced Treasury agents to trace the money in Delaney Square back to him.

Therefore, the only way DeMarco could have known that he'd invested in the Boston project was if someone had told him. None of Castro's fellow investors would have told him, and Sean Callahan certainly wouldn't have, leaving only one other person that he could think of: Callahan's ex-wife, Adele. The other thing that convinced him that Adele was DeMarco's source was that Adele had called Danielle just a day ago to chat with her—and the coincidence of DeMarco showing up at his home following that phone call was certainly not a coincidence.

So. What should he do about all this?

There was no way that he was going to make the Cayman group call in its loans to Callahan. There was no way he was going to disrupt the project in any way that could adversely affect its completion and eventual profitability. Which meant that he'd have to exercise the second option that DeMarco had given him and force Callahan out of the project so Callahan didn't turn a profit, which was apparently all Mahoney wanted. The problem with that solution, however, was that it was too complicated. He knew Callahan wouldn't walk away from Delaney Square without a fight, and he might involve lawyers and even law enforcement if Castro tried to force him out.

Which led to a third option, one that DeMarco apparently hadn't considered. He really preferred not to exercise the third option but unfortunately Mahoney and DeMarco weren't giving him any other choice.

And then one other thing occurred to him: he couldn't let DeMarco or Mahoney have this sort of hold over him. He certainly wasn't going to do anything to John Mahoney; he would never be so foolhardy as to directly threaten or kill a United States congressman. At the same time he needed to send Mahoney a message, one that would convince him to leave him alone in the future.

He recalled DeMarco's little speech about egos and how he shouldn't allow his own ego to cause him to do something foolish. So was taking some action against DeMarco ego driven or was it a pragmatic thing to do? He finally decided he didn't care, and by the time he finished his wine he'd devised a way to make DeMarco pay for meddling in his business.

He left his lovely, peaceful courtyard, walked into the house, and headed toward his den. On the way he passed the media room and could hear his wife talking to their daughter in New York. He shook his head. His wife and his daughter talked almost every day.

From the desk in his den, he removed one of several prepaid cell phones. He doubted anyone was monitoring his calls but he preferred there not be a record of him making a call to DeMarco. He took out the note DeMarco had sent him and called DeMarco's number.

"I've decided to accommodate your employer," Castro said.

"I'm glad to hear that," DeMarco said.

The smugness in DeMarco's voice made Castro squeeze the phone so hard he was surprised he didn't crack the screen.

"It will take me a few days, however. This is a complicated matter."

"I understand," DeMarco said.

"And I would like you to return to Boston."

"Why?"

"Because I'm not sure how I intend to proceed, and I may need your assistance there. I also may need the assistance of your employer. I just don't know yet."

DeMarco immediately said, "I don't see how I can be of any help to you. And there's no way in hell my boss is going to help you. From here on in, it's all between you and Callahan."

"Mr. DeMarco, you're the one who came to me, and I'm willing to do what you want. The least you can do is assist me if I feel that's necessary."

"I'll think about it," DeMarco said, and hung up.

He couldn't *believe* the man had just hung up on him.

Using the same phone, he sent an encrypted text message to his cousin: "I have a small problem and would appreciate it if you would allow la Leona to assist me. Thank you." It irritated him that he had to *ask* his cousin for help; there was a time when he would have simply issued an order.

⎯⎯⎯◆⎯⎯⎯

DeMarco had still been sitting in the lobby bar at the Marriott when Castro called. He'd been thinking about going to the terrace bistro for a late dinner as Castro's goons had prevented him from eating earlier. But after he spoke to Castro, he didn't feel much like eating.

DeMarco didn't like the idea of going back to Boston, and Castro asking him to go there felt completely wrong. His instincts were screaming at him to run for home. He couldn't imagine any way that Castro would need his help with Callahan. Castro would either tell the Cayman company to call in Callahan's loans or he'd tell Callahan to back out of Delaney Square. There was nothing DeMarco could do—or *would* do—to assist Castro. He wanted to tell Castro to go screw himself. On the other hand, since it had been his idea to force Castro to deal with Callahan, and since both he and Mahoney wanted Callahan to pay for what he'd done . . .

Tomorrow he'd call Mahoney and talk it over with him. It was too late back in D.C. to call him now. And he'd call Mahoney from the airport. He was getting the hell out of Mexico.

The following morning, sitting in the departure lounge at the airport, DeMarco phoned Mahoney.

"I met with . . . the Mexican."

DeMarco needed to be careful speaking on a cell phone. "Things went well, I think."

"You think?" Mahoney said.

"He's agreed to do what I want with regard to the man in Boston. The thing is, the Mexican wants me to go back to Boston in case he needs me there to help him, and I'm not sure that's a good idea."

"Well, in for a penny, in for a pound," Mahoney said, and hung up.

Fuckin' Mahoney. He'd been hoping Mahoney would tell him to return to Washington, and instead he gets: *In for a penny, in for a pound.*

He called Castro back, calling the number that had called him the night before, but his call went to voice mail. He left a message saying, "I'm returning to Boston today and I'll assist you in whatever way I can." Then he added, in case the call was being monitored, "As long as it's legal."

26

Castro dispatched four men—and one woman—to Boston. The person in charge was the woman: Maria Vasquez, la Leona.

Castro suspected that Maria Vasquez had a genius-level IQ. She'd been born dirt poor in a barrio in Mexico City, the fifth of six children, and by the time she was sixteen she was the mistress to a Mexico City politician. With her looks, and lacking a decent education and family connections, that should have been her fate: to either be a prostitute or a mistress to some wealthy man, and by the time she was fifty she would be discarded and forced to do whatever cast-off mistresses without money did.

But Maria Vasquez was much too bright to allow that to happen to her. She dumped the politician when she was eighteen and deliberately set her sights on José Luis Guerrero—the man who ran the drug cartel that employed Javier Castro, and who Castro later killed to assume command. She became Guerrero's mistress but Guerrero—and Castro had always admired him for this—was a man who recognized talent when he saw it. He'd recognized Javier Castro's talent and he recognized Maria Vasquez's. She soon became one of Guerrero's principal advisers and when Guerrero tired of her sexually, he began to use her to plan and execute operations for him. After Castro took control, he used her too, and now his cousin, Paulo, was using her. After one particularly complex operation where Maria dispatched a heavily protected federal police captain who'd become an annoyance, Paulo—one of the least poetic men that Castro knew—said, "She was like a lioness taking down a gazelle." From that point forward she became la Leona—the Lioness. The woman was brilliant—and Castro couldn't help but wonder where her talents would take her in the future.

Three of Maria's men were now watching Sean Callahan, and Maria and the fourth man were watching DeMarco. Callahan's movements were unpredictable. He had an office on Exeter Street, not far from Copley Plaza, and he spent some time there but he also attended meetings at the offices of lawyers and architects and bankers; he visited the Delaney Street project and another project that was nearing completion in Quincy; he played golf one afternoon with three other men. Each day he returned to his mansion on Beacon Hill around seven p.m., and three out of the four nights Castro's people were watching him, he and his lovely young wife went out to dinner or attended some social function. One important and salient fact was that the people who worked for Callahan in the office on Exeter Street always left the office before seven p.m.

DeMarco's movements were, in some ways, more predicable than Callahan's. He appeared to have nothing to do in Boston so he spent his days entertaining himself: walking around the city, sitting by the hotel pool reading novels, going to a theater to watch a show. One day he went to Fenway to watch the Red Sox play in a day game. But every evening he would stop in some bar, either the one at the Park Plaza or one within walking distance of his hotel, and have several drinks and eat dinner before he returned to his room.

To make sure DeMarco stayed in Boston, Castro called him once and told him that things were moving forward but that he needed a little more time.

"It's obviously complicated," Castro said. "My lawyers have drawn up papers for Callahan to sign with regard to his withdrawal as an active participant in Delaney Square. He won't want to sign the documents, of course, but he will. Nonetheless, the documents need to be bulletproof, as you Americans say, and they can't allow him any wiggle room to sue or renege on the agreement or take any other sort of legal action at a later date."

"Yeah, I understand," DeMarco said. "But why do I have to be here?"

"I'm not sure you do at this point," Castro said, "but I think I'll have this wrapped up in the next two days, and until then I'd appreciate it if you would stand by. Let me remind you again that you're the one who's asked for my assistance in this matter, so I would think that you'd want to stay until our business is concluded."

"Yeah, okay, but just a couple more days. Then I'm out of here."

DeMarco was going out of his mind with boredom. If he was in Boston of his own choosing, he might have viewed his time there as a vacation and enjoyed himself. But he wasn't in Boston by choice and the ongoing heat wave was brutal and he'd seen enough of Boston over the years that he didn't have any great desire to explore the city. He attended another Red Sox game—once again paying an exorbitant amount for a shitty ticket in the cheap seats—but other than that, he just milled around, reading, taking walks, and watching whatever was on television.

He thought about driving up to Portsmouth to see Elinore. Portsmouth was only about two hours away—but he was afraid to leave Boston in case Castro actually needed him for something. The other thing, if he was really being honest about it, was that he didn't really want to see Elinore if she hadn't improved since the last time he saw her; that was just too depressing. He did call Elinore's daughter to inquire how her mother was doing, but she told him it was none of his business and not to call again. How in the world did such a lovely person as Elinore Dobbs end up with such a bitch for a daughter?

It occurred to him that he'd forgotten all about the other thing that he was supposed to be handling for Mahoney: Congressman Sims and his possibly bogus Purple Heart. So he called Emma to see if she'd made any progress. The first thing she said to him was: "Are you okay?"

The last time he'd spoken to her, he'd just had the tar whaled out of him by the McNultys.

"Yeah, I'm fine."

"What's happening with those guys who attacked you?"

"They had an unfortunate run-in with the law. They were caught with a boxful of assault rifles and are now sitting in a jail cell." He decided to leave out the part where he put the McNultys in the hospital.

"I see," Emma said. She knew DeMarco well enough to know that it wasn't simple bad luck that had befallen the McNultys.

"I just called," DeMarco said, "to see if you'd made any headway regarding Sims."

"Yeah, I did and it's not good. I won't bore you with all the details but I got Neil involved," Emma said.

Neil was an incredibly annoying fellow who was nimble and dangerous when his pudgy fingers were on the keyboard of a computer. If the details of your personal life were stored inside some server, Neil could gain access to them.

"To make a long story short," Emma said, "Neil located an ex-marine named Pat Howard. Howard was one of the few marines sleeping inside the barracks in Lebanon that morning who survived when the bombs went off. According to a couple of sources that Neil found, Sims saved Howard's life.

"When I talked to Howard, I pretended to be a reporter doing a story on congressmen who'd served in the corps. I told him that I'd learned that Congressman Sims had saved his life, and Howard said that was true. He said Sims slithered through a narrow tunnel in the debris, pushed concrete off Howard, and pulled him free even though Sims knew the building was unstable and he could be killed himself."

"That sounds pretty damn valorous to me," DeMarco said.

"I'm not finished," Emma said. "When I asked Howard if he could remember if Sims's right leg was injured, he said yes it was. Even though this happened over thirty years ago, Howard could remember everything that happened that day. In fact, Howard said Sims cut both his legs badly on jagged pieces of rebar dragging him out from under the rubble. But he said Sims cut his legs dragging him *out*; his legs weren't cut before he went in to save Howard."

"Then maybe Sims isn't lying about the Purple Heart," DeMarco said. "He may have been lying about getting stabbed by a piece of flying glass but—"

"I think he's lying," Emma said. "Like I told you before, there's no record of him getting a Heart, and the marines do a better job than the other services with regard to medal record keeping. The other thing is, in order to qualify for a Purple Heart the injury has to be as a *direct* result of enemy action. If Sims had been injured by flying glass when the barracks was bombed, he would have qualified. But injuring himself saving Howard's life means he wasn't, at least technically, injured by the enemy. Although I have to admit it's sort of a gray area, and if he'd been given the Heart I doubt anyone would have questioned the decision.

"Anyway, I asked Howard if he knew if Sims had received a Purple Heart and he said, 'I know he's got one, and he sure as hell deserves it.' But Howard wasn't aware of a formal citation or an award ceremony. So I don't know what else to tell you, Joe. I suspect Sims is lying but I can't prove it."

"Well, shit."

"Yeah, it's a shame. I think what happened is Sims figured he deserved a medal for saving Howard's life and being injured while doing so, but all he got was the general unit citation for serving in Lebanon. So I think when he ran for Congress, he punched up his service record to impress the voters."

DeMarco didn't say anything for a moment, then said, "Okay. I'll tell Mahoney." He wasn't looking forward to that conversation.

"Why don't I talk to Mahoney, Joe? I've got the details on Sims. Plus, this is one time where Mahoney's actually trying to do the right thing."

Mahoney knew that Emma helped DeMarco occasionally—although he didn't usually like it when she did because she was impossible to control. In this case, however, Mahoney and Emma shouldn't be at odds with each other. At least DeMarco hoped not.

"Thanks," DeMarco said. "I appreciate it." And he did; he wasn't anxious to give Mahoney any more bad news.

Now all he had to do was wait for Castro to deal with Callahan so he could get the hell out of Boston.

27

Maria Vasquez called Javier Castro.

"I think we should act tomorrow," she said. "DeMarco's a sure thing, but when it comes to Callahan, I'm going to have to improvise. What I'm saying is I'll have to look for some opportunity after noon when he's alone, and then we'll take him. Then we'll have to hold him until DeMarco is where I want him to be. If an opportunity doesn't present itself tomorrow, then we'll try again the next day."

"What if Callahan's reported missing?" Castro asked. "I'm sure he has things scheduled in the afternoon, and someone will begin looking for him."

"That won't be a problem. We'll make him call whoever he's supposed to be with and give some excuse for why he can't make his appointments."

"Okay," Castro finally said.

He didn't like improvising—but in the end, Callahan made it easy for them.

Sean Callahan was sitting in his office, glad that fucking phone call was over with. It was seven thirty p.m. and he was tired and wanted to go home. Thank God Rachel didn't have anything planned for tonight, so he could just kick back and relax. That was one problem with having such a young wife: sometimes she just wore his old ass out.

He was still in his office because he'd had to talk to a man in Japan, where it was eight a.m. The man was thinking about investing in a project that was still in the pie-in-the-sky stage, and he had money to burn. The problem was the guy thought he could speak English, so instead of using an interpreter, he insisted on speaking himself, which just about drove Sean crazy. He couldn't understand about every other word the guy said, and kept having to ask him to repeat himself.

But other than the irritation of having to talk to the Japanese investor, things were going well and he had no complaints. He'd stopped by Delaney Square earlier in the day, and now that Elinore Dobbs was out of his hair, things were moving forward and the project was almost back on schedule. The only thing he felt bad about was the McNultys. What on earth had possessed those dumb shits to get involved with selling machine guns? Their lawyer had called him about a week ago, saying the brothers wanted to see him, and he'd told the lawyer that he would but wasn't sure when he'd have time to drive up to the Essex County jail. He really didn't want to talk to them but he thought it might be a good idea; they were such maniacs he didn't want to get on their bad side.

He heard the phone ring in the outer office and thought maybe it was Rachel calling to ask where he was, although Rachel usually sent him text messages when she wanted to bug him. He hit the lighted button on his phone and said, "Hello."

"Oh, Mr. Callahan, I didn't mean to disturb you. I was calling to speak to your secretary about scheduling a meeting for next week."

"She's not here," Callahan said. "I'm here by myself and you really need to talk to her about scheduling anything. My calendar's on her computer." Actually, his calendar was in his phone but he didn't feel like dealing with this right now.

"I'll call back tomorrow," the man said.

Callahan wondered where the guy was from—he had an accent—and what meeting he was talking about. Whatever. It was time to go.

He turned out the lights and walked out the door, checking to make sure it was locked. As he was walking down the hall, he noticed three young guys standing by the elevator. They looked Hispanic and were hard-looking SOBs but they were all wearing suits and ties. They didn't look like gangbangers, or anything like that. He wondered who they'd been meeting with in the building. There were a couple lawyers on this floor; maybe they were here to see one of them.

He reached the elevator, nodded at the three men, then noticed the DOWN button wasn't pushed. Why hadn't they pushed the button? Then he found out.

One of the men took out a silenced automatic pistol and pointed it at his chest. "Mr. Callahan, we're going to return to your office. If you do anything foolish, I'll kill you."

He realized then that the guy speaking was the same guy who'd just called asking to speak to his secretary. Who the hell were these people?

They walked back to his office and the man with the gun told him to unlock the door. As he was doing so, Sean said, "I don't keep any money here in my office. But I have about five hundred in my wallet, and credit cards, of course."

The man just prodded him in the back with the gun and said, "Go to your office."

He was told to sit in the chair behind his desk, then the man with the gun said, "Now call your wife and tell her you're going to be very late. Put the phone in speaker mode. If you say anything to alarm your wife, we'll kill you, then go to your house on Beacon Street and rape your wife before we kill her."

"Jesus. What do you guys want?"

"Make the call."

He hit the SPEAKER button on the phone and punched in Rachel's cell phone number. When she answered, he said, "Uh, hi, it's me. I'm going to be pretty late tonight."

"Why? What's going on?"

Sean couldn't help but notice that she didn't sound all that disappointed that he was going to be late.

"I'm supposed to talk to a guy in Japan and he's late calling here."

"At this time of night?" she said.

"It's morning in Japan. Anyway, the guy's been delayed and I need to wait for his call, then after I talk to him I may need to go see one of my lawyers. So I'll be late."

"Okay," Rachel said. "I'll see you when I see you."

He started to say I love you, but she'd already hung up.

◆

DeMarco changed into a pair of dress slacks for dinner and a nice short-sleeved blue shirt that he thought matched his eyes. He'd been wearing shorts and a T-shirt all day because of the heat but decided to dress up a bit for dinner, as he wasn't sure where he planned to go. He'd have a drink in the hotel bar and chat with the bartender—a kid named Sam who he was getting to know way too well—about where he might dine this evening.

The lounge in the Park Plaza hotel was a rather funky place, but DeMarco had grown used to it. There was a dark bar with enough high-backed stools for a dozen drinkers—which was normal enough—but in the seating area were low tables surrounded by armchairs patterned with cloth resembling a giraffe's hide. The oddest thing was the photos: large photos of models who—based on the women's hairstyles—looked like they might be from the late fifties or early sixties. The men in the photos wore suits with narrow ties and fedoras and carried umbrellas and had dark-framed Clark Kent glasses. The most striking photo was of a pretty brunette with a Jackie Kennedy hairdo wearing a hat, a polka-dot dress, high heels, and holding two Hula-Hoops in her white-gloved hands. DeMarco wondered if the Hula-Hoops were supposed to be symbolic of something.

He took a seat at the bar and Sam—a young stud who looked like a serious weightlifter—came over to take his order. Sam had so many muscles in his neck it made his head look particularly small; it made DeMarco think of the Michael Keaton character in *Beetlejuice* whose head was shrunk by a witch doctor.

"Your usual?" Sam asked.

"Yeah, why not," DeMarco said.

Sam brought him a Stoli martini with a lemon twist, and said, "So how was your day?"

DeMarco figured Sam didn't want to hear him bitch about Boston and the heat and the fact he had an asshole for a boss, so he said, "Great."

DeMarco toasted the photo of the lady with the Hula-Hoops, and was just taking the first sip of his martini when he heard a woman standing next to him say, "Janet, you do this all the time. Why do you do this? We make plans and then that jerk calls and you drop everything and run to him. He's never going to leave his wife, and you know it!" There was a brief pause, and she said, "No, Janet, I don't want to hear it. Good-bye."

As she was talking she'd taken a seat on the barstool next to DeMarco and dropped a large purse on the bar that landed with a thump like it contained a bowling ball. DeMarco turned to look at her, initially irritated she was talking so loud and practically in his ear—and then he saw what she looked like. *Wow!*

She was absolutely gorgeous. She was probably thirty-five, about five foot six and built: heavy breasts pressing against the thin material of a white sleeveless blouse and slim, tanned legs emerging from a black skirt that was halfway up her thighs when she was sitting. She had honey-colored blond hair that reached her shoulders and a complexion that also made him think of honey.

She turned to DeMarco, looking exasperated, and said, "My sister. She was supposed to meet me here for a drink and we were going to have dinner together, and then she stands me up. She's going out with this married guy and . . . Oh, never mind. I'm sorry." Then she looked around and said, "Does this place have a bartender? I need a drink."

DeMarco saw Sam and waved like crazy. He did not want this woman to leave. "Hey, Sam! Sam!"

Sam ambled over and DeMarco said, "This lady desperately needs a drink."

"What would you like, miss?" Sam said.

"I'll have a vodka gimlet."

"And it's on me, Sam," DeMarco said. "She's having a bad day, and it's the least I can do."

"Oh, you don't have to do that," she said, touching DeMarco's forearm with a soft, warm hand.

"I'm Joe," he said.

"Maria," she said.

Maria said that she did marketing for a pharmaceutical company. DeMarco and Emma had once had a nearly fatal experience investigating a pharmaceutical company, and he consequently did not hold the industry in high esteem. But Maria could have said that she euthanized parakeets for a living and he would have forgiven her. He'd thought her eyes were brown, but it turned out they were more green than brown, and she had the most perfect lips he'd ever seen.

He told her he was a lawyer, and although he lived in D.C., he was in Boston all the time—*all* the time—on business. When she asked what kind of law he practiced he said he didn't exactly practice law; he was more of a political troubleshooter. She seemed suitably impressed—and God knows he would have done handstands to impress her.

They finished their drinks and he said, "I was just about to go out to dinner. There's an Italian place a couple blocks from here. I've been there before and it's good. I was thinking since your sister stood you up . . ."

"I'd love to," she said, again touching his forearm. "Let me just go touch up my makeup."

She didn't need makeup.

"I'll meet you in the lobby in five minutes," she said.

He waited two minutes and walked out to the lobby and a couple minutes later she was coming toward him, like a vision on high heels. God, what a body she had. She took his arm and as they walked toward the door, he felt a little pinch in his right arm, the arm she was holding.

"Ow," he said.

"Is something wrong?" she said.

"No, I just felt something." They proceeded toward the lobby doors and he noticed he was feeling lightheaded. He didn't understand it; he'd only had one drink. He took a few more steps and his legs started to feel rubbery and he felt like he was about to pass out. "I think I need to sit . . ."

The last thing he remembered was two men standing next to him— he didn't know where Maria had gone—and they were supporting him, helping him walk toward the door.

28

DeMarco came to sitting in a leather chair, one with armrests. The room he was in was dark, but there was some light coming from a room behind him that made it possible for him to see a man sitting in a chair across from him, behind a desk. He also noticed that there was something heavy in his lap, and he was holding whatever it was.

He started to ask the man who he was and how he got to wherever he was, and then, for a moment, he thought he was going to throw up. He closed his eyes and swallowed a couple of times, trying not to vomit. When he opened his eyes, the walls of the room seemed to be moving. It was like he was sitting on a wooden horse in a carousel, and as the carousel went around, the world spun past him. He'd been drunk before but he knew he wasn't drunk now; whatever he was experiencing wasn't alcohol induced.

He closed his eyes again, trying to understand what was happening. He remembered being at the Park Plaza bar. He remembered talking to the bartender, Sam. Then he remembered Maria—gorgeous Maria. He remembered as he was walking through the lobby with her to leave for dinner, he began to feel lightheaded. Then a couple of guys he didn't know came up to him, and helped him walk so he wouldn't fall. But what was he doing here?

He asked the man sitting behind the desk: "Where am I?" His words were so slurred he could barely understand what he'd just said, so maybe the man behind the desk hadn't understood him, because he didn't respond. He tried to stand and when he did, whatever he'd been holding in his lap fell to the floor and landed with a thump—the thump reminding him of when Maria had put her big purse on the bar at the Park Plaza. He looked down to see what had fallen from his lap. What the hell? It was a gun, a big revolver with a shiny four-inch barrel and a walnut grip. It was so big he thought it might be a .357 Magnum. What the hell was he doing with a gun in his lap?

He pushed down on the armrests of the chair and forced himself to his feet, but when he was standing, he couldn't remain upright, and swayed backward and collapsed back into the chair. Goddamnit, what the hell was wrong with him? He closed his eyes, took several deep breaths, and tried to stand again. This time he didn't fall back into the chair but only because he placed his hands on the desk to help him remain upright. And when he did, he was closer to the silent man sitting behind the desk—and he saw it was Sean Callahan. It took another second to realize that Callahan had a large, circular bloodstain on the front of his shirt.

Callahan was dead.

The shock of seeing Callahan made him step backward and he again landed in the chair where he'd been sitting—but the shock also helped him focus. It took him only a couple of seconds to realize what had happened; his body wasn't functioning properly—he could barely stand, he could hardly speak, and his vision was blurred—but his mind seemed to be working okay.

For whatever reason, Castro had decided to kill Callahan and frame him for Callahan's murder. Maria—or whoever she was—had been sent by Castro to seduce him, and with her looks it hadn't been hard for her at all. As they were leaving the Park Plaza, she'd injected him with some kind of drug that knocked him out; he remembered the sharp pinch in his arm right before he started to feel woozy. He also remembered Maria telling him she worked for a pharmaceutical company—her idea of a joke, perhaps. Then they—Maria and the two men who'd helped him out of the Park Plaza—brought him to wherever he was now, probably Sean Callahan's office. Then they killed Callahan—and maybe at the time he'd been sitting unconscious in the chair in front of Callahan's desk—and placed the murder weapon in his hand.

He looked at his watch. He had to blink a couple of times and hold the watch about four inches from his eyes to see the hands on the dial. It was almost ten p.m. He'd left the Park Plaza bar with Maria about seven thirty. So he'd been out for two and a half hours—and he had a feeling that any minute now a couple of cops were going to come through the door and see him sitting there, a gun at his feet, and Callahan's corpse across from him.

He needed to get out of this room. Now.

He stood up, wobbled, then used his shirttail to wipe the desk where he'd placed his hands and wiped the armrests on the chair where he'd been sitting. If his fingerprints were elsewhere in the room he couldn't do anything about that. Now what should he do with the gun, which also had his fingerprints on it? If Callahan had been shot in the side of the head, he might have been able to place the gun in Callahan's hand and hope the cops would think Callahan had committed suicide. But Callahan hadn't been shot in the head; he'd been shot in the chest. DeMarco started to wipe the gun with his shirttail, then thought: *What if they pressed my thumb down on the bullets to make it look like I'd loaded the gun?*

He didn't have time to remove the bullets and wipe them; he didn't have any more time, period, to spend in this room. He had to take the gun with him. The only good news was that the gun was a revolver and not an automatic so he didn't have to get down on his knees and hunt around for shell casings. He shoved the gun into the back of his pants and pulled his shirttail over it.

He took a last look at Callahan—*You poor arrogant bastard,* he thought—and staggered toward the door. He'd been drunk many times, and he could remember being so drunk on one or two occasions that he lurched from side to side as he walked—and that's what he was doing now, moving like a sailor trying to walk on the deck of a ship that was bouncing on ocean waves. As he passed through the door of Callahan's office, his right shoulder hit the doorframe but he didn't touch it with his hands. He walked through a room outside Callahan's office where his secretary most likely sat, staggered down a short hallway until he came to another door, and used his shirt to open the door so he wouldn't leave prints. He expected to see three or four cops dressed in SWAT gear standing in the hallway, but didn't. He was sure the cops were on their way, however.

He didn't know what floor he was on but he wasn't going to take the elevator since he was afraid the elevator might have a surveillance camera. He'd take one of the fire escape stairways. Then it occurred to him there could be surveillance cameras in the hallway or in the stairwells, although he didn't see any in the hallway. Then he had another thought: if there were surveillance cameras, he bet Castro's guys had disabled them so there wouldn't be a record of them carrying him into the building and into Callahan's office. At least he hoped that was the case.

He found the stairwell at the end of the hall, pushed through the door, and holding his shirttail against the handrail, started downward. If he hadn't been holding the handrail, he would have tumbled down the stairs. It turned out he was on the third floor and when he came to the street level, he reached a fire door, one of those doors with a bar across it and a sign that said if he opened the door he was going to set off an alarm. Well, there wasn't anything he could do about that. He pushed on the door lever, expecting to hear an alarm like a screaming banshee, but there was no alarm. He suspected the pros Castro used had disabled the alarm.

He found himself out on a busy street—he had no idea which street or where he was in relation to his hotel—and started walking. He had to get as far away from Callahan's office building as he could and he needed to get rid of the gun. He could hear sirens in the distance, but didn't know if that was the cops headed in his direction or not. In a city the size of Boston, you could always hear sirens. But DeMarco was positive that within the last few minutes, someone had made a 911 call and claimed to have heard shots coming from Callahan's office.

The other thing that concerned him was street security cameras. These days there were cameras everywhere. But again, there wasn't anything he could do about that, other than stay off the busier streets, like Boylston. If he could stick to the less heavily traveled streets, he might be okay.

He walked to the end of the block and took a right, even though he didn't know where he was or where he was going. He just wanted to get farther away from Callahan's building. But where the hell was he? He looked for a street sign and didn't see one.

He had to get rid of the damn gun. He wasn't going to throw it down a storm drain or put it in a trash can; every episode of *Law & Order* he'd ever seen showed cops looking in trash cans and storm drains on the streets near a murder scene. He came to a pizza place and glanced inside. There were four young guys who looked like college kids at the counter and the pizza guy had his back to the counter as he shoved a pie into the oven. Nobody noticed DeMarco walk in and stagger down a short hallway to the restroom. He could hear the college kids talking too loudly. They sounded as drunk as he appeared to be.

He pushed into the restroom, went into the single stall, and latched the door behind him. He took the top off the tank behind the toilet bowl and placed the gun inside it, like some people put a brick in their toilet tank to minimize water usage. He figured one of these days the toilet would malfunction and some plumber was going to get a surprise. All he could do was hope that didn't happen anytime soon.

He wanted to sit down on the toilet and think and recover some more from the effects of the drug, but he needed to get farther away from the murder scene and he didn't want the cops to catch him in the place where he'd hidden the gun. He walked down the hall and could hear the drunken college kids whooping about something, and when he walked into the dining area of the pizza place, they were still at the counter and the pizza guy was making change for their order. One kid turned as he lurched toward the door but barely glanced at him, and then he was through the door and back on the street.

He had to get back to his hotel. He couldn't catch a cab as the cops might check with cab companies and a driver might remember a barely-able-to-walk drunk getting into his cab near Callahan's office and taking a ride to the Park Plaza. He started walking again, then finally saw a building he recognized and realized he was three or four blocks from Copley Square but was walking in the wrong direction. He was headed west and needed to be going east. He turned at the next corner and started back in the direction of his hotel, staying off the busier streets as best he could. He'd gone about two blocks when he saw a BPD patrol car coming down the street in his direction. He didn't want to do anything that might look suspicious—such as turn his back to the cop car—so he put his head down and just kept walking, praying the cop wouldn't stop. He didn't.

He kept walking, wishing he had some sort of a disguise, like a hooded sweatshirt. But who the hell wears a hooded sweatshirt when it's eighty degrees and humid outside? And he still wasn't all that steady on his feet, but he wasn't staggering, as he'd been earlier. A block later he came to a bar and saw a kid standing outside smoking. The kid—like about every third person you see on the streets of Boston—was wearing a Red Sox cap.

He walked up to the kid and said, "I'll give you a hundred bucks for that cap."

"Are you shittin' me," the kid said.

"No."

"Are you drunk?"

"Yeah. So you want a hundred bucks for the hat or not?"

"Shit, yeah," the kid said.

DeMarco took out his wallet and with some effort extracted five twenties, took the cap from the kid, jammed it down on his head, and staggered away. It wasn't much of a disguise but he felt better for it. If he kept his head down the bill of the ball cap partially obscured his face, making him less recognizable if he was picked up on a camera. He hoped. As he was walking he heard the kid call out, "Good luck to you, man. I hope you make it to wherever you're going."

From your lips to God's ears, DeMarco thought.

Almost an hour after he left Callahan's office, DeMarco arrived back at the Park Plaza. Just before he reached the hotel entrance, he deposited his costly Red Sox cap in a trash can. He didn't want any cameras in the hotel lobby to see him wearing the cap.

He took the elevator to the ninth floor, leaning his head against the door as the elevator rose. The hallway leading to his room seemed about a hundred miles long, but he finally made it, opened the door with the key card, and collapsed onto the bed.

As he lay there he thought: *Why did Castro do it? Why did he kill Sean Callahan and decide to frame me for his murder?*

He'd given Castro two options. Option one: call in the loans he'd made to Callahan so Callahan wouldn't be able to complete the project. Option two: simply force Callahan to walk away from Delaney Square and give up any stake he had in it. He'd told Castro that if he didn't do one of those two things, Treasury agents were going to start digging into the money behind Delaney Square, then start freezing money and seizing assets. Well, Castro had selected option three: he killed Callahan.

DeMarco could understand why Castro had decided to kill Callahan: killing the man was the simplest solution to the problem, much simpler than forcing Callahan to sign documents that made it appear as if he'd voluntarily decided to give up his interest in Delaney Square. In fact, DeMarco had unintentionally suggested this solution to Castro. He remembered telling Castro that if he could force Callahan to walk away from the project, it would be no different than if Callahan had resigned: the project would be finished by Callahan's company even if Callahan were no longer around to manage the company. But he hadn't intended—or expected—Castro to kill the man.

But why frame him for Callahan's murder? Castro had to know that if DeMarco was caught, and even if he was convicted, he was going to point the finger at Castro and his fiscal connection to Delaney Square. But maybe Castro wasn't so worried about that now that he'd been forewarned that the financing behind Delaney Square might be investigated. Maybe Castro figured he could completely obscure the money trail and he wasn't concerned about a bunch of government accountants playing with spreadsheets.

There was also another possible reason Castro had done what he did. Maybe, and regardless of the possible consequences, Castro had decided to teach DeMarco a lesson, the lesson being: fuck with me and you end up in jail for life, no matter who you work for. If DeMarco had been found sitting in Callahan's office with a gun in his hand, there was nothing Mahoney would have been able to do to save him. Castro was also sending a message to John Mahoney by framing DeMarco. He was telling Mahoney: See how easy it was for me to take your guy off the board. So no matter who you are—no matter how powerful and protected you think you are—maybe I'll come after you if you don't leave me alone.

Whatever the case, if DeMarco survived this night, he was not going to have anything more to do with Javier Castro.

29

DeMarco woke up feeling tired and groggy. He'd barely slept, expecting that at any minute the cops were going to break down the door and arrest him. Thanks to the drug Maria had injected into him, his head was throbbing like he had the worst hangover in the history of hangovers. He staggered to the bathroom, ripped open an Alka-Seltzer packet, dropped the magic tablets into a plastic glass filled with water, and drank the mixture before the Alka-Seltzer even stopped fizzing.

He looked into the mirror: he looked like hell. Unshaven, his hair in disarray, his eyes bloodshot. He remembered the romance writer—the one who didn't look like Amy Adams—telling him he had a brutal villain's face and the way he looked right now, he had to agree with her. He also noticed he was wearing the same clothes that he'd had on the night before as he hadn't undressed before he collapsed onto the bed. And then a thought occurred to him: *Gunshot residue!*

What if they shot Callahan by holding the gun in his hand and forcing his finger down on the trigger? He could have gunshot residue on his hand and arm and clothes. There could also be minute particles of Callahan's blood on his clothes. Shit! He stripped off his clothes as fast as he could—the last time he probably took his clothes off that fast was the first time he got laid—and jumped into the shower. He turned the water on as hot as he could stand it and scrubbed himself, rubbing like he was trying to remove his skin.

He got dressed in shorts, a T-shirt, and flip-flops. He put the clothes he'd worn last night—including his shoes—into a bag from the closet intended for laundry, shoved some cash and his phone into a pocket, and headed for the door. Then he thought: *The bedspread!* What if he'd rubbed gunshot residue on the bedspread? He called down to the front desk and said he needed his bed changed immediately. "I, uh, got sick last night so could you send a maid up right away." Then he ripped everything off the bed—the bedspread, sheets, and pillowcases—and dumped them out in the hall.

He wondered how many other things he was failing to think of. He didn't have a lot of practice when it came to destroying evidence. His biggest concern was that a surveillance camera in or near Callahan's building had captured his image—but if that was the case, there wasn't anything he could do about it.

As he left the hotel carrying the bag that contained his clothes, he wondered why the police hadn't caught him last night. Castro's people should have known about how long he'd remain unconscious from the drug pretty Maria had shot into him. But they wouldn't have wanted the cops to enter Callahan's office and find him passed out in a chair; if he was unconscious when they found him that might tend to support a claim that he'd been drugged and framed. No, Maria and her pals would have wanted the cops to walk into Callahan's office with DeMarco conscious, holding the gun in his hand, maybe even leaving Callahan's office. If they got really lucky, DeMarco in his drug-induced state might have raised the gun, not even realizing what he was doing, and the cops might have blown his ass away.

So why didn't it work out that way? They must have miscalculated how long he'd be out, or didn't give him the correct dosage to match his body weight. Whatever the case, they'd screwed up.

He supposed there was another possibility, and that was that Castro hadn't intended for him to be caught, but that didn't make any sense. Why go to all the trouble to frame him for Callahan's murder, then allow him to get away? No, Castro's people had just waited too long before they called the cops—and he was just lucky they did.

He walked about four blocks from the hotel, randomly selected a trash can, and shoved the bag containing his clothes inside it. Near where he was standing was a Starbucks, and at that moment nothing sounded better than coffee. He ordered a large coffee and took a seat at an outside table.

He was thinking: *Now what?* And just then a BPD patrol car stopped in front of Starbucks and two big cops stepped out of the car. He waited for them to walk up to him and tell him to stand so they could slap on the handcuffs, but they walked past his table without even glancing at him and into the coffee shop. His heart was hammering so hard he was surprised it didn't burst through his chest, like the critter in *Alien*. The cops left Starbucks five minutes later, again not looking at him. He hoped that meant they didn't have his picture on some look-out-for-this-raving-lunatic-killer bulletin.

He was now back to: *Now what?*

One thing he should do was see if Callahan's death had been reported. Using his cell phone, he looked at the online *Boston Globe* and local TV station websites, figuring that the murder of a prominent businessman would have made the news. All he found was one small article in the *Globe* saying the police, responding to a 911 call, had found the body of a man in an office on Exeter Street. The man had been shot, but his name had not yet been released pending notification of next of kin. The article noted that the body had been found at approximately ten p.m. Approximately ten p.m. was when DeMarco had regained consciousness. So they obviously found the body a little after ten—but probably not much after ten. He was one lucky SOB.

He'd like to know what the police knew. If the article had given Callahan's name, he could have called up his pal, Detective Fitzgerald, and talked to him. But no way was he going to do that now. How could he explain to Fitzgerald how he knew that Callahan was dead?

He also needed to call Mahoney and tell him what had happened, but that meant going through the whole rigmarole of finding a pay phone and telling Mahoney to call him back from a pay phone. It just pissed him off that you could never be sure who might be listening to your phone calls these days. He finished his coffee and had started walking back to the hotel to call Mahoney when his cell phone rang. He didn't recognize the number.

"Hello," he said.

"What did you do!" a woman shrieked. "What in the hell did you do?"

"Who is this?"

"It's Adele Tomlin, you son of a bitch! I *told* you not to tell Javier that I talked to you about him. I *told* you!"

"I didn't," DeMarco said. "I told him that I learned about his connection to Delaney Square by following the money trail to a company in the Caymans. I never mentioned your name."

"Then how did he know?"

"What makes you think he knows?"

"Last night two men came to my house. They broke in about two in the morning while I was sleeping. They dragged me out of bed and showed me a picture of a woman who'd had her nose cut off. Her fucking *nose* had been cut off! They told me if I ever talked to anyone again about Javier that I was going to end up looking like the woman in the picture."

"Jesus," DeMarco said.

"*Jesus*? That's all you have to say? Jesus!"

"Look, Adele, you're going to be all right. You're safe. This whole business with Castro and Sean is over with. Just don't ever talk about Castro again."

"How do you know it's over with?"

She was going to hear about Callahan's death soon enough, so he decided he might as well tell her. "Castro had Sean killed last night."

"Oh, my God!"

"But that means it's all over with. Castro's not going to do anything to you. If he had wanted to do something, the guys he sent last night wouldn't have shown you a picture. They would have killed you. He just sent them there to scare you."

"But what if someone else talks about him and Delaney Square? He'll think I'm the source. I mean, my God, you should have seen that woman's face."

"Adele . . ."

"I have to get out of here. I have to go someplace where he can't find me. You've ruined my life, you bastard."

DeMarco almost told her that there was probably no place on the planet she could go where Javier Castro couldn't find her, but she'd already hung up.

———◆◆◆———

DeMarco walked back to the Park Plaza, went to the bank of pay phones, and called Mahoney's office. When Mahoney's secretary answered, he said, "Mavis, tell Mahoney to call me as soon as possible. It's urgent and it's bad news. I'm going to give you the number of a pay phone. Give it to Mahoney and tell him to use a pay phone when he calls me back."

Mavis didn't say anything for a moment, then said, "Is he in danger?"

DeMarco was convinced that Mavis, who'd worked for Mahoney for thirty years, was in love with the selfish, corrupt son of a bitch. And although he didn't believe that Mahoney was in any danger, in order to minimize the time he'd have to wait for the man to call him back, he said, "Maybe."

Mahoney called ten minutes later.

To make sure he had Mahoney's undivided attention he said, "Javier Castro had Sean Callahan killed last night and tried to frame me for his murder." He then went on to tell Mahoney everything that had happened—how he'd been drugged, came to in Callahan's office with the gun that killed Callahan in his hand, and how he was lucky he hadn't been caught. At least not yet. He also told him what had happened to Adele Tomlin, who was now terrified out of her mind and fleeing to someplace where she thought she could hide from Castro. Mahoney's response, while he was telling the story, was mostly swear words: *Son of a bitch! You gotta be shittin' me. Fuck me!*

When he finished, Mahoney managed to utter a complete sentence: "So what are you going to do?"

"What am *I* going to do?" DeMarco repeated. "Well, if I'm not arrested, I'm going to get on the next plane back to D.C. This thing's over with, boss, and everybody lost except you and Javier Castro."

"What the hell does that mean?" Mahoney said.

"It means Elinore Dobbs didn't win. She's in a nursing home, staring at a wall, and can barely remember her own name. The McNultys didn't win. They're going to jail for ten years. And Sean Callahan definitely didn't win. But Javier Castro is going to make God knows how many millions off Delaney Square, so I'd call him a winner."

"But what did that crack about me winning mean?"

"It means you got what you wanted. You wanted Callahan to pay for what he did to Elinore Dobbs—and he paid with his life."

"Hey! Fuck you," Mahoney screamed. "I didn't want Callahan killed and I didn't tell you to go lean on Castro the way you did. That was your own bright idea."

DeMarco started to say that he wouldn't have gone after Castro at all if Mahoney hadn't been pushing him, but he knew that wasn't really the case. It had been his idea to blackmail Castro—not Mahoney's—and he really couldn't blame anyone but himself for what had happened. He took a breath and said, "You're right. I shouldn't have said that."

When Mahoney didn't respond to his apology, DeMarco said, "One thing you could do is wait until Callahan's death is reported on the news, then call someone in the BPD, like Superintendent O'Rourke, and ask him what he knows about the murder. Then let me know so in case I need to, I can book a flight to someplace that doesn't have an extradition treaty with the United States."

"I'll think about it," Mahoney said, and hung up.

◆◆◆

DeMarco headed toward the elevators to go up to his room and pack when his cell phone rang. Again he didn't recognize the number and wondered if it was Adele calling him back. It wasn't.

"This is Fitzgerald," the caller said.

What did Detective Fitzgerald want? Was he calling to tell him that Callahan had been killed? Or was he calling to tell him that he should go to the nearest police station and turn himself in? He turned out to be half right.

"Did you hear that Sean Callahan was killed last night?"

"What!" DeMarco said.

"Yeah. He was found shot to death in his office."

"My God! What happened? Who did it?"

"We don't know who did it. Got a nine-one-one call, and some woman said she heard a shot fired that sounded as if it came from Callahan's office. We sent a couple guys over there and they found his body."

"Who was the woman who called it in?"

"We don't know. She had a Hispanic accent and we think she might be one of the people that clean Callahan's building but they all denied calling about shots being fired. They said they finished cleaning Callahan's floor a couple hours before we got the call."

"Couldn't you trace the call?"

"It came from a phone in a bar about a block from Callahan's office, and nobody remembered seeing anyone who looked Hispanic or like a cleaning lady in the bar."

Maria didn't look obviously Hispanic, and she sure as hell didn't look like a cleaning lady, but DeMarco wasn't going to ask if anyone in the bar had spotted a blonde with a heart-stopping body.

DeMarco knew he couldn't afford to sound too curious, but he had to ask: "You didn't get anybody on a surveillance camera who might have done it?"

"No. It's an old building and the only cameras in the place are in the elevators, but about seven last night, like three hours before the nine-one-one call, some guy wearing a ball cap and sunglasses, and holding his hand over the lower part of his face, spray painted the lenses."

"I'll be damned," DeMarco said but he was really thinking: *Thank God.*

"We figured a douchebag like Callahan, who'd pull the kind of shit he pulled on that old lady, probably had lots of enemies. By the way, where were you last night about ten?"

"Me?" DeMarco the Innocent said. "In my room at the hotel. I had a couple drinks in the bar. In fact, I met some gal in the bar around seven and thought for a minute I was going to get lucky but she had to go meet her sister. Then I just went back to my room and watched TV."

DeMarco was thinking that if he'd been caught on a street camera last night, he'd amend the story he just gave Fitzgerald, saying that he'd taken a walk before going back to his room. He hoped like hell that he didn't have to amend his story.

"Why are you still here in Boston, anyway?" Fitzgerald asked.

"My boss is running for reelection. He's always running for reelection. So I was just helping out with some campaign shit. I'm heading back to D.C. today."

That is, I'm heading back today if somebody doesn't arrest me.

"But Callahan wasn't the only reason I called," Fitzgerald said. "Before I heard about Callahan, I got a call from the McNultys. I don't know why they called me. I guess it was because I set up that meeting for you with them at the jail and they didn't know how to get ahold of you.

"Anyway, whichever one called, Roy or Ray, I think the guy was crying. He told me he wanted to take that deal you offered and testify against Callahan. When I asked him why he'd changed his mind, he said he'd heard that there's a policy where they don't put brothers together in the same prison. I don't know who told him this or if he's even right, but those two jackoffs are terrified of being sent to different prisons. I was going to let you know, but then I heard about Callahan, so there's no point now in making a deal with the McNultys."

DeMarco didn't know what to say, but right now the fate of Roy and Ray McNulty was the last thing on his mind. He concluded the call by thanking Fitzgerald for his help—and saying that he hoped he never saw him again. Or maybe it was Fitzgerald who said he hoped he never saw DeMarco again.

DeMarco reached his room and was glad to see that the maid had made up his bed, meaning that the bedspread he'd slept on was hopefully being laundered. He'd started toward the bathroom when a voice said, "Hi, Joe."

Christ! He whipped his head around to see who'd just spoken. It was a woman sitting in a chair by the window. The blinds were closed and she was sitting in a shadow, so he couldn't really see her face but he knew who it was. He wondered if she was holding a gun.

"I told the maid I was your wife," Maria Vasquez said, "and she let me into the room. People are way too trusting of a pretty woman."

"What do you want?" he asked.

"Joe, why do you think you weren't arrested last night for murdering Mr. Callahan?"

"Because you screwed up and I was able to get away before the cops got there."

Maria smiled and shook her head. "Joe, Joe, come on. Do you think I would have made that kind of mistake? The reason you weren't arrested was because Mr. Castro didn't want you arrested last night. But who knows what the future might bring? Who knows what witnesses might come forward to say they saw you leaving the building? And the murder weapon. It's no longer in the toilet tank of the pizza parlor. One of my people followed you and retrieved it. It would be a shame if the police were to execute a search warrant on your home in Washington and find that gun."

DeMarco didn't say anything for a moment because he couldn't think of anything to say. "What do you want?" he asked again.

"I just want to make sure you got the message, Joe."

"What message is that?"

"That you are never, ever again to interfere with Mr. Castro's plans. If you do, you might be arrested for Mr. Callahan's murder. Or maybe, Mr. Castro might conclude the simplest thing to do is to send me to deal with you the way I dealt with Mr. Callahan. The other thing you need to do is pass on a message to your employer."

Maria stood up. Because she'd been sitting in a dark corner of the room, he hadn't been able to see her face well. Now he could. She was one of the most beautiful women he'd ever met—and she was scaring the living shit out of him.

"You need to tell Mr. Mahoney that Mr. Castro would never be so foolhardy as to do something to a United States congressman, especially one as powerful as John Mahoney. But the problem is that there are other people invested in Delaney Square, and some of these people . . . Joe, I'm sure you've read about the way things are in Mexico, how the cartels murder politicians and judges and cops and whoever else gets in their way. Well, some of these people, after a while, they start to think they can do anything. These people are not so . . . analytical. They just might believe that they can take action against a man like Mahoney, no matter who he is, and Mr. Castro would not be able to stop them. Do you understand, Joe?"

"Yeah, I understand."

"Good." She walked over to DeMarco and gave him a soft kiss on the lips. "Take care, Joe."

30

DeMarco was sitting in the departure area, waiting for his plane to board. He was exhausted as he hadn't slept well, and he just wanted to get on the plane and close his eyes and fall asleep.

DeMarco had had assignments go bad before—nobody bats a thousand—but never as bad as this one had gone. He'd failed to protect Elinore Dobbs, and now, and maybe thanks to him, she would spend her remaining days staring at a wall. And although he'd made the McNultys and Sean Callahan pay for what they did to her, he'd never intended that Callahan be killed. Then, because he'd pushed Javier Castro into a corner, there was now an ex–cartel boss with a lethal female assassin who might frame him for Callahan's murder at some time in the future. Could things have possibly gone any worse?

His phone rang, interrupting his depressing reverie; he didn't recognize the number. All he could tell was that it wasn't a Boston, New York, or D.C. area code. He wondered if it could be Adele Tomlin calling to curse him again from wherever she was hiding, terrified that Castro's men were going to make her face look like a Halloween pumpkin. He almost didn't answer the call, then changed his mind.

"Hello?" he said

"DeMarco, you son of a bitch! Why did you let her do it?"

"What? Who is this?"

"It's Elinore."

"Elinore! You sound like you're all right. Thank God!"

"Of course I'm all right. I just got a little bump on my noggin."

"It was more than a little bump, Elinore. I didn't think you were ever going to be okay again."

"Well, I'm fine. The swelling or whatever it was went down. Now answer my question. Why did you let my damn daughter take that deal from Callahan?"

"I couldn't stop her, Elinore. You were incapacitated and she had power of attorney. And face it, you got a good deal. You got enough money from Callahan that you can go live wherever you want."

"I didn't want to move! I told you I was taking a stand against Callahan."

"I know but . . . Anyway, there're a couple things you should know. The McNultys are going to prison."

"For what they did to me?"

"No, for trying to sell machine guns."

"Machine guns?"

"Yeah, the cops found them with a bunch of guns and they're going away for a long time. I guess someone must have ratted them out."

"Good."

"And Sean Callahan is dead."

"Dead?"

"Yeah, somebody shot him. The police don't know who."

"Well, I'm actually sorry to hear that. I never wanted him to die, but it was probably somebody he screwed in one of his slimy business deals."

"I'm sure you're right. And I'm sorry this turned out the way it did, but in the long run, you made out okay. You were going to have to move off Delaney Street in three years anyway, and now you can find a nice place to live, wherever you want. Hell, you can move into another building some developer like Callahan is trying to renovate."

"You know, I just might do that."

"Elinore, I was kidding."

"I know you were. But I'm not."

◆

DeMarco walked into Mahoney's office and told Mavis he needed to see the big man. He wanted to give Mahoney the good news that Elinore was okay, feeling feistier than ever, and ready to take on the world. He also wanted to let him know about his last encounter with pretty Maria—or whatever her name was.

Mavis said that he'd have to wait, as Mahoney was currently meeting with Congressman Sims. And DeMarco thought: *Great.* He could just imagine the mood Mahoney would be in after that meeting.

Ten minutes later, Sims left Mahoney's office. He was a big lumbering man in his fifties, and probably weighed sixty pounds more than he had when he was a young marine in Lebanon. He looked shell-shocked; he didn't appear to even see DeMarco and Mavis as he left.

DeMarco walked into Mahoney's office to find Mahoney drinking bourbon, staring morosely out at the National Mall.

"How'd it go with Sims?" DeMarco asked.

Without looking at DeMarco, Mahoney said, "I asked him if he'd really been given a Purple Heart, and eventually he told me the truth. He said, just like Emma thought, that he figured he deserved one and during his first campaign, on the spur of the moment, he lied. Then after that, he was stuck with it. So I told him he had to set things straight, that you can't lie about something like the Heart.

"But I told him that when he did, I was going to be there, standing beside him. And that guy whose life he saved, he'd be there, too, and he'd tell how Sims had risked his life and got all cut up doing so. I'd say that Sims was a decent man and a brave one, too, but he just made a poor decision in the heat of a campaign."

Mahoney polished off the drink in hand and swiveled his chair around to face DeMarco. "But none of that's going to happen. Sims is going to resign. He said he's not going to spend the next year watching his opponent's campaign ads trash him. He said he wasn't going to subject his wife and kids to that kind of humiliation."

"Are you going to tell anyone about him not receiving the Purple Heart?" DeMarco asked.

"No. Not if he resigns. And I'm sure he'll never bring it up again." Mahoney paused. "Fucking politics in this country has become so nasty and cutthroat. There was a time when Sims could have owned up to what he did, and people might have forgiven him. But not these days."

Mahoney refilled his glass with Wild Turkey. "So what good news have you got for me, now that I just lost the Democrats the only congressional district we had in Alabama?"

DeMarco looked at the bundle of contradictions sitting before him. He would never be able to understand Mahoney.

"Actually, I do have some good news," DeMarco said, and told him about the phone call he'd received from Elinore.

"Thank God, she's okay," Mahoney said. "As for what happened to Callahan . . . Well, when you lie down with dogs you're liable to wake up with fleas."

And that, DeMarco thought, was going to be Sean Callahan's epitaph.

Then DeMarco told Mahoney about the warning Castro's lady gunslinger had given him, that if he ever went after Javier Castro again, DeMarco was likely to be framed for Callahan's murder. Mahoney's reaction to this statement was: "Aw, he won't do shit."

Easy for you to say.

"She also said that if you go after Castro, some of Castro's cartel friends who are also invested in Delaney Square might come after you."

"She said that, did she?" Mahoney said.

The way Mahoney said this, DeMarco thought: *Oh, no.* He knew immediately what Mahoney was going to do next.

Mahoney picked up his phone, punched a button, and said, "Mavis, I want a meeting tomorrow with the head of the DEA. There's a bunch of Mexican drug dealers laundering money through a development in Boston and I want the bastards strung up by their balls."

He put down the phone and said, "I'll show them they can't threaten a United States congressman."

DeMarco closed his eyes and prayed: *Dear Lord, please save me from this maniac.* Didn't Mahoney realize that screwing with Castro could get them both killed?

Epilogue

———◆◆◆———

Javier Castro knew he was going to die. What he didn't know was how agonizing his death would be. It was almost laughable that a man would actually pray to be shot in the head but that was what he prayed for now: a bullet in the head rather than being tortured for hours, his body mutilated, his heart finally bursting when it could no longer endure the waves of pain.

He was in a barn someplace in Mexico but he didn't know exactly where. There were four empty horse stalls, saddles and bridles hanging from hooks, bales of hay stacked near one wall, straw covering a dirt floor. Leaning against one wall was a pitchfork and he hoped that's where it stayed. He was bound to a chair with a rope, his hands handcuffed behind his back. His hands had been cuffed for the last six hours and he no longer had any feeling in his fingers. Standing near the barn's double doors were two men—two of his former bodyguards, men who'd betrayed him. He'd been sitting in the barn for over an hour, waiting, he assumed, for his crazy cousin Paulo to arrive.

For the last six months, he'd been living in a home in Belize. He'd purchased it in a manner he thought was untraceable from the estate of a Russian oil baron who'd fallen out of favor with Putin. And he bought it because it was a virtual fortress with high walls and a sophisticated security system that included motion detectors, cameras, and a safe room—an impregnable vault that only an expert with explosives would be able to crack open. He figured the only way anyone would be able to breach the home's security system and get past four men armed with Uzis was if there was a traitor in his ranks—and he turned out to be right about this.

Last night, while he was sleeping, la Leona, Maria Vasquez, had entered his bedroom accompanied by two of his bodyguards, men who had been loyal to him for years. She prodded him gently awake with a slim finger, and with his bodyguards pointing pistols at him, ordered him to get dressed. Maria had been dressed in black—a short black jacket, a black turtleneck sweater, tight black jeans, and black Reeboks. She looked like a cat burglar—or maybe the way a beautiful actress playing a cat burglar would look. He suspected Maria had met with his bodyguards when they were sent out for supplies, and she either bribed them to help her or threatened family members who still resided in Mexico.

How brilliant Maria had found him in Belize he didn't know. The only good news was that his wife wasn't with him because when the American investigation started to damage the cartel, he insisted his wife and daughter go live in a small place he owned in Switzerland—a place the Americans couldn't confiscate—and had been paying a security firm thousands of dollars a day to protect them.

As he was dressing, he said to Maria, "Whatever Paulo's paying you, I'll triple it."

"Please, Javier," she said. "Don't embarrass yourself."

As they left the house, he saw the bodies of his other two bodyguards lying on the floor. Both men had been shot in the back, he assumed with silenced weapons, as he hadn't heard shots. He also assumed that the two bodyguards helping Maria had killed them and then let her into the house.

He was handcuffed, placed in a large black SUV, then driven to an airstrip on private land where a small jet was waiting. On board the plane, Maria showed him a list of banks where he kept cash; the only way she could have gotten the list was from his lawyer or his personal accountant, and God knows what she did to them to make them co-operate. When she asked him to provide the passwords and security information needed to transfer money out of the accounts, he did so without hesitation. If he hadn't given her the information voluntarily, he knew he'd be tortured until he did.

The money in the accounts amounted to about 120 million; all the rest of his assets were in real estate or tied up in businesses or stock held in various companies, and Maria knew this. Those assets would be harder for his cousin to appropriate and maybe he wouldn't bother. Also not on Maria's list was 25 million he kept in gold bullion buried beneath the courtyard in his Mexico City home, for no one but he and his wife knew about the gold. There was at least some consolation in knowing his wife and daughter wouldn't be left penniless. After he gave her the bank account information, Maria spent a little time on a computer, most likely verifying information he gave her or transfer-ring the money out of his accounts, then she slept like a baby until the plane landed, not a worry in the world, nothing troubling her conscience at all.

The plane landed at a private airport in Sinaloa that the cartel used. A hood was placed over his head before he left the plane, and then he was placed in another SUV that was waiting on the runway. From there they drove to the barn where he was now sitting, bound to a chair, waiting for his cousin to come and kill him. While he sat there, his unfaithful bodyguards watched him, looking regretful. He thought about railing at them for being the treasonous, ungrateful dogs they were, but didn't bother. He didn't know where Maria had gone, most likely to pick up his cousin.

Javier Castro's troubles began seven months earlier, almost immediately after he thought he had dealt successfully with the Callahan
problem. A federal task force led by the DEA, with help provided by
the U.S. Treasury and Justice Departments, started looking at money
coming into and going out of the Cayman firm he'd used for investing
in Delaney Square. Thanks to the help of one of the Cayman executives
who cooperated to avoid a jail sentence, the U.S. government was able
to identify a number of properties and bank accounts in the United
States where the cartel had placed considerable sums.

To date, the U.S. government had seized over three hundred million
in cartel-owned real estate in the United States, including his daughter's condo in New York. Also seized were three jets, each worth approximately twenty-five million, and a number of U.S. bank accounts
holding approximately four hundred million dollars. These accounts
belonged not only to members of his cousin's cartel but judges, cops,
and politicians who had helped the cartel over the years. A final problem caused by the investigation was that the cartel now had cash stack-
ing up in warehouses on both sides of the border, moldering, because
it was afraid to move the money.

The U.S. government also got an injunction to stop work on Delaney
Square until the investigation was completed, and when the U.S. bank
that had loaned money to Callahan for Delaney Square learned he
had partially financed the project with money coming from a Mexican
drug cartel, the U.S. bank, at least temporarily, had refused to make
the additional loans needed to complete the project. Now in the place
where Elinore Dobbs's old apartment building had once stood there
was nothing more than a large hole in the ground. No new structure
would be rising from the hole anytime soon.

When the DEA money-laundering investigation began, Javier talked
to a source he'd been paying in the DEA for years, and his source told
him that Congressman John Mahoney was the one who'd initiated
the investigation, and he did so because he'd been threatened by Javier

Castro. It was outrageous! He'd done exactly what Mahoney had wanted when it came to Callahan, and he'd never threatened Mahoney—or at least, that's the way he saw it. All he did was have Maria Vasquez tell DeMarco that if Mahoney didn't leave the cartel alone, people like his insane cousin might come after Mahoney—but he never said that *he* would retaliate against Mahoney.

He realized now—now that it was too late—that he should not have killed Callahan; he should have just forced him to walk away from Delaney Square as DeMarco had suggested. Furthermore, he should never have tried to intimidate Mahoney by showing how easily he could frame DeMarco for Callahan's murder. Mahoney clearly didn't care about what happened to DeMarco; DeMarco was just hired help to him. All Mahoney cared about was proving that he was too power-ful to be intimidated. The man was a dangerous egomaniac, and his egomania was going to cost Javier Castro his life, just as it had caused Sean Callahan his.

After the Americans began seizing money and real estate, his cousin went berserk, calling him and screaming at him that it was Javier's responsibility to reimburse everyone who had lost money. He tried to tell Paulo that that was not only unreasonable but also impossible. He didn't have enough money to reimburse everyone— he'd be a pauper if he did, and he had no intention of becoming one. Furthermore, he told his cousin, it wasn't his fault the Americans had been able to identify assets the cartel and the cartel's friends had in the United States. The blame for that lay with the Cayman investment company and the cartel's accountants. He did offer to reimburse Paulo the fifteen million he'd lost on Delaney Square, but that did nothing to mollify the maniac—so he fled to Belize, not knowing what he was going to do next. He'd been hoping he might get lucky and that his cousin would be arrested or killed before too long and he wouldn't have to stay in hiding forever—but luck had not been on his side.

Javier hadn't seen Paulo Castro in almost two years, and when his cousin finally walked into the barn, Javier couldn't believe how bad the man looked. Paulo was tall, almost six four, and when he was young, he'd had the build of a weightlifter who used steroids. Now he just looked like a fifty-year-old fat man. But it wasn't just his body that had declined. Javier had heard rumors that his cousin had started drinking heavily and using cocaine. His face was now bloated, his skin red and blotched, his eyes looking as if he hadn't slept in days. He'd also heard that his cousin had become even more vicious and unpredictable. The slightest annoyance would send him into a towering rage, and Javier had been told that Paulo beat one of his own men to death with a golf club, a man who'd worked for him for years, just because he was late for a meeting. He'd also become extremely paranoid, the paranoia most likely a result of the heavy drinking and drug use, and he'd killed several people because he was convinced that they were talking to the federales about him even though it was highly unlikely that anyone would take such a risk. Paulo Castro had become like a wounded grizzly bear, terrifying everyone within range of his long, sharp claws.

He was surprised, therefore, when Paulo walked into the barn and then just sat down on a bale of hay. He'd expected his cousin to walk up to him and smash him in the face and start screaming at him, but he didn't. He just sat, breathing heavily, and Javier realized the man was so drunk that if he hadn't sat down he would have fallen.

With Paulo were two more bodyguards, bringing the total number of armed bodyguards in the barn to four. Following Paulo into the barn was Maria Vasquez, still dressed as she'd been when she kidnapped him. She looked over at him—sympathetically, he thought—then went and leaned against the wall near the pitchfork. The combination of the pitchfork next to her honey-blond hair, her black attire, and the bright red lipstick she wore made Javier think: *The devil's mistress.*

The last person to enter the barn was Ignacio Rojo. Rojo was in his late sixties, slightly built, wore glasses, and his hands were gnarled from severe arthritis. He was wearing a black suit, as he almost always did, and a white dress shirt with the top button buttoned, no tie. Rojo was the one who managed the cartel's day-to-day operations, Paulo not being a person who had the patience for details. The thing that Javier had always appreciated about Ignacio Rojo when Rojo worked for him was that he was content with his role. He had no desire to be in charge of the cartel, being wise enough to know that the man who wore the crown also wore a target on his back.

Rojo went and stood next to Maria Vasquez but Maria, sensitive to the man's age and arthritic joints, snapped her fingers and said to one of the bodyguards: "Bring that box over here for Señor Rojo to sit on." When Maria spoke, the bodyguard moved like he'd been poked with a cattle prod.

Paulo started to say something, then started sneezing violently. Javier had forgotten about his cousin's allergies. When he stopped sneezing, Paulo said, "Fucking hay. Why are we doing this here?"

"It was convenient," Maria said.

"Convenient for who?" Paulo said.

Maria didn't apologize, which surprised Javier, but then Paulo turned his head to look back at him.

"Cousin," Paulo said. "You've cost me a lot of money. You caused me a lot of aggravation."

Although he knew it was hopeless, Javier said, "Just tell me what I can do to make things right, Paulo."

Paulo laughed—then he started sneezing again. In different circumstances, this might have been comical. This time when he stopped sneezing, he said, "I've got to get out of here."

"You," he said, to one of the bodyguards. "Do you have a knife?"

"Yes, sir," the bodyguard said.

"Go put out his eyes, and cut off his ears. His nose, too. Do it quickly." To Javier, he said, "When he's done with your face, I'm going to have him cut off your head and mail it to your wife. She always treated me like I was a servant."

But the bodyguard didn't move. Instead, he looked over at Maria Vasquez.

"Why in the hell are you looking at her?" Paulo said to the bodyguard. "Do what I told you."

No one answered Paulo, but Ignacio Rojo said to Maria, "Let's be done with this."

"Yes," Maria said. She looked at one of the other bodyguards, a man standing behind Paulo, and nodded. Before Paulo could react, the man pulled out a Beretta and shot Paulo in the back of the head. Fat Paulo landed face-first in the straw on the barn floor.

Javier closed his eyes. He couldn't believe it. Maybe he would survive after all. It appeared as if Maria, with Rojo's concurrence, had decided it was time for her to take over the cartel and Javier was sure that everyone in the organization would appreciate the change in management. The best news for him was that Maria and Rojo were people who could be reasoned with and he might be able to come to an accommodation with them. Maria had already stolen 120 million from him but if she wanted more, he would gladly give it to her.

"Maria, thank you," he said. "Now please tell me what I can do to make things right."

Maria looked at him for what seemed an eternity, then shook her head. "Give me the gun," she said to the man who had killed Paulo. He handed it to her and she walked slowly over to Javier. She was almost forty now but as beautiful as ever, he thought.

"Maria," he said. "I don't care about the money you took from me today. I really don't."

"I'm sorry, Javier," she said. "You say you don't care now, but you're an intelligent man, and a ruthless one. I'm afraid I just wouldn't feel secure with you around." She smiled that sad, sad smile of hers and said, "So much misfortune because of one stubborn old woman."

And then Maria answered Javier's earlier prayer—and shot him in the head.

DeMarco was shoveling the two feet of snow that had fallen on Washington the night before off his front sidewalk. It had been the third heavy snowfall in January, and he wished he could afford to spend the winter in Florida. He was wearing a heavy wool sweater, jeans, and Gore-Tex-lined boots. On his head was a black stocking cap that he knew made him look like a thug. Which made him wonder if the romance writer who had taken his photo in Boston because she thought he looked like Bruno, her menacing villain, had ever published her stupid novel.

As he bent his back to dig another shovelful of snow, he heard snow chains clanking on a vehicle's tires and looked up to see a D.C. Metro Police car coming down the street in his direction—and his heart started beating faster. In the last seven months, ever since Mahoney had convinced the DEA to go after Javier Castro, DeMarco's heart rate increased every time he saw a cop. He wondered if this was the day they were going to arrest him for Sean Callahan's murder. But the cop car didn't stop, and continued along on its noisy way.

His phone rang just then, and by the time he yanked his gloves off and dug the phone out of his jeans, it rang for the fifth time; after the next ring it would go to voice mail. He said hello without looking at the caller ID.

"Joe?" a woman said, her voice low and sexy.

"Yes," he said, wondering who it was.

"It's Maria. You remember me from Boston?"

DeMarco couldn't speak for a moment. "Maria, trust me when I say that I'll never forget you. What do you want?"

"I just wanted to let you know that you can stop worrying."

"You mean about being framed for murder?"

"That's right. You can also tell Mr. Mahoney that he's made his point, and that no one will bother him at any time in the future, no matter what the DEA uncovers in their investigation. As far as the cartel is concerned—or maybe I should say, as far as I'm concerned—what's happened in the last few months is just the cost of doing business. It's time to move on."

"Really," DeMarco said. "And Javier Castro is okay with this? I mean, from what I've heard, he's lost a lot of money."

"Where Javier is now, Joe, he doesn't need money."

That took a moment to sink in. "I see," DeMarco said. "And the gun that was used to . . . You know."

"Oh, the gun. It's been, shall we say, recycled. Don't worry about the gun."

"That's good to hear."

"Well, that's all I called to say, Joe. But if you ever come to Mexico again—it's beautiful where I am right now; the temperature's about eighty, not a cloud in the sky—give me a call. For some reason, I have a hard time getting a date down here, and I'd love to see you again."

Then she laughed and disconnected the call.

Notes and Acknowledgments

———◆———

The idea for this book came from a photo in the *Seattle Times* of an elderly woman wearing yellow rain gear and protesting against a developer trying to evict tenants from a building in the Ballard neighborhood of Seattle. She was the original Elinore Dobbs.

The story in the book about a multimillionaire landlord given hundreds of citations for not maintaining apartments—while suffering no serious legal or financial consequences—was inspired by an article I found online. I included this story in the book to make the point that in real life developers/landlords like Sean Callahan can often act with impunity when it comes to tenants' rights.

The fictional Delaney Square in this book is modeled after a real development in Boston called Boston Landing, which is a five-hundred-million-dollar development occupying fourteen acres, and includes a corporate headquarters for New Balance, a hotel, a sports complex, and four office buildings. As far as I know, the developer didn't do anything nasty and underhanded like Sean Callahan.

I particularly want to thank Gerry LaCaille. Gerry has been involved with developments in Seattle and he was incredibly generous with his time, educating me on the financial aspects of large projects. The whole process is a whole lot more complicated than the way I describe it in the book and if any of what I've written is incorrect, the fault lies with me and not Mr. LaCaille.

I also want to thank Robert Kirschner, a friend and civil engineer, for advising me on large construction projects and such things as fall protection violations. Bob also gave me some advice recently on adding a few strategically placed two-by-fours under my deck to keep it from moving around when folks walk on it—which is a whole different story.

Regarding drug cartels laundering massive amounts of money and the U.S. government seizing assets, a lot has been reported on this subject. A 2008 NPR article reported that the Justice Department, in a four-year period, seized $1.6 billion in assets related to drug trafficking. Even better, my wonderful editor at Grove Atlantic, Jamison Stoltz, sent me a link to an article in which HSBC Bank, which is headquartered in London and has offices in eighty countries around the world, was fined $1.9 billion for charges related to Latin American drug cartels laundering billions of dollars. Specifically, the article noted that the bank "failed to monitor"—whatever the hell that means—*$670 billion* in wire transfers and purchases of more than $9.4 billion in U.S. currency. So, as noted in the book, we're talking big bucks—and, as always appears to be the case, the bankers get fines that are a drop in the bucket to them and the bankers themselves never seem to go to jail.

Regarding the Stolen Valor Act, I was shocked that people lying about military service and unearned military medals occurred so frequently and so blatantly. Can you even imagine walking into a room wearing a Congressional Medal of Honor you never earned? I wasn't so surprised that people were committing fraud through bogus claims of military service—like the guy I mention in the book who scammed the VA for two hundred grand—as someone out there is always finding a clever way to commit fraud. I also wasn't so surprised that Congress could come together to pass the first Stolen Valor Act. Who in their political right mind would vote against such a law? Then after the Supremes overturned the law in 2012, I was amazed at how a Congress that can't seem to agree on anything worked so rapidly to pass a second Stolen Valor Act in 2013. How come these guys can't ever come together on other really important things?

One other item of interest. I was asked recently at an event if I really believed that folks in Congress are as corrupt as I often make them out to be in my books. Well, just as my editor and I were working together to finish this book, former Speaker of the House Dennis Hastert was arrested for lying to the FBI about paying someone over $1 million (of a promised $3.5 million) in hush money to apparently cover up some sort of sexual misconduct. At the time I wrote this paragraph, all the facts weren't in, but three things about the Hastert case interested me. First, although my character Mahoney is based in many ways—his appearance, being from Boston, being a Democrat—on former speaker Tip O'Neill, former Republican speaker Hastert also bears a striking physical similarity to my Mahoney. Second, when Hastert started in Congress his net worth was said to be only about $270,000. How did he amass enough money to pay someone $3.5 million? Lastly, Hastert was just the latest in a long line of politicians to be indicted for one thing or another. While researching this book I came across one congressman (a Democrat) indicted on sixteen federal counts for "solicitation of bribes, wire fraud, money laundering, obstruction of justice, racketeering, and conspiracy." Just reading the counts of the indictment, you'd think the person arrested was a Mafia hood, not a United States congressman. So is Congress the bed of corruption I seem to think it is? Maybe not, but the institution is corrupt enough that I may never run out of ideas for books.

Lastly, I want to thank my son, Keith, for flying to Boston with me and assisting me with my research as we walked about the city and looked at the places mentioned in this book: the Park Plaza Hotel, Copley Plaza, the Warren Tavern, the Lansdowne Pub, Christian Science

Plaza—and Fenway, of course. We also drove to Rhode Island, where I found Pine Orchard Road after driving around for about three hours, although I modified the locale somewhat for DeMarco's encounter with the McNultys. The most memorable part of the trip may have been the Italian dinner in the North End, where my son spoke in Italian with all the waiters while I stuffed my face.